ARE YOU GOD OR HIS MAILMAN

CHIBUZOR OBASI

Flagbo Press

ISBN-10: 0988780216
ISBN-13: 978-0-9887802-1-7

Ω

To my Mom, Mma never ceases praying.

May the paths be loyal to you my child.

-Christiana Obasi

PROLOGUE
One

It was eight o'clock in the morning. The air was fresh and the rising sun was warm on the skin. At Saint Patrick's Elementary the headmaster is addressing the morning assembly. The school had done that for over sixty five years. The students start their day at the school with a march pass. A group of students selected from elementary four, five and six made up the school band. The rest of the students marched three to four times round the assembly ground. As part of program the children were taught how to respond in cases of emergency. They showed them how to make emergency calls, perform CPR for heart conditions, and to take cover in many other situations. Some mornings, light hearted jokes with important messages were added.

The parent teacher association had debated if they should stop the exercise. But the headmaster seemed to have a superior argument. Amongst other things she said the exercise helped the kids stay awake and focused during the morning periods. Studies conducted by the school proved her right. Most of the kids felt sleepy within the first two hours of class on days when there were no such morning exercises.

Ms. Johnson's every word to the pupils re-echoed through a thin battery operated megaphone.

"Be good students, you are the ambassadors of this great institution, your families, this state and this great nation," she said.

The nation was no longer that great but the kids needed hear it. It gave them hope and motivation. Saint Patrick Elementary was no doubt one of the best elementary schools in the state. It was one of the mission schools that was taken over by the state, but later returned to the church again. It had most of the sons and daughters of the well to do in the state. But the students drove to school in the morning with their parents or in the school bus. If the tough conditions were not directly felt in their homes, they saw it on the streets on the way to school every morning.

They saw kids their age hawking wares on their heads as early as seven in the morning. They saw beggars on the streets. They saw the chaos in the crowded streets, cars bumping into one another, people jumping into moving buses on busy roads and people being run-over by vehicles. Each day the drive to and from school was a lesson on life and society for the kids.

The country's GDP had fallen. It reflected on the tables in most homes. Milk, bread, eggs, cereals and newspapers gradually disappeared on those tables. The kids got used to it. If it was not in their homes they heard other kids talk about it. The headmaster knew the pupils were adjusting to social as well as their dietary needs. She wanted them to be good examples. She would take nothing less from the teachers.

After several years in the school Ms. Johnson still managed to refuse gifts from parents of her students. They knew that conditions were hard and it hit the poor teachers bad. But she found a way to turndown gifts. Although she appreciated their understanding she didn't like the idea of taking gifts. She loved the freedom to do her duties the best she could.

Mr. Ete Udoh, a teacher at the school. He had been there for a few months before Mr. Dogood was employed. He seemed quiet edgy and unease since Mr. Dogood told him about his class theatre project. Dogood was not sure if it was envy or his recent lack of competitive spirit.

Before his class that morning Mr. Dogood walked pass Udoh on the corridor. "Hi" he said. The response was cold.

Mr. Dogood turned backed and began to address him.

"If I don't tell you this, I may be lying to you. I will walk away if you were a petty trader and we were at your store in Sabongari. But that you are Nigerian with a Bachelor's degree in this age and time and a teacher at that, I'll explain to you."

His eyes blinked urging him on. He seemed to have told him something that he needed. But his stubborn air of pride took over him again. Dogood stood his ground and continued.

"I will do this with a sense of duty, shame, disappointment and love for our beloved country. The pledge and Anthem we recite every morning says 'may the labors of our heroes past not be in vain.' Over forty now, it is time we retired that vanquished or not vanquished idea, and faced the truth. Udoh, in this country you should know better. I am sure throughout your primary, secondary even university education in Nigeria you never came across a book that treated the history of Nigeria beyond the conquests of Usman Dan Fudio. Today more than forty years after Biafra, the likes of Book Haram still dictate what happens, when it happens or not, while tearing those "old wounds and spilling the blood of innocence daily."

Udoh's mouth shaped like that of one about to throw a bomb shell of racism, tribalism and other isms, Mr. Dogood caught him off before he even started.

"Udoh, I know you don't see success as failure. In 2008, I was in New York helping work on videos for a cause which highlights issues of social and international justice. This year "Kony 2012" is out. And I consider charges of racism or tribalism seriously ill-informed. Children and peoples of the world are joining forces just as campaigns like 'Aids or Cancer Awareness Walks.' We are riding together. It is no one's Whitehorse."

Though Udoh did not say much after that, the import of what Dogood told him sank in.

"Udoh, sustained thought is like hewing firewood. But one is harder."

He nodded in agreement and thanked him for explaining. They all went to their classes.

Jane was the age of joggling reasons together. Her grandfather rarely went out of the peninsula after he arrived there. But as long as there was breath, there are a few vows and things that only a man owed him-self. Mr. Stone Sr. had an unchecked bucket list. A visit to the cathedral of Saint Mary in Asom Ethiopia was one. It was believed Melik Sheba's son with Solomon had taken the Arc of the covenant there. Instead of being king in that land he had taken the essence with him. Many important men in many great circles had long had conflicted feelings about what that meant. To who or where it truly belonged. Mr. Stone was one of such men. For a man making peace with his God, there was no better time. Off he went. Once there, if it belonged to the men who had left with Moses or those who stayed back, made no more sense. Beholding the site, he was fulfilled. He came back and completed his temple of mysteries.

Jane was that age. She had gone round the obelisks. Like baby Jesus she was making discoveries, using the lost years. At age twelve he too had known the secrets of the holy temples of the pyramids. The lost years of the Christ had been spent in a school in Ashmuni, Egypt.

It was in those studies that it became easy to understand, the religion only came back. It had been. She saw why her people had embraced it again. It was their beliefs and ways of life. It only went through changes. Jane made a sign on her forehead. The trinity has always been with them.

Two

All day Ms. Johnson went round inspecting classes. She wanted to know what the teachers were teaching and how good they were doing. Her attention was captured by Mr. Dogood's elementary six class. A student was addressing another student in the front of the class. She listened in.

"Ms. Stone three days ago I went to lay a wreath on the tomb of the Unknown Soldier. The soldier I don't know. But I knew your grandfather. I know your father. In every age and time, the pursuit of the true meaning of liberty, preservation of life and the future have provoked generations to confront their fears. Men who fought in wars and civil revolts knew one thing. They knew it would be foolish if the future had to confront the same things they faced. We may never know all who watered our trees of liberty. But we appreciate your grandfather's efforts in establishing schools, libraries, newspapers, our independence and democratic system, rule of law and great scholarly works. Please accept this medal on his behalf."

Jane stepped forward moved close to the boy speaking. Bowed her head and accepted a medal and a hand shake from the president. The crowd being played by the class cheered and clapped their hands. On the gold medal was written,

"In honor of your great contributions, Mr. Sylvester Stone."

It was the drama class. In the play the protagonist receives an overdue honor on behalf of her family from the president of the country. Ms. Johnson was intrigued by the brilliance and acting of the young cast. It was a better way to end her day. She went in and sat down to enjoy the rest of the show.

What neither Ms. Johnson nor anyone else expected was the news that came four hours after the close of school that day. A terror group has struck somewhere. A school bus taking students home had been hijacked. The kids were being held hostage in an unknown location.

Ada had picked up her son and daughter as well as her sister in law's two kids. She was watching the kids and arranging the room. From the DVD player she removed one of those movies her husband referred to as moimoi and akara pictures. She looked at the case, puts it inside. She could never get him to sit through that one. But she liked it.

Her daughter was excited as she told the kids about their play at school. Their dog Mr. Wiggle was wiggling his tail.

Out of that joy, Jane playing "Ms. Stone," again picks up the phone to speak with her friend who had played the president.

"Mr. President." The frantic voice at the other end said the boy was not home yet. Looking at her face, her mother took the phone from her. Everyone was in great shock. The entire country was glued to their television.

Kidnapping was becoming a common crime in the country. But no one would expect anyone in their right minds would target those innocent kids. The kidnappers were demanding ransoms.

"What has the world come to?" was the question on everyone's lips. It was only a few days after a gunman opened fire and killed about twenty school children and several others in an elementary school in America. The news of that was yet to die down.

CHAPTER
≈1≈

For the very first time in his adult life fate stirred his life, destiny was the captain of his ship. Mr. Sylvester Stone was a very meticulous man. He never really left anything to chance. But since he got aboard the first charter plane from New York he seemed to have changed a great deal. The pilot of the jet himself was surprised.

As the plane steadied on high altitudes of about 37000 feet above sea level, he pulled out a scratch paper from his breast pocket. He began to read. It read like a preparatory note for that journey. It was not. It was to take his mind off anything that might seem unfamiliar. He had always known that the day would come when he would find himself on that path. He had in fact prayed for it in the past twenty four months, as he sat at The Camp.

He focused his attention on the little piece of paper in his hand. It was his attempt to see life from eyes of a younger Somali friend he met in prison. For him it seemed like a role reversal. He needed to handle it very well. He read out loud.

"The day was young and bright,

A peep through the window,

Oh how the sound of the early morning bird is gone."

Mr. Stone paused. It was the life of a young boy transfixed from his home in Africa to the life of solitude in America, after he had just seen a gleam of the glitters of that heavenly city. He continued to read.

"Feeling crippled and shivering to the bones,

Once he saw the sunrise and set,

Numbers he thought, wishes and wills."

As he continued to read, the poem reminded him of his own life's journey. And for a moment his mind went back to the boy who had given him that poem. He had seen him on TV, smiling all the way to prison. He wondered what was inside him that made him so happy. Mr. Stone could not understand.

"A man without a worry," Mr. Stone said to himself.

When he arrived at the prison, he befriended him.

Now Mr. Stone was sure he was somewhere in the African air space. He felt he was at a safe distance. He did not worry about being caught as he did while in New York. He was relaxed. Maybe it was the work of that piece of paper he read. He seemed high on something. He felt a sense of freedom. He was no longer in any eminent danger. There was a smile on his face. He wondered how nature and fate seemed to be in perfect harmony with the order of things in certain places and time.

CHAPTER
≈2≈

After ten years there, Mr. Stone was settled on the Peninsula. He had gotten used to the life that gave his Somali friend the power to smile in the face of trials and tribulations.

Despite all the challenges of, civil wars, dictatorships, hunger, famines and drought, some he read in newspapers, heard on radio, seen on TV or witnessed within his neighborhood and countries around. He wished he had come to live there earlier. He woke up everyday a freeman. He watched the sunrise and set. He went to hunt and came back to the stone house. When he felt like it, he went into the busy cities, sat in bars and restaurants. He loved the place. With great admiration he watched the African women shake their voluptuous behinds when they walked.

Mr. Stone always wanted to hunt deer. A few times he went to Arizona with friends to hunt. But he could not compare the fun he was having in the tropical forest. He relished the meat, but it was the beauty of the forest that gave him much more pleasure. The gentle breeze and fresh smell of the bush after the rain was wonderful. Even during the harmattan, the tropics mild winter was the best nature can offer. At times he just sat there and took in enough before driving back.

That morning he got ready, got into his pick-up truck and drove. East or west he drove a little further each time. If variety was the spice of life each drive further down the forest proved it. As he drove he heard sounds of gun shots in the distance. He looked at his watch, checked how long he has been driving.

CHAPTER ≈3≈

The earth was scorched and the wind was dry. The dry and dusty air was hostile to the nostrils. Death and drought persisted in the land though it hungered for freshness.

The tall black woman and her two children were on the run. The boy was strapped to her back and his sister was in her arms. They had walked barefoot for days and weeks. Each footfall on the scorched earth was no longer friendly to her or her daughter. It brought with it a piercing pain, hunger and memory. Each step seemed like a journey to nowhere, to a land of no return. But they continued. It was a step away from death, if they did not walk into any.

She was a woman whose every step was embraced by the earth. The grains of sands longed for her footprints. A woman blessed with many wonders. But she was on the run. They walked and rested under any tree they could find. The trees still standing were those that withstood all weather conditions. The trees themselves were barely alive. They looked more like the weary travelers. The woman and her children spent their nights under the trees, and any kind of shade they found.

Their days were spent in bushes, roads and narrow paths. It was a journey neither the tall black women nor her children planed nor prayed for. They walked out of the mouth of death. They escaped it. But it still lurked in the shadows. It was a walk that no one would be expecting any soul to be making from that direction.

CHAPTER
≈4≈

The town has been left for dead and defeated. According to soldiers who took care of the last air raid and those who went on foot making sure every house, hut and shade were set ablaze, it was a mission accomplished.

The last batch of men who came out waited for a few days. After the enemy forces have left before they arrived. To their surprise, unlike in other places where they showed restraints. There they had shown none. There were no signs of men killed or women raped. What they saw was different. There were no signs, not a sign of life. The men trembled, shook their head and held themselves in their grief.

The men were demoralized. But they remembered their covenants and hung on. The news was a sad one. They felt their greatest failure had taken place. They wept. They went back into the bushes and disappeared.

No one expected that there was still any form of life left there. One week after, Ngozika and her children crawled out of the hole. Their hut had fallen over them. The unceasing air raid that lasted for two days forced the hut into a hole in the ground. The mud walls of the hut could resist the fire power of rifles and bullets. But not the earth quaking mortars and bombs dropped from the air. It sunk the hut beneath the earth.

Underground they clung to each other. And feared they would die. Ngozika pleaded with her children not to cry, that it would get them noticed. Days later when every sound had died down they started making their way out. Once outside they adjusted their eyes to the sun light. They began running as fast as their feet could carry them.

CHAPTER
≈5≈

Though her name was Ngozika, she looked different. Her physical appearance had a lot of dissimilarities with most people in the town. She was a tall slim woman, about six feet five inches. Her dark silky shiny long hairs were always braided. Her cheeks were smooth. Her face showed no facial marks. Nothing to suggest she was from the other Niger neighborhood either. Only one or two people had been known to have come that far to live there from that part of land. The town's people every now and then made comments about her looks.

"Ngozika is beautiful woman." They would say.

But what they did not fail to say, was that they doubted where her beauty came from. They took her for an outsider. And she would only laugh off such remarks. She would put in her own jokes.

"Ngozika was no outsider" she always said, in a funnier dialect.

But if she was, she was settled. Ngozika was approaching fifty years of age. Her children were seven and three. She was a symbol of something that she did not know, something that was beyond her. It was something that was beyond her age. She was the beautiful black woman.

Tata the wise old woman, one of the oldest people in the town, claimed to know her bloodline. She told people that she was of the blood line of the woman who came to the pond season after season. Her name was Ugoala. They both shared a unique and unspoiled beauty. Their beauty drove men insane when it did not lead them to their death. The women's eyes bore the likeness of the moon. Their skin radiated like the sun. Their beauty was ravishing like stars of the night sky.

Tata was one of the survivors of that terrible flood. If anyone knew the story of the place it was Tata.

"Ugoala the prophetess had a child. She left that child to her mother. She wanted to lead a new life of her own. She did not want the baby to encumber her. When she took the baby to her mother, she told her, "Here is your mother. I did not ask her to visit me." Her grandmother did the same the year she became pregnant. She said reincarnation was only a force to distract her."

Some lives are linked and connected by ancient echoes across the corridors of time. In her daughter she had seen her grandmother, an incarnate of the feminine divine element. She was one in the trinity, the beautiful woman- who came to the pond. "But Ugo did not want to be held back. She wanted a life different from her great grandmother's and their ancestors."

Those before her carried the calabash of life for the earth. They passed it down generation after generation. They spoke about themselves in the plural "we." But she wanted to say "I." Ugo wanted the power to be totally on her own, liberated from the ties of those before her. And there she was running and breaking away from it.

The baby was a reincarnate of the grandmother.

"She was a child that should not have come when she did." Tata said.

Her mother took the baby happily and began to nurse her. She showered her with praises. She called her the spring's beauty and the summer's dream. She was Okochi, Anyanwu ututu and the morning dew. She grew into a beautiful woman. Before her mother knew it, men from far and near sought her hand in marriage.

Ngozika's bloodline had trails of beauty and mystery. Nkwoeke committed suicide when Ugo turned down his persistent advances. He came home one day, climbed the palm tree. There he sang and wept.

"My mind is clean, my intentions pure, and my love is genuine.

I am the keeper of memories.

Am afraid I have not moved into the future.

I am going back from the present.

Oh cherished memories. Oh preserved moments.

Oh Beautiful one. I have loved you again and again."

After those sad love songs, he gradually leaned back knowing it was the end. Nkwoeke took his own life.

He was a coward. The people called him a coward. It is only those cowards in their frustrations and fear of life who invoke god or love in their suicidal intents. In their madness they seek to take the world with them. It is the satanic act and forbidden by his people. He took no with him, but the memory of his love.

Tata was disappointed. In his bid to escape the strong hold of love and life, he has taken the life he did create.

"Never reject yourself even if the world rejected you."

It was a common saying in the town. His was ended. He is no longer part of that town.

Ije; the migrant, voluntarily joined the slave ship. Because Ugo would not marry him, he became friends with the captain. It happened one afternoon when he came back from visiting her and the baby they had together. He followed the ship and sailed to sea. If he could not conquer her he would conquer the sea. May be then she would find him worthy. It was two seasons before the flood. The migrant went away and never came back.

CHAPTER
≈6≈

Tata was a woman blessed with tales and vision. If theirs was a monarch she and her sister Ulari were close to the throne. But they were simple women with no interest in history. But they had seen the spiral passage of time.

They knew the queens who crossed the Rivers and those who crossed the deserts. Sheba did. When she did she was never a virgin nor pretended to be one. The sisters followed the tides from the rise of the sun to its setting. Wherever the wind blew east, west, north or south they know where dust would settle- even the whirlwinds.

Tata knew the stories of many people. She recalled the things happening in faraway places. She talked about the river wars, the cold, economy and governments in distant lands. She called sex the channel to the future and children were that future. "Ada Abirika" she called out, "..beware of hostage takers." She worried about those who manipulated the human energy center and body systems. She warned of greedy persons and groups who would toil with the destiny of their countrymen and mankind.

"The virgin earth cries out." She warned about the destruction of the earth by man.

She said Ugoala foretold the birth of a prince in the Arabian Peninsula.

"Looking up in the night sky the position of the moon and the stars, she saw a youth of happiness and fame."

Tata said Ugo became speechless as she spoke of his adult life.

"He would be a man of great friendship and faith, with a symbol of great contradiction. He would be loved and hated. He would extend his hands of friendship to the rejected. In the beautiful cities of Jeddah and Dubai structures will bear his image and likeness. In his ranches would be the rarest and strangest breeds of horses. On New York's Wall Street he would be a leading stock holder, a silent partner in the global media empire. They would call him the Sheik."

At dawn the next day Tata recalls, "Ugo turned her face away from the pond, backing the rising sun. She was heard announcing the departure of families from Europe in small ships to the new world. One of the sons of those families in years to come after traversing great seas will follow channels of the Nile through the Congo to the Niger and would come to the land where she stood to seek shelter and a safe haven."

"The earth lays bare and the moon over her, a man in search of peace will find her beauty."

Tata remembered the flood and about the love between a man and a woman. "Ogbe was a man in love and on constant trips. He did not believe in falling in love. He said love ought to grow, when the seeds of love are sown. It was to be nurtured till it blossomed. That season he was not there to nurture it nor watch it blossom. He came back one day to meet an empty house. His bride and the love of his life was nowhere to be found. The flood submerged their house. She was gone. The love of his life was gone. He had nothing to live for, he said." Tata remembers.

Ugo foretold the traveling trader who found water in the desert. But Tata saw a traveling businessman whom the nation has become his homestead. His abode was everything home. But the place he called home was in his heart. He would have a son. That son would be a true fulfillment of his dreams. Then the time came. The pain of labor was over. The cry of a baby and the voice of a mother were heard. It was a baby boy. The smile on the face of her mother spoke of centuries love reconnected. The husband bent gently, kissed her on the forehead. Took the baby gently in both hands, looked up to the sky. "His name is Chukwuemaka." With both hands held the baby to his heart. Then he handed him back to his wife. Ojukwu was the name of the businessman. It was dry season in the hilly north. And it was around the 1930s.

Tata was a young woman then.

"The baby was the semblance of everything foretold." The little bundle grew fast, smart, intelligent and energetic."

On days when Tata spoke she stood before the lake.

"I am an image of the maker, I look beyond the sea, and I watch the sun go westward. Many rivers flow into the sea, but the sea is never full. Please hear my speech, listen to my words. My tongue speaks in my mouth. I am the mouth that ate salt and pepper. I am made of clay. The hands of the Almighty formed me and gave me the breath of life. My parents called me Tata. My words come from upright heart my lips utter pure knowledge. The old man saw the sea. He warned the waters would rise. He warned of the flood. The bird flew, after the rain they saw the rainbow. But the flood that destroyed our home was spoken of by the beautiful woman who came to the pond. I wanted to cry but my tears dried before they came."

CHAPTER
≈7≈

As Ngozika walked she held the girl seven by the hand. The boy was three. He was on her back. She had taken a container of water when she left the town. Though it was empty now, she still held onto it. She hoped to refill it when she came close to water. But there seemed to be none, Ngozika still hoped upon hope. She saw death and knew that death was terror. It had rejected her and her children. She was determined to walk to safety. "Ngozika will walk, if she walked to death, so be it." She consoled herself. She did not want to dwell with the ghost of destruction nor of the dead. Though they have been walking and exhausted, somehow something urged them on.

Their days of fasting were paying off. There had been days when they went without food. It was when things could still be called normal. She had told them it connected the body and the spirit. It takes the body through that cycle of cleaning and healing. "You become strong in body and spirit." Save for the headaches and dizziness caused by low sugar, they were doing ok.

She was not exhausted. Her children were still surviving from the water, and several other things they picked up along the way. They ate anything they believed to be edible. If it had some form of water and freshness, it was food. That was before they entered the scorched part of the land. It seemed they were walking into a desert. Something had told her to follow the direction of light. She might be able to walk into some kind of help. She looked east, west north and south and continued. Relief agencies or other refugees may not be far away. She kept hope alive, singing them to sleep when it was safe to. Yet she feared greatly that her son might be the first to give up the ghost. He was already beginning to show signs of fatigue. The girl seemed to understand fully well what they were faced with. She was not afraid, if she was she did not show it.

Ngozika could tell a dead soul in a dying frame. Though she had seen death and shaken hands with it. She knew that in a war situation everyone was not a monster. There might still be human beings left. There may still be people whose jobs were not solely to steal and destroy. She knew there were soldiers looking for women to rape or to sleep with. There were many looking for whom to make their lovers or take as slaves. Those were nowhere in sight. She was on a lonely road. Ngozika was ready to do anything to keep her children alive. She hoped the white painted truck with the logo of two leaves on it would come their way. There was no sign of it. There were no signs of helicopters that hovered over her hut.

The joy of being alive was enveloped in fear. The woman who sang to her kids "Is this world a beautiful place." Also felt deep within her marrows, the entitlement some people felt and enjoyed. She hummed the words, "When they call to tell you how they see the world. They come into your kitchen, into your bedrooms, they pull you by your hair, but when you call them, you're on your own, the world can do without you, one less burden."

What she feared the most was death on that road. It was better to have some form of human contact before dying. She didn't want to die of a slow and painful death, though she has been there and back. She wondered what kind of war it was, that left everyone dead except for herself and her two burdens.

"Who else is fighting in this war? Is there another war or warriors other than the men that entered the covenant to protect this land, who were now either dead or fled to safety?" She queried.

The heat was intensifying as each dawn became day break and the sun above brightened. Their sorrow was so much. She prayed for the nights to come. Now they were under a tree with only a few leaves. On a branch of the tree was a bird's nest. In the nest were three eggs. She did not immediately see them or did but ignored it. Around the tree she picked and smelled the leaves. The smell was not bad. She tasted it on her lips. The taste was okay. She chewed it for water and strength. Her son was watching her.

Her daughter, who fell asleep on her back, was now lying on the ground where she placed her to sleep, while she stretched her back and looked around for food. They were out of any kind of supplies. Their only hope was anything they could find there. The water container was empty. The last refill was at the mouth of the river, before they crossed it with an old canoe that looked more like a raft. They had made their way close enough to the road. It was where they could easily be sighted, if any help was coming.

She continued to chew on the leaves. Her son stretched out his hands. She hesitated before eventually handing him a few of the leaves. They both chewed not exchanging any words. After a little while he fell asleep, curled up on the ground. Ngozika hoped he would wake up. Then she drifted away. She was in a deep slumber.

CHAPTER
≈8≈

The three bodies lay motionless. They could be passed for dead. After all, death was the prevailing situation. And all men had become merchants of death. Before she drifted away into her sleep she held herself up enough. She refused to sleep, and feared it was death. If it was death she wanted to cover or bury her children's bodies, before her own death. She did not want them to be eaten by vultures or other animals. She was too weak to do anything. But Ngozika managed to say a prayer. "Lord" she cried out, "if you know that which you will do for me do it now when am alive, because the dead don't praise you."

As she closed her eyes she dreamt a dream. In her dream two strange animals devoured her body and her children's. The animals were however not vultures. That would have woken her up dripping in sweats. She shifted and changed sides, on the hard ground under the shade of the tree. She moved from her left to her right, using her right arm to support her head. Then she went back to sleep.

An animal eventually came. It was an antelope. It was running towards their direction. She was startled and she woke up. She hurriedly cleared her eyes, did not remember much. Ngozika moved over to shake her son who turned reluctantly. She walked over and woke her daughter up. They were all awake. It was not death after all, she thought.

The antelope had stopped abruptly. It did not move, fixed its eyes on her and she did the same. In that split moment she went back memory lane. The antelope had appeared to her in the past. In an intense and prolonged look, its facial features became human. She could not recollect when, how or where she saw it before. But she was sure it was the same antelope. It had the eyes that could only remind her of her grandmother. The woman she grew up with.

Her grandmother died in her care. When she was a little girl she took her and taught her all she knew. She did not grow up with her mother. Her mother had gone away after giving birth to her. Her grandmother nursed her. And she grew in her care and love. Before she died, she promised to always be with her, wherever she went. Ngozika was holding her in her arms when she died. She cried. She shook her body as her ghost journeyed into eternity. It was her saddest loss. She learnt what it meant to lose a loved one. Even in death their bound grew. Ngozika often dwelled in those last moments they spent together.

Where her grandmother came from the antelope was neither hunted nor eaten. The town had taken its name after the animal.

Ngozika tried to clear her eyes again. She wanted to be sure that she was not still in a dream. She remembered that the last thing she saw was the antelope. She saw it take the form of an old woman. She knew the message. She looked up and saw a huge tall man.

He was a hunter after the antelope. He had seen the antelope stop at the foot of the tree. He approached it, aiming at his target. The hunter came to a halt. It was a dying woman and her children under the tree. There was no antelope there. As he came closer his taste for hunting and killing were instantly gone. He loathed himself. He went closer assuring them there was no problem.

"I'm not going to hurt you," he said in low tone.

He bent over the little boy and touched his head. He had fever. He held him up and asked his mother to bring the little girl and come with him. She gladly did. They walked back to his pick-up truck. He got them in and took them to his house, which was not very far away. As they drove her mind continued to wonder. He did not want to exhaust her any further with questions. She wanted to ask questions. But she could not find the words to start with. So they drove quietly with the two kids going back to sleep.

On getting to his house he asked her to make them food. He showed her things in his kitchen. On the stove was the roasted antelope. He killed it a day before in his hunting expedition. What they needed was food. A shower would be civilization, but first food. She woke her kids and fed them. He brought them a jug filled with water and placed it on the table. It was cold water. As he placed it on the table, it seemed heavier than his usual glass jug. He looked at it a second time to be sure it was the same jug he has used most times. It was. There was nothing different.

As he decided to leave the room his eyes moved from the table, to the faces that the woman was feeding. It struck him. He didn't know their names. And the woman has not bothered to talk about herself or her children. She seemed a little hesitant. In the past, if no one knew nothing about her, she had never failed make the names of her children known. It was her legacy. She had nothing and has given them nothing but their names. Ada was the name of the girl. She called the boy Ulu. Ulu was an unusual name for a first son. That was a part many came to wonder about.

She did not explain to strangers. Those who knew her had come to accept certain things the way they were.

CHAPTER
≈9≈

The water on the table looked like a little lake than a pitcher of water. The container was the cleanest she had seen in months. The water seemed to be in a gradual and constant motion. The woman told him her name and her children's. He told them about himself. But left out the story of how he came to live on the peninsula.

He was a veteran of several wars. He was tired of wars after seeing many deaths and destruction.

"Wars never solve any problems." He told them.

He spoke as though he was speaking to grown-ups, as he continued to look at the seven and three year olds.

He lived in a town on the border of Nigeria and Cameroun. His house was not too far from where the war was being fought. As far as he wanted to remove himself from everyday life, somehow he saw himself involved.

Mr. Stone asked how far she had come. She could not say. Ngozika did not know. All she knew was that she had left death behind. And that was what mattered.

"I have been on the road for many days." She could not recall.

"The desert offered us passage. The wild offered us leaves and fruits, till you got to us." She was grateful.

They continued to talk. She listened, studying the kind of man he was. He was a kind man, who has seen much in life. If he had the power he would stop all wars. That was not the power that almighty has bestowed on any man.

"Even the prince of peace was never able to make wars disappear from the earth." He said.

It was a burdensome task he understood. She was convinced he was doing a lot. At least that was what she thought.

The children went back to sleep. They hadn't eaten that much in a long time. She went into the place that she was shown earlier as the bathroom. She removed what she had on as clothes. As she looked around she did not find anywhere to place them. She wanted to throw them away. She needed some clothes to wear. She wanted to ask for something to wear before she went into the bathroom. He was not thinking of it.

He appeared to live alone. There was no sight of anything belonging to a woman in that house. Even the bathroom, it was bare. She had a lot in her mind. Thinking of those was a distraction. She heard a voice outside.

He did not know that she was ready to take a shower. He only thought she was going to use the place briefly.

"I am sorry." He apologized.

"There are towels and clothes on the rack outside the bathroom door." He informed her that she could use them.

When she finished her shower, she opened the door gently. The water dripping from her dark beautiful skin instantly made her on object of desire. A little shy she tiptoed and picked up the towel and clothes. They smelled fresh. They filled her with life. She went back into the bathroom. She dried herself up and then put on the clothes.

It was night. She helped her kids to the bathroom. She washed and cleaned them up with the same towel that she had used. Back in the living room she had some oversized clothes on the couch waiting for the kids. She was delighted. She has walked into life in the midst of war and death.

She was getting ready to tuck them to sleep on the couch for the night when Sylvester Stone walked into the room. He took them just as he had picked them up from under the tree. He took them to the bedroom. He placed the two kids on a large bed. The empty bedroom had not been used in a long time. Maybe it was meant to serve purposes like this one, he thought. He bid the woman and her children good night and proceeded to the adjacent room.

That one was his bedroom. Every night he took the time to make it dim and every morning he pulled the blinds for the bright daylight. He enjoyed the peace and quiet where he lived. He enjoyed his hunting and the songs from the birds in the mornings and late evenings. He has actually gotten used to the raven that comes close to his bedroom windows every morning. Since he became aware of it, the bird had not missed his routine. It came every morning tweeting. It asked the same question of him each morning,

"It's daybreak."

"Did you get up this morning?"

In response he would throw them wheat from his little storeroom when he got out of bed. That ritual continued. He could no longer make the difference. He was no longer sure if the birds would come if it was not for the food. They had duties that they were performing for each other, he would rationalize.

In his two bedroom stone house, Mr. Stone who has come there to build himself a quiet life often avoided the rest of the world. Though he went out of his way to help anyone in need, he preferred to stay on his own. Since he got there he often referred to himself as, "a man in the quest for peace, who must first develop the peace from within."

He was actually looking for peace of mind. He arrived on that piece of land years ago. He first came to the city, while searching for a proper hide out. He was a man used to the life of the city and had lived in biggest and nosiest cities in the world. He has made money and made mistakes too. He paid his dues in both cases, he would say. He doesn't take pride in talking about his own tales. And he never really did apart from in a situation as he has found himself now.

Any man would, she was a tall beautiful black woman. She was ten years younger than he was, almost starving to death with those innocent looking kids.

Something appealed to his male instinct. He felt disarmed and needed to relate to her. He wanted to make her understand that she was welcome. If she wanted to stay, she was free to make that place a home like he has. He arrived there about her age and has been there for twelve years.

CHAPTER
≈10≈

It was their second day. Her children looked happy. And they were recovering from malnutrition. For her she has just had enough of the war. And for a moment the war seemed bit far away. She knew she lost all her friends and people whom she has come to regard as family.

But life has already made her the woman she was. Her grandmother's death, her relationship with her mother and men have taught her that life were to be led in phases. Every relationship only lasted as long as it should. Apart from her children, she had come to take life as nothing other than a dance that lasts only for its season. They were great kids, she loved them. She never wanted to see them as a mistake. She was going to see them dance their seasons dance the best they can. In the past, there were times when all she wanted was to be important to someone. But that was then.

The intervention of the antelope and Sylvester Stone gave her a new hope. Those kids would grow up as humans. They would grow to tell the story of their survival.

"I owe my life and the lives of my kids to you." She said as they sat in the living room on that second day.

Sylvester was not a big fan of travel literature. But he kept a dairy. He sneaked into his room fished out his dairy. There were a few pages where he repeatedly noted, "These contents were personal thoughts." Beside those he began, "their escape, like Mary and the Child, their survival, like Moses floating to the house of Pharaoh." For a lack of better imagery he scribbled down something about beauty and trust in the note, and then covered his pen.

Without intending to his eyes moved to the next page. He began to read it. Those were his thoughts on dictatorial rule and wars. He had written-

"The worst form of dictatorship is the one that impoverishes a people and continually devalues their worth. Slavery and colonial regimes may not have set out to do this. But the present global financial and economic system perpetuates it. Africa and the third world remains a patient. The medical experts and sympathizers like the IMF and the World Bank would not let die nor heal. "

He closed it and came out to join her again. He knew he wanted to say more about her in that note. He wanted to capture that moment but he seemed to have been stopped. What he wrote was better than nothing. He did not go in to write down how much she owed him. He wanted to put down in words that powerful feeling and surge of interest in life that Ngozika and those little angels had sparked in him.

CHAPTER ≈11≈

Mr. Stone was alone child. He did not grow up in the care and love of his own family. As the flood devastated families, homes and love lives in Alaukwe Imo, in Europe it was the cold and the economic down turn that seriously affected families. The bitterness wreaked havoc. Lives and families were no longer what they used to be. Men were abandoning their wives and kids. Their responsibilities and families came last in their lists of to do.

One of such men who took to the streets leaving his wife and eight months old baby was Zit, the father of Sylvester Stone. He had lost his job. He could not feed his family nor afford to keep his wife and kid warm. He took to the streets and to the bottles, barely visiting them. His excuse was that work kept him from coming. He took with him the only thing Sylvester could call family love.

Sylvester did not see his father again after his first birthday. His mother fed him with the help of the church and odd jobs she was able to do.

Though now and then people told tales of his father, he has grown up knowing there was no such person. He did not care. He hated any association with his father. He hated the middle name which he had given him with a passion. He called him Christopher at birth. It was 1933- the year before the Second World War. The story was that he was enlisted to fight in the war.

The only time Zit spoke about his family with pride was in relation to leaving for the war. That still was not often. At least those times it seemed he was fighting for a cause. But those who knew him doubted strongly if he was ever sober to be enlisted. He never came back.

Members of his extended family moved to the new world early enough. His uncle, his wife and children moved in little boat that ducked somewhere in Louisiana.

On his mother's side his grandmother was save from the stalk. And in the new world she found the true meaning of redemption. She was about to be placed on the stalk when his uncle a well-known pirate broke into the chamber where she was being held and rescued her.

They set her on a boat heading north. Throughout the journey she never forgot her cat which was thrown into a well by the crowd. The poor cat did not start haunting the village, not till her last days and after. She finally died of hunger, darkness and dejection in the well. The cat was her dead cousin's cat. It was a special breed and a gift from a prince of Egypt. Every night it was heard making strange noise around the village. Some years later that woman who was almost burnt for witchcraft became a respected member of community of nuns. She spent most of her days and nights in prayer. She prayed and fasted. She asked god to forgive the men who labeled her a witch.

She was labeled because she would not cheat on her husband with a man of higher social standing. Her sister had suffered a similar fate before her. She was declared mad by a head doctor. After that whatever they did with her no one knew.

The new world was magical. It held a salvation she did not know existed. She could not thank the almighty enough when she prayed. When she faced the altar, she could only thank god for the blessings of the new world.

Zit and his parents were not very fortunate enough. Their dreams of escaped never materialized. His father made several attempts, but was not really capable to putting his family on a boat or ship leaving for the new world. They finally gave up. They stayed and worked for the king for bread and shelter. They were born into that system. They lived with it. They worked the land for the king.

CHAPTER
≈12≈

Ada and Ulu came into the living room as their mother was going into the kitchen to fix a pot of soup. The little boy sat beside the older man. He was happy. They were becoming more comfortable with him. He would love and care for them.

Mr. Stone noticed a band on the right wrist of the little boy. He wondered why his mother didn't remove that. She removed everything they had on when she gave them their first bath in his house. He gave them some fresh cloth to wear. Why did she leave that? It was then that he took a closer look at the band. He saw a time and tradition older than the fellow that had it on. It was a royal bead. It was Ulu's bound with his great grandmother.

Ngozika told him about the bead. It was from his great grandmother. She had prophesied he would be born. She kept it and waited. She waited and on her dying bed she handed it over to her granddaughter. "Give it to my mother's womb. He will come. Let him keep it." She said. It was to be given to that kid whenever he came.

A few years later that child was eventually born. On his seventh day, his mother slipped the bead onto his wrist. He quickly got used to it. And like an adult he often admired it. He wore the gift from his great grandmother faithfully. They shared a bound that came to mature as he grew up. He came to love a mother he did not know. He had faith in the beads, as in the words of the woman who had handed it down to him. Those words were first spoken to him on the day he got those beads. On his seventh day on earth, Ngozika went round the tree where his son's umbilical cord was buried seven times. Seven times she repeated those words. They were words of wisdom. They became dreams. And he would pursue them. When he played hide and seek with the other kids, it became his magic wand.

Though Mr. Stone always looked like a contented man, those moments, that reminded him of family made him feel like a child. He missed the childhood he never enjoyed. He had everything money could buy. But he felt that emptiness all his life. He had money in several bank accounts. He still had a large chunk of his money in his stone house. He had money he was no longer interested in making the way he has made in the past. And he was not interested in telling anyone about it. He had no childhood to remember.

Mr. Stone has not in all of his life seen himself trust anyone. But he felt different with this woman from a war torn country. A woman whose life he just pulled from the teeth of death. He has been with several women. It was only a few of them that he has been able to stay with, without constantly having to look over his shoulders. He feared that the women were all after his wealth. Whenever he met a woman he feared he was being set up. He feared people from his past, friends and enemies alike. But there was Ngozika, a woman who could fit into his game hunting life style. She does not seem like one who would bother about his wealth. Or where the bulk of the money he spent came from. To him she did not ask too much questions. That was the life he wanted, it was the life he led.

Ngozika's story of survival, part of which he witnessed was compelling. His interaction with them, led to him building an imaginary world for the four of them. He was happy. And they seemed happy and growing healthy. He wanted it to remain that way.

CHAPTER
≈13≈

The children were running around the house, playing outside. A neighbor's dog was playing with a squirrel on a short tree. The little boy, who was throwing stones at the bird on the wall stopped. He started watching the dog and squirrel.

He missed his dog. His dog was playing outside during the raid on their compound. His sister was singing to the bird. Mr. Stone who had been watching from the window was captivated by the scene outside. He came out and joined them. He tried to hum the song that the little girl was singing. The little boy dropped his stones. They all began to sing.

"Nwa-nnunu no na osisi, na elu osisi, kwerem ukwe.
Nwa-nnunu no na elu osisi, na osisi, kwerem ukwe
Little bird on the tree, on the tree, sing a song for me
Little bird on the tree, on the tree, sing a song for me"

They sang the chorus over and over again. The little bird perched from branch to branch on the tree picking on the flowers. It seemed to be enjoying the song. Mr. Stone lost himself in the joy of childhood again. He was delighted, learning a new song, a new language and life again. He wanted to be as carefree as the bird on the tree and the children singing the song.

CHAPTER
≈14≈

Though Ulu was still a child, the world his mother was choosing was not one he thought he would fit in very well into. And he was not aware of, nor cared about the imaginary one that Mr. Stone had built.

He had a free spirit. As much as he did not like the war he did not see Mr. Stone's place as the escape he wanted. He did not fancy the way Mr. Stone stared at his mother at times. There were days when he would sneak out of the house, to listen to the sounds of gunfights coming from a distance. In his mind, it was his war that was being fought. He would throw pebbles into the lake. He wished they hit the enemies. He threw in sticks and smiled as they floated on the water. He was intrigued by it. He watched the lake and thought of distant places.

The war had continued. When Mr. Stone went to town from his border home he get newspapers and magazines talking about the gains and losses in the war. He often came back and found Ngozika glued to the radio listening to the war stories. She prayed in her mind. She prayed that the ghost of the dead of the land found peace.

Her prayers and thoughts were mostly wandering. Often she recalled the faces of friends and people she knew. She was sure they did not make it out. She knew of the stories of people getting help. They were on the other part of the country. It was not her people. If her people were getting any help, she and her two children would long be dead before anyone reached them. Her town was destroyed beyond imagination. And the vultures even feared to come near it. There was nothing actually to attract the vultures – people were burnt beyond the reach of any scavenger. Those who survived died gradual deaths. It was from that death that she resurrected.

Mr. Stone helped her and her children understand the war. And the reason for which he says, "Wars solve no problems." She read the newspapers and magazine. Listening to the radio one day, she had the urge to go. She wanted to go away. She wanted to go to the people in need at the battlefields. She felt she could nurse the wounded in the war. But looking at her children, she appreciated the safety of Mr. Stone's walls. She leaned back. Her shadows cast on the wall. It was shadow on the space of beauty and peace. In the distances, where her soul calls her, hunger stretched its claws like those of a crab. It lured little boys and girls with no crimes to pay for, to eternal sleep.

Ngozika wanted to go. Her people had been pushed to the wall. It was natural for one pushed to the wall to kick, to cry or fight. They were fighting in the fields. In her case she stood there looking at her own shadow on the wall. She did not kick or cry. But many times her eyes turned red and she only shook her head. The thoughts of those children in the next room outweighed.

The land was wasted, and so were her people. Weeks before the war a man met his wife in the garden where trees, leaves and flowers spoke of the beauty of nature. They played with the Lilies of the valley, rowed on beautiful patches of the earth in the garden. It was beautiful, it was scenic. It shone of love. They ran around like a people without worry. They were in love. They fell on the grasses, row over each other until they consummated their relationship.

Months later a beautiful girl was born. They called her names that spoke of the beauty of her birth place. She was beautiful. She carried an aura of peace and innocence about her.

Such was the product of a field that today is littered with bones, corpses and the dying. The beauty nurtured by nature, man and the woman is today faced with overnight destruction. Her thoughts raced. But she consoled herself, "Life is a web. It is a continuing cycle of lives, needs and consumption, struggles and regeneration, an unending web. Once in a while fate weakens the visible and invisible hands that have tilted its balance. One man alone could be the only agent needed to reset the whole network." She hoped that, that salvation would eventual come to free her people.

CHAPTER
≈15≈

The war went on, and destruction continued in the bushes and fields. Men were fighting to defend their dignity. There were nothing more to defend. The homes were empty. The towns were only filled with ghosts. But towns and men have risen from ashes of wars, and someone has to tell the tale. A man has to embrace the rhythm of life.

Omenka was a lucky and gifted man. He was in the battlefield. He remembered the lessons from his father. His father told him as a young man to "choose his battles well, never fight a man who has nothing to lose." About battles he was not sure of winning he said, "Never underestimate yourself. If all fails let it be the tale of the tortoise and the lion, 'here let it be known that two giants fought.' And above all my son never be your own victim."

His mind was on those words. He understood the drum beats of the wars and loyalty in friendship. It was loyalty, love and patriotic spirit that have moved him to take arms.

Omenka did not look back. He placed his steps with great care. When he got to where his friend was, he held him and cried. They were many men, but few soldiers on their side. Those other side overpowered them with superior and sophisticated weapons. They kept them retreating. The battle was heavier by the minutes and so were the causalities. The remaining men were exhausted as was their weapons.

Ahamefula; Oke Oji, the Great Iroko, their leader, who had commanded and encouraged the men was filled with fear. He told them to run for their lives. There was no safe place in that field. He fired his last rounds as he ran with Omenka. But they were hit by a forceful return fire. Within a few seconds Omenka saw many dead than he has seen his entire life. His friend was down. He stopped, watched his Aham. He tried to calm him down. But the pain was enormous. Tom Omenka lifted Ahamefula Ejikeme. And puts him on his shoulders. Blood was dripping all over him. He was his best friend.

The enemies were advancing. He ran as fast as his legs could carry him with the load on his back and the blood covering his face. He looked back. And knew he would not make it out of there alive. But he continued, turning his head and looking back. Again he compared the speed of his movement to those of the advancing enemy soldiers. His friend became aware of the danger to the two of them. He wouldn't make it. He was destroyed by the bullets. Aham asked to be put down.

"The great tree has fallen." He tried to mumble.

They both knew it was a painful decision. He puts him down and ran. He went back to him, tried to pick him up. His eyes spoke of the fear in his heart. But he urged him to go, told him to be strong. But he knew that that was not the solution. He was almost dead. He could not leave him there. They both knew that. There was no help in sight. Tom Omenka was looking in all directions. He hoped something would happen and that help would come. But he was alone with Ahamefula Ejikeme.

He wanted something to relief him of the task that he was about to face. Eme knew there was no time. He cried and asked his friend not to leave him. He did not want be captured nor die in the hands of the enemies. To Omenka the moment he feared most had come. He had no options. His friend has made the final call. He was duty bound to oblige. He was a strong man, bullet ridden. But his head hadn't touched the ground. Fear, anger and frustration griped Tom Omenka. He had no time.

He pulled out his gun, said a prayer.

It happened. Tears filled his eyes. But he could not cry. The man lying there was his friend and leader, what would he tell his people? He pulled out his machete.

As he did it flashed through his mind. Several weeks before, different sides in the conflict enjoyed a ceasefire. It was a weekend in which they partied. The troops shared drinks, cigarettes and other goodies. The beverages showed the sources of supports for the different warring groups. Throughout the weekend it was a feeling of comradeship. The killings were the last things they wanted to resume. Though to some in the battle, it was like any other job, they got paid to kill. It was their job. Some had joined the army for one insatiable desire. It was a thirst for blood and to kill. After years of practice, they knew if there was one place where their desire would both be glorified and honored, it was the Army. They enlisted. It was after that weekend that some of the fighters understood for the first time why they were fighting. It was their first opportunity and possibility to question some of those reasons.

Omenka came home a hero. He stood and watched. He watched his friend was being given full burial rites. The rituals at burial were those of a hero. It was like watching men cause the earth to quake. Clouds came and the dead spoke.

The mourners were more or less jubilating. They cut down branches of trees, and trunks of banana plants waving palm leaves. Some climbed palm trees and made sure all the palms fronts pointing to the sky, bowed low to the force of the earth. By the time they came down all the fronts were pointing downwards. The people danced around the village. They clang their swords, singing songs of the brave warrior. It was the war dance.

The Ese-Elu was being played at the family compound. It was the symbol of the male achievement. A great male was being sent to join the spirit of the ancestors. Gunshots were fired into the air. It was to clear the way for the one coming. He was great. The people were engulfed in the ceremonies. One only wonders if he was their sole loss in the war. No, but the living celebrated the dead. And the dead they hope prepared a place for them in the land of their ancestors. The land of the departed was one place they would all go to one day. The rite of passage was accorded men and women, and more so, if seen as great and heroic. Above all it was a time when the bodies of great men and heroes disappeared in battle fields.

As the Ese played, men lined up brandishing their guns, swords and machetes. They danced in a long queue. The oldest among the close relatives led the group of mourners. He takes the first turn to recount the great deeds of the man being buried. The man's son did not make it home from the war. So he could not be the next in line. Other relatives went on to eulogize the dead. They danced and responded to the questions posed by the leader of the drummers. Through the small lines of accompanying assorted musical instruments the talking drum posed audible questions. Every man on the line listened carefully as not to miss the question that was being asked.

CHAPTER
≈16≈

Wind of the news had to gotten out of the town. Men spoke about the death of a leader. Heaven opened its gates and the rain poured down. There were thunderbolts. Newspapers and magazines carried the story, he was a great leader.

The news said the young ojukwu, the Moses of his people was in attendance. But was out of public view. Ojukwu was a born a leader. His people would rally around him. Eme was one of his great men. He was their Moses. He was their strength. The war was a burden he took graciously. With fine officers like Eme, he knew it was a duty. He went from the seat of a regional governor to the leader a young struggling new nation. As the military band and war songs played on radio, he his voice was courage.

Ngozika read about the burial. She hailed the dead man, the leader and her people. "May the great sounds of the Uko accompany this soul when it departs this earth" Ngozika wished. The Uko - the female version of the Ese would be played for great women. She has heard her grandmother talk and sing about the great feminine elegy. It was music and dance that celebrated the lives of women of great accomplishment. She heard her sing songs about it and its praise. She replayed those songs in her mind.

One day she sang the song and the antelope appeared. Her eyes reflected a bright light. Then she fell into a trance. She uttered the words that came forth in her mouth:

"From the hilltops I look down,
Seeing the plane lands and valleys,
Through the length and breadth of this earth,
They ask.
How long are the tunnels?
We know, deep down daylight fades.
A walk from where we came,
Through the hunters' path,
To where Aladimma holds on mountain tops,
Masked spirits alternate fate on hills
and seats of the divine.
In distant and nearby clans,
The Epke dance draws the long masquerade to dance.
From the savannah and beyond the sea.
Music from the cloud
Here we have seen,
These dance steps we see again, rhythms of fire.

ARE YOU GOD OR HIS MAILMAN

Long nights spent looking into the night,
Mirroring dark horizons
We look into the Calabash,
The water reflects flat lands and valleys,
Mile and miles away.
But who beats the Uko that we hear?
Who leads the women's procession?
What protest match is that on the path?
A dirge, voices go high!
Then we hear them submerged
In the sound of the great Uko.
Like a strange symphonies, from far away, they ask.
Who is she in the moon
Bright and battle ready
The forest bears witness to the tunes
Footsteps and falls, sounds in harmony.
It is not the Ikoro, of a quiet night.
Eyes and ears wide open,
New feet and dancers we train fit for the dance.
In accurate steps for every moon and age.
A line of new dancers bears the eagles' feather sky high
Following a procession-singing farewell
And in echoes and re-echoes of the sounds,

The hills and the caves resound

In echoes of their Gods."

Ngozika sang and danced. Her steps moved like those of a riotous goddess as she danced. For the first time she thought of herself as something other than a beautiful woman. She herself had seen the dead hero. She felt a sense of self, history and linage. She felt great and beautiful. She had become a voice. She told herself when she woke up.

Ngozika wished the men and women will celebrate her life and death as she saw them celebrate. She said her death ought to be celebrated with the music and dances of jubilation not of sorrow.

Again she stood up and started to dance. "It is a dance of life, a gift of the living to the dead, mother earth receive your daughter," she said.

Life came from the earth and there it goes to after its earthly stay. It was proper it went with the best of the moods provided by the living. Ngozika spread her arms and began to shake her hips and legs. Everything on her body was shaking to the rhythms of an unseen singer and drummers. Underneath her the earth shook. Her breasts shook with joy as her face brightened up. She was addicted to the sound playing in her head, to the songs her grandmother sang.

It is a life full of service and glory. It was not the sufferings of the war. The war could not bring that out nor take away. Her children watched her. She was ecstatic to be distracted. Her ecstasy was taking her to a higher ground, though she was celebrating the earth. She lifted her legs one after the other and did again. In a flash, that moment seemed like a repeat of the rhythm and match of the first soldiers she saw leave for war. She lifted her legs and jumped to the music. The music, whose sounds were those of short guns being fired on the other side of the border.

She was happy that she was alive.

Ngozika had seen enough death and dead bodies devoured by vultures. For the Ese to mean much. She had seen them pick the eyes out first and it was enough to make her forget those dreams of hers. Actually they were her grandmother's not hers. But dreams of greatness can be infectious.

She could not help but think of the great things and others that her grandmother told her about. Her grandmother had told her of a woman. She would return to the land of her great ancestors after a hundred years of sojourn and power tussle with men and women, friends and enemies. She heard she would return amidst joy and jubilation to a home she built for herself and her daughters. She would return to show them the act of womanhood.

Ngozika – her thoughts kept drifting and drifting as she watched "how could a great woman's return and her passage not be celebrated with the Ese?" she asked no one in particular. But she wished and inquired more about the great woman from her grandmother. Who she was and when she would come and where.

The room was electric again. She was celebrating. She was celebrating her own death, she said, life was good.

CHAPTER
≈17≈

Ngozika had seen the last batch of enemy soldiers who came to crush their rebellion. It was a rebellion. That was what they called it.

But if only they knew the town and its history, they may have used better terms. If they knew, her people were fighting men. They did not know. Those whose homes they destroyed were a people who despite the flow of the River Niger and strangers had reminded and lived in luxury. They protected themselves over five thousand years. They were a people who lived in style, when they and the rest of the world were yet unborn. They did not know those were among the great voices heard in the past. The marauders did not know, her people kept the tellers of the tales of great men; of the Songhai, Mali and neighboring Empires.

Her people were men who had vowed to defend their people with their lives. Men who had promised blood to make sure their women and children had a future. Now a subdued people, all they wanted was to be left to live in peace in their land. They wanted be treated as humans. They just wanted to live as a people with the rights to a fair share of the blessings of the almighty in that land. They simply wanted to do their business and practice their religion in peace.

The land of her people was a blessing. Their continually being put in margins was no longer acceptable. The men from various parts of the town came out armed and ready to train themselves. They made their own weapons, guns, grenades, launchers and rockets. They had their covenants. It was a blood covenant like they always did when matters of such grave nature came up. They were not going back on their words. They would fight to the last man even if it meant fighting with the swords.

And their swords were no cheap swords. Their local blacksmiths made one of the best in the world. They made them out of bitterness, pain, redness of blood and fire. They fueled flames of their fire with the bones of their departed. The earth's best was to strengthen them in wars. And it would defend them against the unexpected. The ghost of their dead cared for them. They cared for their future, their women's and their children's. The sword was their symbol, they came after warriors who carried arrows. Ngozika continued. She listened to the sound from a distant land.

Her people suffered. They suffered defeats and causalities. They got back again. The people found ways around. It was in that resolve that the declaration of the Ahamefula burial rites was established. It found meaning. It was a burial and living memorial for the fallen heroes. Its performance at different fronts took a new turn. The fallen were all engraved in the hearts of their people. Their sacrifice was for the living. They blessed and praised their dead. The living praised the ancestors.

Ojukwu was shaken. But his people were strong because of him. He was strong because of them. In a war it was difficult to trust. Yet trust was everything. At Mount Sinai Moses got the law for his people. At Aharia, Emeka Ojukwu read and reaffirmed the codes and the declaration of Biafra. It marked the anniversary of the war. In the new spirit of the declaration, the Mbaise people opened their arms to new brothers and sisters. The heartland welcomed other Ndigbo fleeing, hard hit parts of Igbo land. They took them in and shared what little they had with them. Munaonye- the only son, Ibekus, Achebes found new homes. The obasis' held their doors wide open. The Remembers, the Warriors, the Healers, the Teachers were to live and practice the words of the declaration to the letter. The guest families and their host grew together. For years their children did not know the difference. They enjoyed bonds of friendship and legacies of brotherhood. It endured. When they went home they sent them their priests and teachers.

"The remnants saved by grace, multiplied by grace, like the stars of above." That was the way one of those sons was to describe it in later years. Ngozika knew her, their enemies never did.

CHAPTER
≈18≈

Huge smokes were going up- straight into the sky. Over the fire burning outside some men burnt off the wool of a ram. They prepared and cooked it. As the rites continued the men agreed the war had to be fought.

A dog had been killed. Its blood had softened the earth. For thousands of years their people carried out that sacrifice. A dog was sought for and killed for the head of its eyes, as it was called. It sought to connect the spiritual essence of the dog's retina to the worlds it inhabited. The dead man was able to see the living and the dead as he journeyed. The dog belonged to both worlds. That sacrifice has traveled through time. It has gone places, from the head of the black dog carved on both ends of the canoes and ships of those going through the River Niger to those traveling the Nile Valley and to the new worlds of the saints of travelers.

The men counted their loss and gain. The death of the great men was a big loss to them. Those were men who brought them respect.

Inside the compound the Ese continued to play, men and women danced. It was Nwaoge, the child of time, who now led the dance procession. He was of the house of the honey merchant and the tall beautiful black woman Nwanyi-aka. A woman who when young men came for her, she sought the will of Obasi The Mighty One Above whose clothing touches the entire earth. She asked to be shown the one. The Mighty One answered, "My daughter you have the answer you seek in your heart." She had been given a sign.

The maiden called out to her father, "Father, who knows the heart?" She asked. "Nwanyi-aka, my daughter, he answered. 'On the right day the sun will rise at the right time. On that day the earth will bear witness."

That day came. Her parents accepted wine and gave their daughter away to her husband. Then the heavens opened up. And there came a down pour. "This is showers of blessings" they all agreed. The streets became flooded. The bride was lifted shoulder high by her proud brother in laws from her father's compound to her husband's.

In the morning the air was fresh. The dusts had disappeared. The earth was fertile. Everyone bore witness to it. The leaves on trees, the grasses were green. The animals and birds of the air had a new song to the glory of the One Above. The man who was filled with life has seen his joy complete. He was overcome by a sense of fulfillment. He called her, "Love." A house blessed forever with the gift of life, love and voice. "He is a product of that house. A son of the house of love, those beautiful nights and days." The tiny little wooden instruments on the extreme right of the Ese assortments punctuated the introduction.

Nwaoge told of the heroic deeds of their great and beloved brother. Nwaoge was a light complexioned man, average height and slender with the voice of a warrior. He was a good dancer and singer. They said though he never fought in a war, his voice revived dead warriors in battlefields. When he spoke his words came out in high and low pitches adding meaning to every sound that came out of his mouth. His words could heal or kill thousands of miles away, while the healers and warriors did men within their arms reach.

He chose his words carefully. "I stand here not for love of words and the excitement of their sounds. I stand because it is a duty. Our brother has done his. Let us honor him. Let these words and songs we hear honor him, let them flow. Let the earth echo them. Let them flow like a never drying river to the ends of the earth. Let the winds and the mountains listen. Let the hills and valleys echo. Let the forest and the sea roar them. Oh let the earth hear us. Let the heavens hear us. Let our cries come the ears of men." He paused.

The crowd had gathered around him. The men and women outside the compound were now inside. They joined the procession. He continued.

"Our beloved brother on his way to our ancestors will no doubt receive a warm welcome. He has done us proud since the day he was born. He stood up to the powers and the colonial lords with all strength in him till this day." Nwaoge continued.

He enumerated the deeds of the man whose name they celebrated. Though some parts of his dissembled body were somewhere they did not know. He went on to speak about the relationship of Nigeria and their British friends. He called it a one sided relationship.

The relationship was good. Everything was good and fine as long as our British friends in power and boards of multinational corporations received their gift from our lands and sweats of our people. "Our beloved told this country the truth, same ones treating us as their boys today, have never tired of answering master to those who milked the land dry, my brothers." Nwaoge announced with the tone of a man about to make an important announcement.

"That man there was the only man who saw this and said no, he said no, we cannot take it. He said the colonial powers enjoyed receiving the gift of a bride moving to her husband's home continually in all her dealings with the country. It was a relationship of a bride and the groom, he said. The groom waited and kept the best of whatever came from the bride."

He was still dancing as the composition from the Ese played. Nwaoge spoke of the events that led to their gathering that day. He described the country's independence as events that took place as the bride and groom decided to go their separate ways. "After the British took the apparatus of power and gave them to the weapon carrying men of the hills of the north, it was Eme, Ejikeme Ahamefula that morning, before our mourning who sued for peace. For the land we live in have been raped, let us make peace with the mother of the earth, those who do not know us rejoice at their creation of maps and false borders. They have left us to die fighting, they have left us, the lower part of the Niger pacifiers." He said.

He wanted to sing as he recounted. But the Ese which provided guides had given him liberty to recount. Eme was a great man indeed. The usual nine to ten questions protocol was broken. Nwaoge told an epic tale of the man. And the Ese flowed with his tale without questions. The procession danced.

He said it was loyalty and friendship that the two shared that worsened the war. Their friends in parliaments overseas refused to recognize the suffering of men, women and children in a place they claimed to protect. "He called them to come that it was time for their protection. They would not come." He said. They turned their back to those suffering. Like they did not know the genesis of it or were unaware it would happen. Women and children called for protection from death and malnutrition and the world paid no heed.

" Ejikeme called no one listened. He went to the street saw death and could not bear it any longer."

Ekeneme Otipko staggered in. Friends called him "klem the drunken police officer." Attempting his clownish dance moves that had become popular. The speaker paused. The drunk waved his index finger in the air. Cleared his throat. "They robbed Peter to pay Paul before they killed Christ. Ever after, Sam and Ben have robbed Nwankwo to settle themselves." The whole crowd laughed. He was funny as well as a national embarrassment. He knew that.

"My friends have chosen funny over national. You know. It is what they pay for. Another name for those guys in the presidency, legislature even the Judiciary is national embarrassment. I am only an officer on duty." Almost falling to the ground Klem staggered to the corner and sat down. His bottle of Star larger beer tightly clutched with his armpit.

Nwaoge whose oratory was legendary continued to eulogize the man who suffered, died and was brought back for his friends and clan from the battlefield.

Tom Omenka took in everything, he was a tired man. He had done his own part. The part that circumstances has thrown onto him. The power of situations, sometimes it held men hostage. The good and the bad in the human, under certain circumstances tell that the human mind is not totally at liberty to act of its own free will. The cannibal remains a savage from the eyes watching miles away. But put in the same hole he does far worst. He began to look at himself, the war his friend has sacrificed himself in, his role and the role of those they fought against.

The piece of skull was receiving all the praises and the full rite of passage accorded a whole. It was until months ago a vibrant and powerful voice among the nation. He hated the thought that the war was being fought because of the misunderstandings. He expected men with reason, could sit down, discuss and settle. He hated the fact that people turned a blind eyes to the issues. He felt they were simple to understand, if the nations were to co-habit as one. Even that name was ridiculous. He thought to himself. A man and a woman involved in an adulterous act giving a name to a new born was a taboo. What more, give a name to a nation? It questioned the legitimacy of the baby. Nwaoge could not understand it. It beats him. He hated most of all that his great friend who had put in a lot of his time and energy building bridges and trying to understand those little issues had to pay the ultimate price.

Nwaoge was still dancing to the Ese, praising the great deeds of his departed friend when a thunderous lightening shook the gathering. Men yelled, "The departing had encountered the living." Their message to the ancestor had been received. The clouds changed and everywhere was beginning to turn dark. The music and chanting was also taking a louder form. Everyone was uncertain if it was going to rain or not. But they seemed not to be bothered. The women began to whisper to themselves. The men conversed among themselves and someone went up to the music stand. The musician relayed a message. They were to continue, the cloud was a good omen. It was approved. The man whose rite of passage they were performing was truly a great man. And the world knew he was one of its great citizens.

Klem was sure he knew the man talking. The clown walked up to him, took a good look at him. He was sure he was one of the friends at a burial that became known as the "Najia National Burial".

"You are one of them," he shouted, pointing his finger in the air.

It was a tale of three friends at the burial of their friend. The bereaved prepared the body, put him in a coffin. The brother of the late man made space in the coffin. In the space he placed a plate of food. It was rice and nice pieces of meat. One of the friends asked, "my friend, why the food?"

The bereaved man politely answered: "In our culture death is a journey."

The dead man, he explained was embarking on a long journey and would need food on the way. The man who asked the question was move by sympathy. He went and took 50.000 Naira and placed it in coffin beside the plate. "He will need to buy more food when the one he has finish."

The other followed suit, "It is true he would need more when what he has finishes." He said. The friend dropped another 50.000 Naira in the coffin. The third one among the friends seeing this was also touched. He pulled out his wallet and wrote a check of 150.000 Naira. He bent down, placed it in the coffin and took a change of 100.000 Naira.

Despite the solemn mood Klem the drunk would not believe otherwise.

The sound of the music was lowered and everyone listen to Nwaoge speak in a solemn voice. "If the war was to come again they have no choice but to be men," he said. He pointed what the state of affairs in the land has done to their race.

"Some are gone and some would never come back. A man is with no honor when he is on such a trip. Our skins and the blood that flows tie us in our veins. But when we leave on a journey without return the blood dries, our minds and skins tell us whom we are, yet we deny it hiding from ourselves. We are the lost, a people once, kings and queens, and we hold our hat in our hand roaming the streets and kitchens of strangers."

Nwaoge stopped abruptly, looked at is feet and made a few dance steps that brought relief to the solemn faces in the crowd. He said the death of Ahamefula Ejikeme was a symbol. A sign of all that the people are had become and can become. He was a Christ that his land rejected.

He smiled and marveled at what the symbol was capable of. He looked straight, a man in a black clergy collar shirt with a book in his hands. He said he was reminded of a man who suffered greatly, was humiliated and nailed to the cross. On the cross they still made ridicule of him, called him a king, alleging that was his crime. He told his followers who were all hiding by then that he was a king, a son of god. But they knew him, his father was a carpenter. Thus they made him a heavier cross. The cross he said, ever since had become a symbol of an everlasting symbol of strive, victory and kingship. Thousands of years later millions heed a story and the worship of an unknown king whose kingdom they never recognized in his lifetime.

CHAPTER
≈19≈

Ngozika was in a trance. She continued to make her speeches, songs and steps around. A black bird come straight through the window and stopped right in front of her. She was aware of a presence in the room, though she had not seen the bird fly in and stop where it did.

"Those birds do not come into people homes uninvited or without a message." She said.

She feared what terrible message the bird bore. She was sure it was not a good one. She reached out to pick up the bird. But before she did, the bird hops onto her open palms. Her first reaction was to hold the neck of the beast. Look into its shiny eyes as if she was going to force it to speak. It would not speak. She broke its little beak. She was not sure why she did that. Instantly she wished the bird with the raven will fly away. She wished it would not leave a bad message. She wished she hadn't broken its beak.

When her grandmother died it was a hawk. A hawk had landed in front of the family compound. The bird of prey touched ground. It did not go after any chicken or lizard. It rather remained on a spot. It was a sign, the elders immediately read and consulted. They waited for days of busy preparations. It was a sign she did not understand or care about. But the movement of elders, who met time after time to find out what the problem was told her, something was amiss. The visitors and elders consulted to find out what the problem was. It was not entirely strange. They would have been at ease if they had seen a four limbed creature crawl in and stood on the spot where that hawk had landed.

A week later, her grandmother was laid to rest six feet underneath that spot. Neither she nor anyone else knew what happened to the hawk.

Hers was a land that observed many taboos. They did not eat the three-leave yam or the antelope. Like any other, the yam and animal had great myths surrounding them. The antelope was an animal that they have taken their name after. The antelope had its contradictions. It was considered clean, pure, savior, wise, trickster and unclean at the same time. The animal runs swiftly. It is called; the wind, waka about, it heals the spirit of men, it brought them back their youth. In the antelope the old and the new merged.

A goat sighted with the leaves of the three leave yam in its mouth would be instant news. It was the same with a dog being sighted challenging the green snake to a dual, or a python around the water pot of it host. However a message sent with an antelope would have been easier to understand. It would be Mother Nature's time check. Her favored daughters will know it was a call to come home. But the after tossing cowries three times on the earth, the diviner had their answers for them.

Ngozika helped the black bird out of the window. She hoped it would fly away. Once outside it plunged head first. Then it lowed itself and flapped its wings twice.

"You don't know what it means to be free, because freedom is what you have taken for granted." A voice said from a distance.

The raven joined other birds. They spread their wings. One could see the air of freedom. They let themselves fly and drop at the pressure of the air. Then soar again into the empty space. They filled the void with their wings and might. They too were of the earths' bright and beautiful.

Ngozika was still in a trance when Sylvester Stone entered the house. He did not disturb her. He went into the kitchen and fed her kids. He prepared them for bed. They no longer looked malnourished. They were happy in their new home. After getting them to sleep, he came back to the living room. She looked exhausted but attractive in a way he had never seen a woman before. She walked pass him on the couch and his eyes could not resist following the movement and rhythm of her body. She came back and sat on the couch opposite Mr. Stone. His eyes rested her bosom. She did not mind. She reminded herself of the peace she has experienced. She told him, of the end of the wars and of a peaceful future. She told him of her visions.

As Mr. Stone listened he began to wonder what she was talking about. He was just coming from the town. The news of the war was still everywhere. His car radio just gave news of the great assaults on some villages near where her people moved the new headquarters of their government. He had secretly wished the campaign for Lagos was successful. It would have ended the war, he had hoped. He was not in the mood to talk war. He almost told her that, but then she said it was a vision. "I have seen the black bird and the hawk." Ngozika explained.

Mr. Stone was taking in a lot of details. She was dangerously beautiful. He had a great desire for her that moment. He was salivating like a kid waiting for his mother to dish his favorite food from the steaming pot of soup on a cold harmattan day. Ngozika continued to talk about the vision, about peace and a time when her people will live in unity. She spoke of a strong economy where every part of the land produced what they were known for the common good of her people. She spoke of export and a central monetary and banking system and a unified military in West Africa. She spoke of a unified front in the search for cure for diseases and vaccine for malaria.

She spoke of elections in a democratic way that made the trance seem more like a number of legislations passed in a single day.

She was happy and that was what Mr. Stone wished for her. Her beauty set the room aglow. Her dark radiant skin made Mr. Stone's body temperature go up. He was unable to speak or to think properly. He mumbled a few words. Then he went over to sit beside her. He held her hand gently. And his eyes began to open to the future she spoke about. Her body yielded like a fertile land ready for the chief crop of the farming season.

That night Ngozika the tall beautiful dark skinned woman and Mr. Stone the light skinned foreigner, who saved her and her children from death had a peaceful consummation of the bodies. It was warm, it was pleasant and above all it was fiercely rare. Neither Ngozika nor Mr. Stone had imagined the world they were in.

That night Tata was heard, she laughed out loud from somewhere, "ha- ha-ha-ha! It is love. It brings the day and night closer."

"It is the marriage of the moon and the sun. It is almost dark. But the ring of fire is to be watched.

I see a lot of success around. I don't see the challenges.

I've chosen to keep the challenges closer. That way I know one day I may be among the successful.

In the heavens there is a ring of fire. It eclipses the world."

From that union they begot a son. He was light skinned, the color of his hair was black and his eyes were brown. At birth his mother prophesized. "He would hold an important position of power in the future of the war torn country." She said at a time the future of the country would depend on him.

She called him, "Azuogu." Mr. Stone called him, "Sylvester, Stone A. Junior."

On the day of his naming ceremony his mother called out the name she had chosen three times, "Azuogu, Azuogu, Azuogu" she declared.

"Enemies and friends alike will fear you. They will as well love and respect you. You are to speak up for the oppressed, speak tough and act tough. But above all be kind and wise in your decisions." Ngozika proclaimed.

CHAPTER
≈20≈

As years went by Azuogu grew into a tall handsome young man. He was bestowed with his mother's gift of vision and father's economic ingenuity. Friends and enemies began to flock around him. Women loved him. They wanted to just hear him speak while dreaming of holding him in their arms and possessing him. He was eloquent. Words from his mouth created images that would never leave their hearts. They melted at the idea of hearing him speak.

"Mama is father's past going to hurt my future?" Stone Jr. was not sure.

His mother never really answered. Ngozika never said a word about the past or the future of the man that she had come to love.

Ngozika; the Mahogany, has learnt to leave the past behind and to follow the future. The future held a promise for her. There was a lot in the past that she would need to forget. They hold her back. Like a river she flows to the future. The past was a stampede. Mr. Stone had at times wanted to explain his past to her. But he always met a frustration. She was a simple woman, "she did not belong to history." She would say.

Sylvester Stone was a man who lived and loved the world. He had seen all there was to see; the good, the bad, the ugly and their phantoms. He had seen poverty, wealth, power and powerlessness. For years he was on Forbes top 100 most richest and powerful people in the world. He did his charity, he did his crime, and he did his time. He has become a changed man.

His crimes were of varying magnitude and influence. He posed legitimate business fronts in many parts of the world, while he dealt in all forms of dirty businesses. In New York he laundered money with the boys on Wall Street. In Germany he manufactured drugs, drugs that never saw the light of the day. In Moscow he was into renewable energy and oil. In West Africa he was into faceless arms deals and oil bunkering. In Tokyo he was an electronics and computer magnet. He was everywhere in the hospitality business. Hotels and restaurants bore his name. In Dubai the most beautiful recreational facilities in the world had his coat of arms. It was there he went when he rallied the Middle East against the west.

In a world filled with hate and anger. Mr. Stone was well aware that the kingdom of heaven and it stories very well depended on those who hold the keys to this present kingdom. Politics of religion was not always his thing. But now and then he pulls a favor or two for friends. In doing so he even saw further and further into the future. He was not a prophet. He saw what made men peaceful and what made them violent.

"But an ordinary king retold the tales of his god in his tongue, if he in the process created more empires, beyond those who called themselves and others barbarians and lognazims…he Stone was capable of some good too" He looked into the void when the thought hits him.

Mr. Stone saw his name etched somewhere on the corner of the holy book as the son of peace. He called meetings there. Kings and princes from the Kingdoms of Arabia and others around the world reasoned with him.

"Peace, be with you! Blessed, are the peace makers." he greeted them.

If in the holy book, a word carried the meaning of peace the way he saw it that would be enough for him. His eyes were not on any kingdoms. "Why do the heathen rage?" he asked himself in private.

In every front Mr. Stone laundered money, evaded taxes, forged fake shipping documents. He moved money around the world without regard for tax laws. They pedaled influence, using their connection to congress to lobby for federal tax breaks. The tax break brought in money supposedly from companies' subsidiaries overseas. The monies came in billions of dollars with little or no taxes on them. They promised to create employments which they never did. They used their money to buy back company shares. They grew their companies and their shares. They paid handsomely into the campaign funds of the politicians.

He delivered arms and weapons where there were prohibitions, men and women into prostitution in the most unimaginable places in the world. He ordered kidnapping of the high and mighty, kings and queens. He killed for the sake of killing, killing his enemies and enemies of his friends. With a stroke of his pen or a phone call he was capable of shaking the foundation of the global economy. He stopped the flow of crude oil to several countries a few times for the fun of it or mere blackmail. And for days he marveled as he watched the Dow Jones industrial average go up and down. He called himself, "The morning star."

Many countries wanted him. The Americans and the Russians wanted him. He was on their list of most wanted for crimes. But he still mingled and found his way around. Before the spotlight beamed on him he aided TV hosts, radio and newspaper journalists run after scam artists and petty criminals all over the world. The cameras were at his beck and call. Always pulling attention away from where it ought to be. He had the best men and women working for him. They were genius, PhD's in accounting, economics, and psychology and in many other fields. Some were poor, broke like a broken calabash that can hold no water before they came aboard.

One of his boys worked for the CIA. Part of his last assignments was in Iraq, Afghanistan, and Pakistan. He was already enjoying civilian life, but was tired of watching boxing championship fights and seeing 007 over and over, when he met the boss. He suited what he wanted. And he as well was hungry for some different adventure, something deep down inside his heart pushed him towards that path. Life was not always a competition, but sitting there, someone was winning. Someone was always winning. But it was not him.

He loved it when he became part of the team.

Before any deal Mr. Stone's boys took days and months to study their victims and clients. He wanted them to reach their clients at their deepest and most superficial of levels. They had detailed and daring plans he handed to them. It was their tools to make billionaires out of millionaires. Mr. Stone has shown them a road map. And in turn it was what they were going to show their clients. The boys will show them the map of the world. It was the places where Mr. Stone their boss has gone to in the Americas, Europe, in China, India, Russia, and Africa and in the oil fields in the Middle East.

"The map of the world is better shown to a man, whom you have made believe he can conquer it, on an island or in the ocean," Mr. Stone told them.

His cliental ranged from men and women who were Fortune 500 CEO'S.

"To the wealthy money and gifts soon became nothing. But give them happiness. It lasts a life time." That too was another make believe that Mr. Stone peddled with the boys.

They lured those clients into bed and new businesses. In their real investments, he taught them to invest like champions. When they invested they took that advice.

"What mattered is not what they got for the quarters. But something you can hold for the rest of life." He told them.

But in a world where time was of essence, they had to wait for the right time. Giving time its due was a principle. Mr. Stone adored it. Anyone close to him understood that. It was the reason some of his boys never met with him in person. It is the reason S.A Stone Jr. did not go to him with some questions.

CHAPTER
≈21≈

When the time was right, one of their last clients Ms. Karen Stone was made to think she was fixing the time. She was the daughter of one of London's richest guys. The old man having made his money concentrating on just a few businesses was now spreading his tentacles.

She was not aware she was being studied. She had flown in from London to Los Angeles the day before. She had a private suite at the Hayat a few meters from the airport. The suite was close to the presidential suite.

Once inside she relaxed. The sweet fragrance from the candle filled the room. The view from the Window was scenic, the trees; a display of nature's wonderful delight. She could afford it. Everything swung in harmonious rhythms to the gentle breeze. The palm tree waved to the beautiful blue sky. It was joyful, the sun was warm. The music was new age.

It was peaceful. The TV and the Radio turned off. She would listen to tomorrow's news, it may be good.

"For now the whole world could wait. The business at hand was what mattered." The phone clicked.

His aging father was relying on her. She was the most ambitious and reliable of his two girls. Though her father was skeptical about her bid to acquire the over two billion dollar media empire, he admired her independent spirit. He could follow her lead. After all he was just a lucky guy who ran in money, a lot of it. He could follow a daughter who at twenty eight had her Bachelor of Science in Marine Engineering and a Master's in Business Administration.

Mr. Stone was happy he was dealing with the right candidate. He dreaded dealing with her father. He was proud of his boys and their capability. But the old man was worse than a fox.

One of Mr. Stone's boys who followed the case was Yari. He had graduated from college in Budapest. He was a specialist when it came to women. He could not but compare one of the women that they dealt with to his mother.

"The closer you get to a woman's laps the closer you get to her money," he said. "They enclosed their money between their laps that is where the key is." Yari proclaimed.

With his own experiences he proved his theory that the heart held the key and the hip was the lock to his team. His understanding gave him an age. As a little boy he watched his mother get up every morning, prepare to go the market.

Every five o'clock, she woke up prepared her food in the cold morning. She would put on her skirt then took her money holder out. She counted the money thoroughly, arranged them in tens, twenties, fifties and one hundreds before putting them back into the money holder. She tied around her hips from behind, allowing the money to rest in the middle in front of laps. She would them put another piece of clothing over it to conceal the money. After that and her meal she was ready to go.

His mother was a wealthy trader. She concealed her money from those she wanted to conceal it from. "The hip was a bank," he would hear his mother say. Other women said it too when they exchange goods or services that were not to be settled immediately with cash. Yari knew that as a fact. And he used it as a skill with the rich and the comfortable. It was the knowledge that he and his colleagues have used to unlock wealth and secrets.

The women they have come to know working with Mr. Stone were women who carried their money in plastic cards and bank accounts. They were women whose cards and purses were always on their hips front or back. They were women who when they dropped the panties on the floor in their homes or in the hotel rooms dropped millions of dollars along. They were women like the girl occupying the suite next to the presidential suite.

"The closer they got to unlock those laps the closer they got to wealth," he said.

"Once unlocked, you could be making those life-changing calls yourselves lying on a bed," Yari noted.

The world has become easier with a telephone call from a room or a swipe of a card millions was transferred. Their business involved a lot of travels. And they did on short notices too. At times they travelled with falsified documents that gave them new names and citizenships.

In a deal he recruited his three cousins. It was usually not something he brought family into like that. Mr. Stone discouraged it. But he had sought the help of Cousin Mike. It was Mike who insisted in bringing the other two. Mike as mean as he looked, his laughter was infectious and more intoxicating than any wine. He could not refuse him. The plot was hatched in London. It involved a network of safe houses and illicit bank accounts around the globe. For four week they globetrotted in private jets from London, the Middle East, Southern Africa, Kosovo to Canada and back to London. It was a successful trip.

One thing Yari also knew well was to never sidetrack the mob boss. Mr. Stone was always in the know. No one dealt him a bad hand and got free from his cold brutal hands. A few times his boss's friends decided what countries to run down. And they did after discussions of the contracts to rebuild them. It was all that was necessary. A war could be declared in any place. It was a strategy from old, modified a little. Mr. Stone had no problems, as long as he and his boys were aware. He was a man whose sitting in on such meetings guaranteed some levels of success. Maintaining defense contracts and the supply of arms were vital.

"There had always been something to gain from war" He would tell his boys.

Those were the words that captivated a young ambitious Nigerian boy. He was selling life insurance to African politicians and black migrants in London. It was the late 60's. He had exceptional talent, reaped the benefit of hard work, drive and opportunity. The hard work of the entire family paid off on him. When he left home, his father told him, "When you dine with the devil, you eat with a long spoon. You even keep your knife handy in case you need it." Those words guided him many days and many nights. The boss had what he wanted. He would dine with him spoon, fork and knife, if he had the opportunity. Months later the boy met Mr. Stone and was introduced into oil brokerage. "Son, the world is your River. It is your stage, swim in it. Dredge it." Mr. Stone told him. True to his words Mr. Stone showed him the ropes and his empire spread across the globe.

Beyond the politics of words, only a few generals knew the true reasons why they went to war in the places they fight. The boots on the ground were the least in the know. Mr. Stone was a man who insisted his boys knew what they did and why they did them. Sometimes it was just pay back as was in his dealing with the fox and his daughter.

When the FBI eventually apprehended Mr. Stone on a cross border trip, he nodded his head and applauded the guy who arrested him. The arresting officer himself put a call to his superior and announced, "We have got the Octopus."

His superior a stern man who barely managed a smile to his wife and only son at home burst out in a loud jubilant laughter. And the whole office instantly came alive like a market place. Before long the story was everywhere in the news. The tabloids said his biggest crime was his American targets. But Mr. Stone's lawyers were all over applying for his bail. Prosecutors were busy piling up charges after charges.

He was a flight risk and there was no judge who would grant him bail.

CHAPTER
≈22≈

Sylvester Stone rested his feet on the wall in his cell, getting used to prison. When he appeared in court for a plea hearing he pleaded not guilty. At the end of the day he was back to his eight by six cell room at the Camp, reading newspapers. His arrest was headline in all major dailies and weeklies.

"This publicity is not good," he said.

Days went by he conferred with his lawyers. He had another plan. In the court the next hearing he changed his plea, to everyone's surprise but his lawyers and close friends. The judge and prosecution hoped at least for a deal that would bring in more people in. But he simply was not entering into any. He was saving everyone's time, he said. Ten days later he was sentenced.

In prison he had friends on both sides. As a federal guest he was treated more lightly. Once there he met with friends with whom he did businesses with many years ago. It was friends caught when he could have been caught. His friends were in position of power on the inside. He would discuss life in prison, old times, play games and read the papers with them. They went for their meals together and shared jokes. They treated him fair. In his cell he counted days and nights, hours, minutes and seconds.

His Somali cellmate often tried to make him relax, when he notices the concentration on his facial muscles. He made him laugh. Karim was a man who believed that at a stage in life, a man ought to give up the act of defending himself against accusations of his own stupidity. He waited as he urged others to, for maybe, someday nature would prove otherwise. Karim took life as it came day after day. After a few months in prison, he began to craft letters to console his young wife. He made jokes about himself. In some he really frightened her.

He wrote, "There are days and nights when no one is able to make the difference between men and women here."

She would not even be able to recognize him, he told her. She worried that prison had turned him into a monster. One early morning he reproduced the conversation he had with her. He posted it on a corner of the wall. When Mr. Stone saw it, he marveled at their passion for life and each other. And though Mr. Stone was not well versed to give lessons on prison life, he felt great sympathy for the couple. Finally he made up his mind to talk to him about it. Karim after listening to Mr. Stone, asked him to read the conversation from bottom to the top. When he did he could not believe what he had just read. Then he asked him if his wife was aware of that.

"It is our little joke, our lives had been interrupted by pain and pleasures several times" he answered. The old man had a good laugh and great relief.

CHAPTER
≈23≈

After a year in prison Mr. Stone was still cool with the guys inside and friends outside. They were working hard on his behalf trying to reach a deal. They waited, they plotted, and they used money and gifts. They used intimidation, blackmail, and above all friendship built over the years.

Finally, somehow a deal was reached. There was a blue print for his freedom. The time line was the eve of the New Year. That New Year would be ushering him into the third year in prison if he does not make it. When he looked at the blue print, he vowed nothing was going to keep him behind those walls beyond that midnight.

In the blue print he was to be moved to an undisclosed location once he was on the outside. He knew that the society was sick. It was not him. He knew what stocks the corporate heads that ran the prisons traded on Wall Street. Remaining there, he was just a number in another cooked up economic abstraction. Two million were already there half of whom did not belong there. He did not belong there. "In fact no one belongs here." Mr. Stone barked when he was angry. He placed a finger on a corner of the map. The first move was west. Then he traced it till it was time to go south. In the blue print Mr. Stone saw the stagnant ponds as well as the fastest flowing rivers in the world.

In the courts prosecutors and former clients still frustrated judges with suits after suits, charges after charges, anytime they felt they had discovered a trail left by Mr. Stone. Arrests were made, those arrested were soon let go. Mr. Stone left no criminal trails that would endanger those who worked for him.

In his second year, when it seemed the news media lost the interest in Mr. Stone, there was still an investigative journalist, who followed every lead and every arrest. His name was Morale. He worked as a freelance for the Los Angeles times. He had a great love for such diggings. He hoped to trace the man's last cent. Whatever it took, he was willing to give.

But Mr. Stone was not an easy man. He anticipated such a time, day and people. One morning he was surprised to find a screaming front page story about him. The large banner read; "The last Treasure of The Mob Boss Discovered." It had a picture of him on the side. After reading the story Mr. Stone raved. He was angered by it. There was no truth in the story and there was no discovery of any treasure. For the first time in a long time, the inmates saw him look like a man with no hope. A phone call from his lawyer saved him from having a heart attack. If there was anything new or true in the story, it was nothing new to the media or the people working on the case on either side. It was filled with speculations, but it sold the papers.

Morale the Journalist was looking for a lead. He was tired of arrests that led to nowhere. He was hoping that someone somewhere knew something. There would be a man in the street who was disaffected with the boss. "After a year there was likely to be such a person," Morale theorized. He was convinced the man was still a billionaire. He was still investigating.

"I will not abandon you." He was not in doubt. But his friend did not know what else to say. And Mr. Stone needed the assurance. Both men valued true friendships. He hung the telephone. The call came in from an Island. Though the line was properly encrypted the prison system had found a way of at least tracing calls to their places of origin.

CHAPTER
≈24≈

Mr. Stone celebrated thanksgiving again in prison, eating turkey with friends, Indians, blacks and whites. Silent night came and prisoners sang in belief that a savior would be born. Mr. Stone was never a churchgoer, his experience was as a child, and he did not believe much in the teachings of the churches. He however believed in God, the love of God and neighbor. He did not however understand the idea of a child pedigree and a virgin birth all taking place in the brutal Middle East. "The politics of the lands and the status of women," he mused has recorded humanities most violent deaths.

But he was in prison and the word savior meant more to him than previously. The thoughts of that little child, that boy who suffered excruciating pain on the cross and died at the prime of his youth began to occupy his mind.

"Kingdoms and kings have passed away. Still people of all shades and color, tones and tongues chanted and bowed before images of him every day of the week." Mr. Stone recalled a preacher tell him once.

Singing when he was in high spirit was not a problem to him. So Mr. Stone sang the silent night, with a tone that his cellmates ridiculed. But he did not mind. As he sang the songs he began to believe. That night was coming in which even if there were no more virgins left anywhere in the world, a savoir was surely coming for him. Faithfully he was waiting. Because that savoir will get him out of prison and back into freedom.

In fact, thought of the idea of a virgin revolted him, when it flashed through his mind as it was. Despite his new found faith he still snapped. Were they not those who served him drinks topless in bars and restaurants? Were they not those who danced naked on tables in every bar?

"They danced and one could see their intestines through their anus. Were they not?" He asked without expecting an answer from anyone. But he loved those girls who worked for tips. He got whatever special additional service he wanted.

"A savoir will come, woman or no woman." He concluded

His anger was partly due to the error, which he associates with the reason responsible for capture. His arrest was due to the miscalculation of his secretary.

"If she had worked on the border security, things would have been different. And I would not be sitting in that hell I'm sitting now." He wanted to curse. But restrained himself.

His anger was visible on his face. He took a deep breath and smiled. He knew that not far within him, he loved and respected women. "They are the heaven on earth. Any one sincere enough can remember, at least, at one point in their lives, whether rich or poor." He managed another smile.

In prison the Negro spirituals the black slaves sang long ago in the plantations made more meaning to him too. He hummed the tones and at times was tempted to sing out. Once he saw himself singing, "Swing low sweet chariot, coming to carry me home."

Time went by fast when he sang. He occupied his mind with redemption and thoughts of the coming night. He sat there like a man in a trance. Suddenly the prison walls seemed like they were moving. His eyes were filled with tears. He was transported back to the last time he attended a church service. He was still a boy then. He eyes zeroed in on the face of the black woman on the altar singing "swing low sweet chariot." He shivered and his whole body was filled with chills.

He sang out louder and the whole prison chorused in unison. For a moment he was transported beyond those prison walls. His mind was free. He was finally free from bondage. He seemed at peace with himself, an unlikely expectation from a man piloting a physical escape from prison. The picture of that little innocent boy whose whole attention was focused on the singer, while the preacher got headache talking about sin and repentance, became real in his head again. Then there was silence, the chorus died down. Mr. Stone looked around, felt himself and was still behind bars. The clock was ticking.

The guy occupying the cell opposite held the bars on his door with both hands. He seemed to have been there all along watching Mr. Stone. He was doing time for kidnaping a kid. He was just a nice guy who let sympathy get the best of him. He told friends. He was walking down the street one evening a nice smart looking beautiful kid was running after him. At first he was scared, he thought she was a ghost. It was already dark. But the kid kept running towards him. He was already approaching a corner of the street. He makes the corner and he heard the kid say something. When the kid got up to where he was, she wore a nice smile.

She asked him "where is my grandpa?"

He told her he has not seen anyone come that way. The kid wanted to engage him in a conversation. She asked him his name. He was taken aback by her courage. He told her it was late that she should go back. Her reply was that she was scared. He offered to walk her back to the corner of the street. When he did she started another conversation. From then he was not sure of what happened. But the next morning he saw that the kid was asleep on his couch. He was worried, he turned on the TV a kid in the neighborhood had been reported missing. It was a case of kidnapping the reporter concluded. That compounded his problem the child in question slept happily. When she woke up she did not seem disturbed. But he was already a criminal, from that point on there was nothing he could do. The kid was just an innocent girl. She seemed from another planet. He had no story that the justice system would understand.

Mr. Stone had no reason to doubt his story or otherwise. He has remained a nice guy since the first time he saw him. That was before he was transferred to the cell next to his. And still he just went about his business. His other neighbors were big names. They still ran their networks from the inside and got all kinds of favor in the inside.

CHAPTER
≈25≈

The prison warden, Mr. Paul Achichov after thirty years in the system was excited about his retirement. He spent a lot of time during his last days there admiring the pictures of past wardens on the prison's administration building. He marked the spot where his photograph will be placed for history. He deserved it, he often told himself. He started his career in the prisons as a young boy. He went to school while he worked there. He worked his way up from a common prison guard, to the administration building, which swore he would not leave for anything.

Mr. Achichov instead of spending time with his family that evening, stole into the prison building. He was working on his hand over note. He has done an impressive work with his career there. He wanted to dot all his i's and cross all his t's. He did not want anything to mess up the reputation he has built. More so, the man coming to take over from him was a man who respected him. But they had their professional differences.

He was thought as being very bureaucratic. Almost all the inmates in the prison knew him. They met him one time or the other. They met him during his rounds with the guards or during their visits to the administration building. Some who had been there long enough remembered him as, "the boy guard who climbed the ladder."

The new warden was not likely to be known by many of the inmates. He was a man given to technology. He would computerize the prison system. According to him, prisoners ought to be identified and traceable wherever they were in the world and at any time. In one of his proposal which was taken from his PhD dissertation, he suggested a chip that could not be removed to be inserted into the body of every prisoner. He suggested that every prison in the country enlists the services of certified physicians to insert the chip. He wanted it in the body of the prisoners from the first day they arrived at the prisons. Chips and Radio-frequency identification was not his only thing. He had more the old warden dreaded like hell.

Human population and growing crime rates scared him. Its great control was his obsession.

Mr. Achichov had his reservations. "Those ideas would revolutionize prison. But they are very dangerous." He wanted his opinion noted, even if at a later time the prison decided to adapt the new systems. "Haven't we come a long way, from burning em on a stake to one shot injection," the warden said.

He was spending part of his holidays, going back to the office to finish works, he already started. Each evening when he got off from work, he passed through the administration hall. Knowingly or unknowingly, he starred at the spot. "The photograph would be hung here. It would be perfect... When I leave the service." Though his family disapproved of his going to the office when no one knew he was. It made him happy to end his day, every day with a look at the wall in the hall.

CHAPTER
≈26≈

New Year's Eve came, as the world was counting down and so was Mr. Stone. The only difference was that while those at Times Square and elsewhere around the world were getting ready to explode the dark night with the fireworks, Mr. Stone on the other hand was to benefit from a blackout. That blackout was going to be followed by a massive computer crash. That crash would affect the whole prison system and several computer systems worldwide. The entire world counted to zero. And so did Mr. Stone. They popped champagne, he did not. His heart was anxiously beating.

Once on the outside no time was wasted. He moved, his friends moved. Time was not their friend till they could move to safety. But once he was seated behind an Escalade, he felt like a mob boss again. Only that this time he was not the architect of that blue print. He had quietly followed instructions. He obliged, prison teaches patience and he was a fast learner. His identity would do him no good. He had to make a few changes. He obliged again.

A few hours later Mr. Stone was introduced to a young handsome cosmetic surgeon. He was one of the best in the country, he was told. His training from high school through college was financed by a group of Italian mobs who required his services often. He went into a room set up for that purpose with Mr. Stone. It took only some hours and Mr. Stone's appearance changed.

They seemed to be moving fast. But he was still in the same city and building since leaving the jailhouse. Money was moved. But again he was instructed not to bother with finances. In due time he would get his money where he wanted it. He was instructed not to worry how money was spent unless he wanted to leave trails. Leaving a trail was one thing he did not want to do. The money moving at the time were funds used for the services that they saw necessary to his safety. The money they had paid for those services and other things that were procured in the last twenty-four hours. In a few minutes his journey was to start again. He had to relax and get as much rest as he could get.

He tried to relax, practicing what he has learnt in prison as the most efficient ways of relaxation for him. Before long he fell asleep. In his sleep he woke up a new person. A strange face and in a strange land. He saw himself following games in the Savanna.

When he woke up from his sleep, Mr. Stone was airlifted by Flex Jet. It was a charter that would make a few detours before an actual exit. It would come back, before Mr. Stone would board another that would then take him closer to the savanna. From there he did not know what his means of transportation would be. But everything seems to have been carefully taken care of.

When he landed somewhere in the Caribbean, a friend came out and met with him. He assured him there was nothing to worry about.

A few weeks later Mr. Sylvester Stone knew where his final destination was. He would be housed in a stone house, on a peninsula. The house was fixed with secure communications lines.

The peninsula, which seems abandoned for fears. It was chosen for some many reasons. The most traffic there was few men and women who traded in fish. It was on the border of Cameroon and Nigeria. The climate made Mr. Stone feel it was certainly a place to live a quiet life.

That piece of land became a center of a dispute several years after his arrival.

CHAPTER
≈27≈

Tata was a witness. The peninsula was strategic to the war. A land with a large deposit of yet-to be drilled crude oil and other minerals. It was in the session of the country's breakaway republic. The federal government feared the power and wealth in the region. It kept breaking the region up by creating states. The place and people still found common bonds. The peninsula was better a bargaining chip. It was used to negotiate with the Cameroons. It would cut down the growing power of the rebellion. To a great extent that tactic succeeded. The breakaway republic all of a sudden found their friend on a strategic position become hostile. It was a stampede.

Ahamefula Ejikeme; Oke Oji, the Great Iroko was gone and so were the souls of their people wondering in strange lands, driven out by the first flood, the slave ships, colonial occupations, the wars, hunger and starvation that became their punishment. They were a people in transit, they became a wandering people.

It was a sin that souls no longer communed. But the world was full of goings and comings. Some were leaving while some were coming. It was how the peninsula became home to the foreigner. There was birth and there was death. It was the way of life.

CHAPTER
≈28≈

Ngozika had started home schooling Ulu and Ada. Mr. Stone encouraged her to enroll them in the nearby elementary school. "It would help them socialize with kids their age" Mr. Stone told the woman.

As the new school year began they started going to school on the peninsula. They adjusted easily. They were like other kids in the school. Though the war had made them grow up quicker. Their experience escaping the war was years beyond anything in the imagination of their class mates. The two were bright and liked going to school there. They made friends with other kids easily.

Ada was a floater. She got along very well with everyone. She wasted no time in introducing her friends to her brother. She was excited about her stepbrother. She told her friends about him. There were days when Ada did not want to go to school. She wanted to babysit her brother. Her mother allowed her. Ngozika wanted her children to grow up as normal kids. Ada did that till her stepbrother was enrolled in the same school with them.

In school Ada befriended a girl whose family was French speaking. Her name was Dakar Amor. Their friendship encouraged her to take a big interest in learning the language. At the first opportunity she had she registered for the class. As for Ulu he made friends with the big boys in his class. He was little and often needed their protection.

They all walked home from school together. On their way back from school when they were not playing street soccer they were fighting. Ulu liked to play a lot. But even as Ulu played his grades were high.

He had a passion for the wise as little child. In those days he played around with his friends anywhere. The moment he saw Gboh-gboh-gboh the game would cease. It was time to seek the wisdom from the old man who has got it on the street. Gboh-gboh-gboh was their nick name for George. He was a very old man. The hairs on his head were all gray. The children called him the oldest man in the town. He certainly was the oldest active and most liked man around. He and his family were one of the oldest residences of the peninsula. The kids said he was a hundred and something years old. Every morning he walked from his house to his son's bar. It was a regular exercise. People said he did it for his body and brain. He went to the bar, sat there most of the day and told stories.

As kids they did not always have the opportunity to hear him in the bar, so they usually ambushed him. On his way home every day they made him sing or answer their many questions. Ulu and the kids capped their demands by asking him to make them wise. "Gboh-gboh-gboh, make us wise like you."

The old man did not fail them. "If you have endurance you would be wise." He told them.

He asked them to bow their head. As they bowed their heads, "I will make music on your heads." He told them.

"Gboh-gboh-gboh, me first"

"I bless you with the blessing of the wise, the smart and the crook"

He then clinched his fist to frighten them. Then he gets his knuckles ready. Then gently he knocks them on the head with it. He did it in tens, twenties, and thirties. He had a name for each as he repeated the performance. Any act for the children, it thrilled them. They were pleased at the thought of the blessings of an old man. He was about to make them wise like himself.

"Me, me next." The kids urged him on.

The old man played with them till he became tired and asked them to wait till another day. That was their love for wisdom. Papa George was smart and agile old man and the children liked him. They learnt a lot from him. Ulu believed he had the power to make him become like him one day. At least they wanted to grow old and have gray hairs.

As he continued to grow up he did not stop running after men and women perceived to have the same magic as George.

CHAPTER
≈29≈

A few survivors of the war came to live in the peninsula. From time to time Ulu went to meet them to hear about the war, but none was from his town. He wanted to meet people from his town. His mother told him that one of his uncle's was alive. Ulu was pragmatic as a child. What he may have lacked was a clear vision. One day Ulu set out without anyone knowing where he was heading. The only one may have consulted was the band on his wrist. He went to his hometown in Alaukwe. He wanted to see things for himself. He was being pulled by an imaginative and creative force. The same one that made him throw those pebble into the lake or try to swim from one end of it to the other.

When he got to the town, he did not know anyone. The direction he had was very confusing, but somehow he knew it was there that their journey began. He had a power of cognition that spoke beyond his age.

He did not want to be hindered. He was not one to be hindered.

A few years later Ulu left peninsula. Like a rafter on the sea he was floating at the first opportunity. He wanted to be further away from the home. He wanted to see places, peoples and their ways of life. He was tired of running. He was tired of calling places home, because he found shelter in them. The war changed him. He was a little boy who cared for nothing, but playing with his sister, and children his age. He fought the war on his own terms. When he survived the war, he became a man with no home. Now he was a man on the move. He met people and places, made friends some he remembered and some he did not. Ulu believed in brotherhood and shared oneness of the universe. People gave others and things their identities. And to a great extent that made them what they became. But in men there was still a true self-knowledge. Those men identified themselves. All men may be spiritually of the same source, physically their environment continued to influence them. Ulu believed in the wedding between the earth and the heavens. He saw it as night turns into day and day into night. It was the maker reconciling himself with the objects of his creation. Ulu would work his way through schools and colleges around the globe. He was going to understand and know that which he did not.

CHAPTER
≈30≈

Ulu arrived in California, "the sun is beautiful here," he observed. The sands on the beaches were beautiful too. He loved the placed. Ulu was flowing like the River. Like the Mmere Nwa-ite flows mixing only with the fresh the water, searching only for the fresh water.

It was weekend and he was in Los Angeles. There was a party.

A big party thrown a Nigerian in Los Angeles, as expected by the planners' guests came from over fifty states of the United States. They were all well represented. Nigerians worked hard, they also loved to party hard once in a while. The venue was the REX Hotel in Hollywood. It was who is who of the Nigerian America diaspora. And Nigerians did not slack when it came to saying "we are". "We have arrived" is no yahoo, yahoo. Some came in clothes they bought with months' worth of savings, some in car they will never be seen in again. The management and staff of the hotel had seen parties of all types, but it was the most colorful yet. The music, the dance, the food, the drinks, the people and their attire, the Ashirebi in all colors, the women's headgear, the jewelries, families, group of friends, drop dead gorgeous beautiful women, the single girls and the bachelors, it was astonishing.

When the real and the surreal merge a certain beauty exudes. It was usually followed by a certain attraction too. Ulu had attended the party at the invitation of an old acquaintance. After the party he sized himself up. He had seen them, there were his people. The urge to get to know them was high. They were the blood in his veins. He shuffled through his contact from the night. He brought out a card from another old acquaintance he met at the party. He called the friend. And the friend called another friend. The next day he met with two business owner. He had only seen one from a distance at the party.

For the next couple months he sieved the true from the real. He met the city come and go. From there he saw the oceans form dark clouds above, turn from rainbow to receding evening sun. There he met and saw.

Rosa was a Pakistani university professor, in the states searched for job without luck. A Muslim woman, back home she would have easily accepted and joined the home front. After all being a mother and house wife is a full time job. But she kept on searching. There were bills to be paid. Her husband's once booming business had fallen on hard times. And he sold it.

Rosa answered an ad, it was a babysitting job. A Nigerian business woman was looking for a babysitter for her one year old. Though her mom did the interviewing for the job, little girl herself was picky. She had turned down a few Nigerian and Spanish women after a few days on the job.

Rosa's resume was impressive. With seven kids of her own, who have all turned out well, there was a lot the business woman could learn. She could not figure out how she was battling with taking care of one when the woman she was about to employ had done seven all by herself. Well, what she was going to learn was not the issue, her income flow was good. Little Angel was what mattered. Rosa got the job.

Showing up for work next morning Rosa had her head fully covered, a nice shiny gown and a pant that was only showing about six inches from the legs. Her shoes were a little different from the half inch heel her had worn the previous day. It was a flat. And her sole was showing red stockings. The little girl seemed to have an instant liking for the woman.

Rosa brought out her schedule which was not without a few clashes. But it didn't really matter. Rosa had classes to attend at 5.oopm every day since she was taking child development classes at a college nearby. It meant she would leave an hour earlier than her employer would have wanted. It could be accommodated.

Rosa settled down to work and so was the little girl settling to understanding her intriguing new friend. They played, they sang, they ran, the little girl eat and went to sleep. When she woke up Rosa was there. Rosa's was the face she saw. First week passed, second week passed, first month came and was gone the business woman waited for when her daughter would say, "mama no, mama no." But the little girl did not. Instead it was a growing bound.

Though it was not the best job Rosa could be doing she was giving it her best. She was also beginning to feeling at home doing it too. She ate her food in front of the kid. The little girl would not stop stretching her hands for some. And Rosa said part of her five times a day prayers before the kid. It was the closest the Christian mother had come to another religion. She would have liked to do that by herself, but not with her only child.

There seemed to be an unexpressed friction developing. The little Angel seemed to have found a friend. But her mom was not sure. The babysitter herself was used to a larger class full of grown-ups. And no one was saying "mama no."

But Ulu was a traveling man. He didn't watch the masquerade sitting in one place. There are good things the peace and the tranquil. On the other side of the River there was fresh water. He was going to see it. Turning his back, it was the little beauty smiling and her nanny waving. The smile he returned with a giggle. The baby stretched her tiny arms. Her Rosa positioned her. Ulu took her in his arms hugged tight and warmly. She did not want to let go. "She knows you gonna be away for a while." It was the voice of little Angele's mama.

That year California hosted a contest, so much music and color in action. There were marching bands from all over the world. The America Honor Band, Roots of Music Marching Crusader Band, Seminole Warhawk High School Marching Band, Pride of the Blue Grass Lafayette High Sch. All American Cowgirls' Chicks, LA Unified School District Marching Band and even Izimo Japan Marching Band were visiting. Indonesia was present making sense of life with the beauty of flowers. They were old and young talents looking for their place in the world. Music was a language spoken across barriers. Ulu knew where next to go.

CHAPTER
≈31≈

Ulu met and became friends with Ella and Stan. Stan was in and out of college as he was in the bars and liquor stores. He drank anything with alcohol in it. To sober up he would drink soda or continue with alcohol. It cured hangover, he would say. When he was sober he searched for his European heritage. He talked about his smart brother who was in the military. His family served the country.

Stan used to consider his brother the real gun for hire. But the man he met in court a few hours before his meeting with Ella was the real deal. Stan stretched out his arms. They were touching both ends of the sofa. He was fatigued. Ella walked in and wanted to know how his day was.

"Hey how was your day?" She asked.

"I met Mr. Nivo Real. The lawyer has no time to listen to his clients or his opponents." Stan was in court with his landlord. "Nivo calls himself the real bad ass legal gun for hire"

"Who is that?" Ella inquired.

"He's my landlord's attorney."

Nivo was a tall man who liked to intimidate his opponents. In court his many up and down movements and loud laughter seemed to do that. Where he found the opening he smiled himself a deal. He pushed defendants into little tight corners. He would lord it over them and came out swinging.

But in the open he was as venerable as those he put on the spotlight. He loved to think of his court trial and eviction of his clients tenant as a show business.

"Nivo got a thrill out of it. He dragged people to court for no reasons." Stan said. Ella was already laughing.

"In court, nicely dressed in suit, he sought to smile his way to victory. He walked up and down. Sometimes he got his cheap victories."

Stan with his own many experiences has come to understand men like him. He knew the house, he lived in was neither his own nor was the courtroom his showroom. Mr. Nivo Real had several bosses and the number of cases he had in court seemed to increase the number of people, he had to impress. Time was not anyone's friend. His age simply did not fit in well with a new career in showbiz. Not at this time. That morning in court Stan pitched him against all the conflicting interests.

The judge ruled. It was simple. "Pay more attention to your legal duties. They will serve him better."

Mr. Nivo Real was confused. He did not see it coming.

Stan felt a sense victory, but the stress was a lot. It was not the time to celebrate. He needed to get settled first. Ella agreed with him. He needed rest.

Ella was a good listener. It made her able to retain many friends over the years, even Stan. Ella hoped the friendships would pay off one day. She let Stan crash on her couch now and then. And he dropped $100 or $200 which helps her with the bills sometimes. Ella was a sweet beautiful girl. She slept by day and worked by night. She was more productive when it was dark. By day she chased dreams. The men were not part what she chased. She has had her share of being with all the wrong guys. Her mother said those experiences would make her value the right one when he came along.

Ella was a small time successful singer. She sang in bars and night clubs while auditioning for roles in the movie and TVs. Those were not able to pay the bills. They were her dreams. But fortunately she proofread and had other part time jobs. There were days when she was empty. Her soul starved for music. Hers soul starved for love, as she starved for stardom. The new intern at Peter's Studio where she went occasionally thought she was his problem. He could not bear it. She could not understand it. Ella had old gypsy soul.

CHAPTER
≈32≈

Stan was always drunk. He came to identify of himself as, "Stan the drunk." Many times he wondered where he truly came from. Stan had days when he woke up and spent hours in front of the mirror. He examined his eyes, jawbone and the shape of his nose. He was Aryan, he claimed. He tried to determine he was.

But if rumors were true, his great grandmother was supposedly impregnated by a runaway gladiator, before he was caught and put back in the cage.

Opposite the mirror was a painting. The oil on canvas depicts a 1000 years of race mixing, before even his grandfathers were born. It was a copy placed by the original owner of the house.

The painting itself was said to have been commissioned by a brother whose detractors called "the madman of the Middle East." The brother himself was a mix of the old black Sudan and the Arabs of the North. In later years he was murdered by a mad crowd, like the one that killed the Christ. His great grandmother was a lover of a Wiseman Al Jahiz of the house of wisdom. Al Jahiz, who wrote of knowledge and of their people when the river was still clean and the deserts faraway. It was before memories became dust and flew with the sands of the desert. He recorded the love of his people in 816 AD.

The painting recreated that time when blacks of old Sudan showed their Arab women love, treated them to their natural talent for dance with an unmatched gift of rhythm, ability to sing which incurs the envy of angels, when they bore them princes, kings, queens and princesses. It showed their poets and singers, their courage, energy, and generosity, nobility, cheerfulness, good-temperedness and near purity in language. It showed the depicted young Greeks hungry for the taste of knowledge moving to Africa.

Like the castaway, Ulu was the lost one. He had flown in like the River, an outsider, the darker brother. His communion with superior powers kept him on a higher path. He knew it was the same blood, it flowed in their veins. In them were souls. And those souls came back to the same spot in the only universe known to their kind. He left places from where the umbilical cord had grown into plants in some distant lands.

"I have followed the path of the stream; the earth and its people were one." He told them.

He was on transit like everyone on planet earth. He was from the spots where the fragrances of the pond attracted of the healing one.

He stole away many nights into the caves, the magnificent mountaintops, deserts lands, crowded streets and markets squares in search of that oneness and the true image of its maker. He has been to the desert lands in India, where the Fulani and European gypsies trace their root. He had sand samples from where the first human remains were dug up and sands from the holy lands. He had his own curiosity to feed. He went not shopping for intangible cultures for the world, as much as for his own consumption. He understood those identities, their distinctness, and some were in very sad states. Many times one needed to be lost to find the true way. He was on that way. He wandered off wondering what amount of their blood and soul was left in him. It was the rainy season. The leaves and grasses were turning green. He was on the move again.

In the house where they lived with those simple understandings. They were guided by simple codes. It was contained in a very complex painting hung in the living room. On the side of the painting was a plain hand written sign. It read;

"On these faces and beyond you find minds,
In some you find peace, on others intrigue.
In all you find minds that have encountered life beyond its face value.
Do no harm to the earth,
Do no harm to life
Do no harm to the sea,
Do no harm to the wind
Do no harm the trees."

CHAPTER
≈33≈

People at the peninsula thought Ulu vanished as the tin air. No one knew where he was. His mother and sister tried to stop him from leaving but his mind was made up. In Alaukwe, Tata who called him the son of the timber merchant knew that the forest was on fire. "Ulu is his name," the watcher of the lake recalled very well.

"He too is gone. He was the migrant, the sojourner, the preacher, the teacher and the searcher of souls. And if the world was a stage he was a dancer in the sun." Tata said looking up into the sky.

Everyman pursues his own destiny. Every experience is unique and so is every voice. Tata had followed her own footsteps and her voice heard everything re-echoing the sounds of the times.

"There are discordant tones in those voices lost in the dark paths. But Ulu your soles has touched the soul of the earth. You leave footsteps and fingerprints of difference. You speak the earth's tongue. I see the clouds." Tata whispered.

It is man's place to despise his entrapments. In his journey, Tata sees a man seeking to be free. But where he is headed she is not sure.

His great grandmother handed him the ancestral watch; the symbol of what her great ancestors were. In it Tata sees a cycle of goings and comings.

Ulu left when he could not bear the relationship between woman who gave birth to him and his stepfather. Tata said he was meant for leaving. She sat there in front of the lake trying to capture the play of light and dark. In the back and forth movement of the wave, she saw a mix of joy and happiness. Each time it came and went revealing the wet sand, it seemed like a distant and yet lasting illusion. The woman who saw day light and darkness knew that there were things that defied human understanding.

On that day when like a rafter Ulu joined the path of the migrant. Tata looked into the in the sky. She was told by a friend that on that day, "somewhere faraway in the East, a man would be born. That man would be a man of a noble birth. He would be raised in the tradition of the orients."

He was a man in constant search of the meaning of life and death. He quietly sought to know why life began when it did, and ended with the mystery of death. In spite of the opulence around him that man would live for the sole purpose of his search.

He would have the light of a man in the search of the meaning of light in darkness. He had the lantern of a man in search of truth constantly lit in his living room day and night.

That lantern would channel positive energy from around the world to that point where it is lit. Men would seek him from far and wide. They would seek for good and evil. Many would want his blood.

Tata turning her back to the sun, she clears her throat twice "Tofia I have seen the sea of blood…"

"My son no one with a drop of our blood in him should cheer at the death of his brother. This blood flows in our streams, rivers and seas. It is the vegetation. It is the food on the table. It is the car and houses overseas. It is our blood at home and in distant lands. It flows without drying. We bleed." Tata continued.

Years later the man with the lantern would inspire fusions. Cities and schools in San Jose, New Brunswick and Beijing came together. Young folks joined the lions club seeking the light, his inspiration

CHAPTER
≈34≈

Ulu went where the air went, where the water went and where the fire kindled. He carried with him the earth in search of its universal motherhood and love. He was her royal. He recalled and told tales of its beauty.

Ulu studied peoples, their ways present and past. He took tiny notes and marveled at the works of others. He went to universities, museums and religious buildings. He camped in the bushes, on the mountains and street gatherings.

In his world even a caricaturist take hostages with his pencil and paper. At one he observed those sisters sat there on the ground. It was like they were paid to sit there. The caricaturist drew his characters. His characters were mostly those who came to him to be drawn. Others who stood before him somehow became part of his picture. The image of the almighty was hovering all over. The way he moved his pencil on the papers, Ulu could have been captured.

The gathering was a sizable crowd. The cartoonist did not lack who or what to draw. It was a beautiful work he was doing. He was so busy all the time. He could have forgotten to get a picture of those black girls on the floor in front of him.

But he did not. Their veiled faces did not stop him. It may have urged him on.

Ulu hungered for others. And their cultures in his quest the world over. So it was that year, he found himself at a festival of beer drinking. The folks competed on who would drink the most beer. It was held once a year in the month of October. Oktoberfest was what they called it. Ulu marveled at the different shades of what was beautiful and the way man conceived of it.

He mused at the power and beauty of capturing and of recalling.

The guy still drew, this time he was drawing the little girl posing in front of him. She was the smallest and probably the youngest in the gathering. She spent so much time sitting in front of the caricaturist.

Ulu could no longer remember if he had come to the ceremony with her. She sat closest to him. Placed on the paper on the drawing board her face suddenly came alive on it. Her head and face looked older than the rest of the other faces. She too had made art that night. She still had a small tiny body and arms. Ulu did not see her legs. "He was going to make them small." He thought as he walked away.

Those sisters Ulu saw earlier, this time were weaving their hairs. "Nubian braids, art, style and beauty" Ulu thought. He did not talk to either of them. He had the urge to ask, if it was a special role they were playing. But whatever role it was, that first impression did not and could not suggest a key role. As the party went on roles changed for sure.

UIu had never been to the feast in Munich. He was glad he got invited to this time. He did not care to drink any beer before going. The student center was very different. It was big and beautiful. A magician he hung a bag on his right hand side of his shoulder and went around with candies, which he handed to people. Ulu did not see a bottle of beer in the entire hall. It was college hall, college rules.

They ate the food that a professor came out to declare he prepared the sauce. It had no taste that might have been his reason for saying he prepared it. He probably wanted absorb others of any guilt. The interesting aspect of that declaration was that it was taking place immediately after the drama staged by the club came to an end.

UIu could not understand if it was a difference scene of the same play. They enjoyed the food they were served. They could not vouch for his friend who gave him that food. Every food tasted different on each test buds. The bitter leaf soup which was his favorite of his mother's cooking, would even taste different to him now. But it was from there he learnt his first lessons about the chef's hat. It was simple thank you for cooking. And thank you for eating. They were good cooks.

Ulu looked up, the cartoonist was still moving his hands this time very rapidly, the magician was stand still no one laughing at his pranks. The sisters were no longer there. A kind of feeling went instantly right through him. If it was an illusion he could not still phantom it. The night became heavier than he had thought of it. The music on was Nina, she was singing something about allies. He does not remember.

He walks straight through the door, caught up with two girls that shared the same table with. The girls were talking to Fred and Celeste. They introduced him to the siblings. For the rest of the night they stood outside the hall chatting with the friends like they have known one another forever.

Fred came to the party with his sister. It was fiction before it happened to him. His sister was a lover of her own sex. She had them in every form, shape and color. Growing up she was uptight, bullied as a kid, but somehow she found humor as a self-defense mechanism. It was a launching pad from which she turned those who wanted so bad to victimize her as the victim of their own plots.

For Fred, he owed to humanity. Nature sought balance and he was there. Mankind would not go out of extinction. Though he thought those girls were searching for a soul mate in a soulless being. He however gave willingly of himself each time he was called upon. Celeste his sister was not a keeper. Whatever it was she promised, had a fatal force, and soon it all came out to the open.

At last count Fred had given the gift to four. They were lovers, then mothers and now single mothers. He was only twenty, handy and doing the duties. She had gotten them to believe it was going to be a life of feminine happiness forever. A baby fathered by someone they knew and trusted would seal their union.

Fred was never sure what to believe, she had a magic about her. Celeste told him her last girl was ready to murder the spirit in her. He welcomed her. But when she left her multi-million dollar home for the streets, he felt sick. For two years she went from one rehab to another, none of those was able to free her from the heroin and cocaine she shot into her system. Then she hooked up with another girl.

She was the last baby mama. Fred was beginning to feel grown up. His sister was becoming sick of love. She told anyone who cared to ask about her last girlfriend, "those two are somewhere on the potential drug overdose victims waiting list. If the county jail has no space for them, the coroner may as well save them some." She was vulnerable, looking hard to hide it.

Ulu got home and opened the fridge and took a bottle of beer from it. He began drinking it when Joel the musician walked in. He seemed to have forced the door open. The noise was loud. He may not have noticed, after playing that thing all night he would need time to readjust. Ulu did not know why but saw he had an extra load on his hand, plus his trumpet. Ulu sat on the kitchen table he could not invite him to share one bottle of beer. He fixed his eyes on his friend's trumpet. There would be no better subject tonight than Joel telling him about his rehearsal. As they talked, he thought of what the computer and other electronic equipment was going to do to his friend. His teacher was already very old. He had enjoyed his days as a musician and trumpet player. He had played in great orchestra around the world. Joel stood all of the time as they talked. It was not that he did not want to discuss these things. They were his most favorite topics.

CHAPTER
≈35≈

Ella had a set of fabulous art collection in her room. They were on loan from her mother. They were from places she had visited in Mozambique, Tanzania, Nigeria, Uganda, the Sudan, India and Iran. Ella's Mother was a beautiful woman with a beautiful soul. She volunteered with a group of friends on a New Africa initiative. It was an American group of teachers, doctors, artists and entrepreneurs who saw the beauty of the continent. They worked with Africans on health care, education and encouraging fair trade practices.

She often sent Ella letters describing the beauty of places and peoples in areas she was in Africa when she sent her any piece of art. Those letters explained the efforts of the group. They educated people on the continent. "This place is not a raped, abandoned and forgotten piece of land unable to support growth." She wrote in one of her letters. She however expressed her fear that globalization may however do harm there if unfair global trade continued unchecked.

Ella was educated. She knew Africa was not a country. It is a continent and a people. She wanted to learn more about the people and their cultures. She made note of places she would like to visit. She rehearsed songs and speeches. She would wait for a time when her mother's group will be there again. Her mom had explained to her a lot about the people. She mentioned a place in Tanzania were water was offered as a gift to visitors. Water was important and needed there. They did not have enough of it to drink. But out of good heart they offered bottled water to their visitors. Rainfall or its lack had significant impact on the people's daily life.

Ella's favorite piece of art "the giraffe," was from there. She wanted to visit the people with that generous heart. There were several other places she wanted to visit there. The Masai people interested her very much. In one of her songs, she expressed a longing to be held in the arms of a senior Masai warrior. When her mother heard it, she answered her in a voice devoid of any melody, "It is a free world my daughter."

Ella never liked the tone when she spoke that way. She called her mother a dream killer. She said she killed the dreams of men and collected their bone in her pieces of arts, sculptures of different kinds. She killed them in her own dreams and left their children orphans. They were her trophy. And there were days when she truly showed her disapproval. She would watch the smoke go up, look at it and proclaim,

"Now we have a new pope." The voice was more of a chant. She liked to get even with her mother that way.

Ella wanted to make her trip to Africa special whenever she made it. When her mother told her, "The Medical Mission Hospital is our biggest achievement on the continent." She was intrigued by its story. Though she has no medical training or healthcare background she promised to do something.

"It was an abandoned hospital building. A Nigerian Charity led by Imani, a woman I have come to know very well and her friends from the Philippines were working on reviving it, when we came in." Her mother explained.

The miracle of the place started by a call made by the Amazing grace Ministries, a church organization in America. That call brought the different teams together. Works took off on the hospital. The place was cleared, buildings were renovated, equipment cleaned up and new ones bought. Skeletal services started. Then many wealthy individuals and families came to identify with it. It became the place of hope for many, most of all, for those not so well to do. A local newspaper with wide circulations had written an article about it entitled "a miracle in the interiors of Africa." That article got wide attention. A lot of people became interested in the amazing work at the Medical Mission team in the area. That year Dr. Friedman director at a big hospital in California heard of the story and shared it with his Nigerian friend. That was the beginning of another miracle for the hospital. Three times a year the hospital would send aides in; medical equipment, drugs, staff, training and exchange visits with the hospital "in the interiors of Africa." The doctor never failed to remind his staff, "Research is the key to everything" before they set- out on their trip.

"A former American president on his African tour visited the hospital. His foundation was going around the world mending what was broken by the sheer might of office. His initiative was to join forces to fight, hunger, poverty, malaria and HIV in developing countries. The global face of AIDS health care foundation was a happy partner. But throughout the visit some of his African counterparts didn't know or decided not to acknowledge he was in their country. They were home guarding their loots with their lives." Ella's mom concluded with a smile on her face.

"Very interesting mom. You know you're really nice when you want to be." Ella was intrigued by it all. Her enthusiasm grew and she wanted to contribute as well. Her phone clicked. Ella's footsteps were never heard, going out of the main building.

His roommate's door was ajar, he went over and shot it for her. Ulu back in his room lit a candle. He would be fast asleep by the time Ella comes back. He had tried to let her know she would attract intruders if she kept leaving her doors open. But that was not always on her mind. And somehow it has become part of his duty to maintain security within the house. "She might be able to convince the guy she has been sleeping with to come over tonight." Ulu thought. Her appointment with the psychic was 4 pm. She would not know what lies he might be telling her. But whatever it was he told her. He knew she would believe it. Ulu told her he prays. She did not understand that. But he was sure God would hear his prayers, especially, at such nights when she consulted with the mediums. He did not want to disturb himself concerning her or whoever she brought down there that night. At least she may get lucky. One thing was bound to happen.

It was 11.45pm. Mark was in the kitchen, engrossed in his computer game. He hardly noticed Ella come in at first. He raised his head. She was gorgeous. He could have mistaken her for the female character in the game. He was Stunned.

"What?" She asked.

"Hmm, Nothing." Mark answered

"You wanna take me?"

"I got nothing. Nothing working for me." Mark said still looking stunned.

"You do."

"Just this fingers, say, brain."

"Hmm, good for the lucky bitch, whoever she will be."

It was a see through night gown. For a few minutes he wasn't able to concentrate. The sound of the water going down as the toilet flushed helped.

His thoughts raced. Then he concentrated on the female character in his game.

"She rules my nights and my dreams. Yet she is only a dream." He etched that in the game.

CHAPTER
≈36≈

The next morning Ulu got up from sleep. He went into the bathroom. He walked straight into his room. The bathroom was filled with something unusual. It smelt strange. The fridge in the kitchen smelled of garlic.

The first time he saw him, Ulu was going to his room. The tall white boy turned around and says hello. He came out from Ella's room. Ella had complained. She could not sleep, move or stay in the house. She felt her space invaded. There was no doubt they inhabited the space with a few UFOs at certain times of the year. Since the touchdown on the moon and outer planet, the earthlings and their neighbors intermingle. Stan was an identifiable one. Mark came down occasionally as well.

Ulu imagined it would be best, if Ella told her visitors the truth. He looked serious. As if it was clear, some force he did not know anything about pulled his strings there. He felt cool. His gray dress did not help matters. He was ugly. Whatever she saw in him, Ulu thought.

She thought her life was over when those crazy kids told her she would have bad sex for seven years. Going weeks and months without it, she settles for the gray pullover guy.

The space smelt foul. He had dropped a used condom and white tissue paper in the kitchen waste. Ulu couldn't really say what they had been used for. When Ulu saw it, he felt sorry for that lovely angel of the night. He was not always a deep sleeper. He hadn't noticed a thing. If anything happened that night, it might have been some very special technique. He thought. Even that- the house shared information. It could not conceal such joyful moments. Not when angels, demons and saints interacted. Not even the sound of breath. In the morning the sound of the shower in the bathroom that sounded like a heavy downpour was not heard. He had expected someone would use the shower. That might have solved any doubt. But it did not happen. He heard the door shot. They left the apartment.

Ulu continued to work on a project proposal. The state had sent him some projects to review.

Ulu's mind went back to what the cartoonist was doing. He did not ask him if had made pictures of himself or if he had drawn any of his friends. Few of them feared their images being captured while they captured others. If he had any he would have loved to acquire it. Though he was told he did not collect money for that art. But still he had his signature and phone number on all of them. His grandmother's signature was all over him too. On his right wrist there was a band. It was the royal bead his granny bequeathed to him. The communication channels were always open he thought.

At thirty he was beginning to think of the world and his world. Each time he took time to think from where he came. When he did he looked at the bead on his right wrist studiously. He looked at the single beads one after the other. He had worn it for a long time. He has grown with it still there. He would recall the words of the woman whom the gift was from. Those words had become his dreams, and he pursued them.

He wanted those dreams to come true, even if they were only real in the night when he slept.

But the world around him was changing fast. There were new realities. He began to give up some of his dreams. None of his other roommates knew nor understood his deep attachment to the wrist band. Ella though was the closest to understanding them at times.

If he felt disgruntled by things around him, if he felt his dreams were broken. There were those who came before him.

All he needed to do was look harder. He needed to push his researches further. He would find things and people around him. He would find things in him. Somewhere around were his uncles or uncles and aunties he did not know. They were in that land before him. They left traces. Their children and grandchildren were those kids he played with. They were ones that he studied with, worked with and hung out in the clubs with. They shared the same blood. Their blood was the same. But they had been there longer. The world was so mixed, they did not know it.

If he still looked at those beads and think of royalty, there were those who did not know of the blood that follows in their veins. Ella was a careful observer and good companion when she wanted to be.

"Ulu when is your conference paper ready?" Ella asked

"Not until tomorrow evening."

"I see, you are not talking to anyone"

"I have got to finish listening to these tapes and read those books from the library"

"I just wanted to know everything was okay" Ella went back to her room.

Ulu had a load of tapes and books in front of him. His desk was filled with research papers from past conferences and reviews. If he was to recreate the past as he has heard or seen, he needed those hours of solitude. If he was to reconnect the past and the present they were in there. He pulled out a series of materials and began reading through them again.

CHAPTER
≈37≈

The world is a tapestry of those who started that journey. The potter and his band were long gone too. From the finest clay in the world they made the best clay pots. The earth's wonder dust, ashes, sand and water mixed, tested and proved by fire. They carried their finished pots on their heads to the market. They walked for miles, nights and days to distant parts of the land, on their market days, to sell. Their earthenware was always awaited. That knowledge made the trip a lot easier. But not as easier as the songs they sang and the music they made along the way. Music and minds traveled without limits. Once someone raised a song and the rest chorused it. They walked miles without a care in the world. They met in minds. The loads on their heads became lighter than the wind. The band of traders had a constant head count in their call and response. Each member had special names. From it the crowd recognized him or her depending on the song. That name also went hand in hand with the pitch he or she gives to the songs, from the first in line to the last, from the oldest to the youngest.

But one day the marauders came. The band, songs and the earthenware all broke to pieces. Afor, was not heard responding, neither was Ije, Agu, Ohia, nor Ekwenu calling. It all happened very fast. The cry was loud, the voices young and old. It was a loud cry, it continued. The craft was destroyed. The beauty of the pottery was gone and so was the potter. The mass once held together by the clay was dry and broken in pieces. The sounds of the chains and the shackles took the place the music. It became the New Harmony.

True, Ije the migrant left home the season after Ugo refused his marriage advances. He got aboard the slave ship on his own. Passion and love have disappointed him. The ship docked in many ports which would be the final destination for many of the souls on board. He continued to use his charm. It was that which kept him off the chains.

His freedom was not only bought with his friendship with the captain of the ship. He was said to have been told he had to trade to pay for it. Whatever he sold to them no one really knew. They speculated that he was a slave merchant himself. They said his step brother Omenuko a friend of a well know slave trader had sold him to cover his loses. In most part of that long and lonely journey he stayed all by himself. His folks, men with whom he shared kernels and bread fruit with did not trust him. And he feared for his own life. In disperse. He called on the son of David. "If it is you lord, accept an offering, if it is the children of men..." But he was sure god must have exhausted his punishment for them. He could not put a curse on them, he rather blessed them.

It was equally said the man who handed him to captain had instructed him to treat him kindly. He was likely to find him very useful. Alongside working with the captain he kept livestock. He could have raised the money from there. But he paid to be a freeman on the ship.

In his sojourn he met and married Dianna a woman who would later die of breast cancer. He loved her. He wished he could heal her. They had two children. The children grew up healthy, but in a society that was not ready for them. They faced discrimination and out right abuse. It was harder for the boy. They worked hard though never really fully accepted anywhere. Even at the church they attended. The girl became a nurse and worked for a local mission hospital and the boy did anything he could find. "Love all men, even if it is hard." Those were the last words of Dianna to her children before she died. They would never forget the last words of their mother. They both gave a helping to people suffering with cancer anywhere they were accepted.

The life of a sailor was one full of adventures. Ije had become a sailor. His next was writing notes and craftily going off to drop them at the house of Wilberforce. When he dropped them and quietly prayed for an age when there would be neither just slavery nor just war.

He had become friends with him too.

The slaver and repentant captain John H Newton had come back from sea. He survived the stormed. On the pulpit he had become a singer of hymns of grace. Amazing grace-fighting his guilt, seeking forgiveness for souls, thousands gone, some toiling away and others still on the way. It was his poetry. The power of his poetry not his chain that captured young Mister William. The young darling and member of the parliament fell in love. Like any young man his age with his star power and revolutionary spirit something had to be his victim. The power of the pull from the pulpit – the slave trade became his victim. For years William Wilberforce repeatedly presented his abolition bill.

Mr. Wilberforce hated the trade in humans. He heard men kill themselves, rather than get on that ship or on the cold farms.

Even as he was thinking about it somewhere people were captured, forced on board, being killed,

A newsletter on his door steps as he came back with his unattended-to-bill, was a story of another man who killed himself. He was tired of running from those who captured his brother. He had watched him go. His brother was aboard the Pegasus that slave ship took off from the west coast of Africa. The human consignment was heading to Europe, America and the West Indies. Mr. Wilberforce and his friends continued to make concerted efforts to end the trade. He saw the bitterness on the faces of captured men as well as on the faces of the dealers. Each day as he went back to the law makers, he asked.

"Of what use are these folks to you if in South Carolina walked into the river?" He was not joking.

Those men, women and children were not testing to see if they had become Christ or his follower able to walk on the water. No their experience in the ship for months had given them a taste of what life on the cold land would be as captives of other men. They preferred to meet their creator. He knew his people were hard hearted. Even when the calamity of Ibo landing was clearly ringing in their heads and the song "walking in the water" pricked their hearts they hoped the local dealers did not bring them those Igbo slaves. But they were not willing to give up the trade. He told them, "You know these men, women and children would rather become Jonah in the belly of the fish that become slaves."

For decades Mr. Wilberforce fought the British legislature till the folks saw the sin in the trade in humans. The fight was in his blood. He was of a line of great Christian men who bought and freed British and Saxon slaves.

Those whose cries and sorrows were drowning in the Brownlow were queens, kings, Ezes, Obas and noble bloods. Among those who had long sailed were Queen Amina captured on a trip, Oba Ovaruwem, The Crown Prince of Nri, King Jaja the Amayanabo of the Opobo kingdom and their faithful subjects. Their people revered by them, till the enemy ship took them into slavery. Their new homes were curial to the life they led. The things they became and their life in bondage in Europe and American farms were strange.

It was the life. It was the history that Ije the migrant found himself entangled with. He had conquered the sea. He would give his life to stop the trade. So he continued to work with groups fighting the trade. While he fought the cold and the trade, his daughter with the beautiful woman grew up knowing nothing about him. When he thought of the place he came from, he consoled himself.

"No man has won every war, somewhere, sometime he lost a battle. It is life." He would conclude.

Somewhere near Istanbul were a group of men who fought gallantly. They forestalled their own kidnapping. But they were thousands of nautical miles from home, years away. They stirred the slave ship. Where it anchored it was safe. There they made a home. Their names they managed to retain. Their languages faded away, they learnt a new one.

CHAPTER
≈38≈

It was 2:00 am. Ulu heard a knock on the door. He knew it was not the trumpet player. He had quietly crept into his room about 12:00 am. It was unlike Ulu to leave his door unlocked. In the past he walked right into his room and locked the door. His light was on. The computer he used had its peculiar light and noise.

He did not want to answer the door. It was definitely Ella's new friend. And he did not try to imagine why he was at his door. He still did not understand nor place that guy. The actions and words of the guy in gray earlier were weirder than he expected. He couldn't tell which among the two the real trouble was. And which would be in the future. The trumpet player was fast asleep. If it was the same guy from that morning, he did not want to confront him. He had told him it was all right that he was intervening for his friend. That was all he wanted to do with him. He did not want to have anything to do with him again and not at that time of the night.

The sound died down. He resumed work on the computer. He thought of the past days when Ella had come into his room and they spent some time together talking. They talked just about anything. His mind went off roaming. He had to finish what he was doing. He hadn't completely decided what his next action would be so he shut down the computer. Went into the kitchen and took a glass of water. At this time Ella or her friend would have probably noticed that he was still awake. He came back into his room and switched off the light and went to bed.

When he got up he took a pen to sign the post card he got for Chris his friend. It was great he sent him the link to the university web page. His picture on it was very interesting, though he had no idea he was appearing there. He could not sign it. The few lines he added to the card were increasingly being peopled by strangers. It has got a trumpet player, Ella, and the strange boyfriend. He wondered if Chris would understand how these folks have wandered into his story.

He read the card again, left it on the table. He switched on laptop. Then he remembered their jokes about laptop and the laps of their favorite girls. He decided to send him an email. He wrote him about the Oktoberfest that had no beer. He did not mention the girls, the three Germans he met. Had they been Spanish or Italians he would not have omitted it.

He did not really understand what it was that drove his friend crazy about those girls. Something about them made him go bananas. He really loved those dark hair girls, descendant of Saint Augustine's ancestors and cousins of Hannibal the great- the moor. When he had one, Liza was her name. He treated her like a beauty queen from the movies. He took to movies, feasted her in and around Europe. He took her to the Vatican where he showed and told her the stranger secrets of the paintings of Michael Angelo. And then to Munich, he had discovered she was the best girl to go to see Michael Jackson History world tour with. There in the crowd he tossed her up and down, dancing to "It doesn't matter if you are black or white." Their love lasted for forty days and forty nights. When he lost her, he played "the night is my companion" for months.

His blonde date plan would bore him, so he left it out too.

The night before a friend of his came in. She stayed till 3:00am. When she came in she was soaked wet. There was a down pour outside. He gave her a towel. He was watching boxing bout being televised live from Las Vegas on TV. An Olympic gold medalist, proudly wearing his stars and stripes was terribly beating his opponent. When he finally knocks Mr.

Rezi out, he bent down beside him. As he did, the loud and excited crowd held their breath for a moment. Then he told the man who has made a lot noise about coming to teach him a lesson, "there is something which has made this country and other great ones what they are, let that magic rub-off on you and enjoy the rest of your stay here." Mr. Rezi was on the ground with his hands around his head, if he was conscious enough to hear him, there could be no better teacher.

During his Olympic days he was fond of telling the media how fortunate he was. "I could be wearing these colors elsewhere. But fortunately I represent my country in a sport where the rest of the world cheers and the only one who cries is this man here."

Indeed he brought happiness to viewers and took pride home. The TV was on a commercial break. Ulu turns to his visitor who had already made herself comfortable.

She dried herself and changed into one of his shirts.

The rain and the fight that night took him years back when he was a child. His mother told him stories. One was of animals after it rained. It had just finished raining the eagle looked at her eaglets almost soaked wet, "today is another lesson" she said. He had forgotten the exact stories, it was very long ago when they sat and listened to tales by moonlight. But he recalled she told him that rain was a life giving force and of fragrances after the rain. He missed the sound of the tropical rain on the rooftop. He remembered very well running around naked and singing as it rained with little care.

That night after the fight they told stories and talked till they got tired of talking. She had given him two very important books. She wanted to take a test which she encourages him to take as well.

Till he met her all his Asians friends were mainly males. And those heroes he met in comic books and films. They did not talk too much. He learnt a few Chinese words, though it was hard and they were reluctant to teach him. He wanted to learn. Sometimes he remembered lines and even full passages from the books or films. He was particularly fond of one, it went something like, "…It's the year of the locust. I am in search of myself. But here I have created a riddle and ripples in the water. I am hungry to see its poetry and its politics. I watched it. There is nothing absurd about it. It's the year of the locust."

"You don't learn a language with something like that," she told him. He had informed her that after his first language, every other language he learnt was an act of survival. It was not mere leisure or the pleasure of learning.

But they were very shy people even in the class rooms. It seemed a hard one to deal with.

Outside the air was fresh. It has stopped raining. It was breezy.

As she was leaving she inquired about his roommates. The trumpeter had gone to New York. He picked up his black suit as a perfect fit for the outing. It was after he finished watching cartoon network's adaption of the temptations of Christ. Before leaving the house he kept repeating a particular line from the film. From the way he said it, he was not particularly fond of the line. "I have got the world in my hands. I want to sell you their souls."

The friend he went out with dressed the same way as he was. They were going for an all Cuban music show. He played in gigs to feed himself, while he waited on his big dream and a beautiful girl.

Ulu could not say much about the tall Ella. If she was inside she might have been sleeping for eighteen hours. That was the case the last time. He was surprised, the last time that he had to ask her. After her knock on the door the past night he did not hear or notice anything from her till he went to the university in the morning. He could still hear the noise from the fan in her room. If anything has happened, it would make you not think about it, other than that some substance was at work. She had been on some doses by the way. Unlike before he could not check on her. He would have knocked to see if she was doing fine, but since the guy in gray pullover at breakfast came. He decided that she was not any of his business. Things get along well that way too.

CHAPTER
≈39≈

It was Saturday the Trumpeter, Ella, Stan, Mark and Ulu were on their way back from a football game. They stopped at a store. Ulu went to get a phone card. "It must be something from the game." His friends joked. If it wasn't he didn't usually get his cards from down there. His options at the store were very limited. Attempts to reach his home land with a card from there would end up frustrating him.

His friends' joke was about the corner store. It was the starting point of a now big Hollywood star. It was on the corner of the street where the 90210 wanna be resident stayed, yelling at female celebrities, "are you single? Marry me please!"

Ulu wanted to hear the voice of his mother, her sister and his friend the French girl.

The French girl was his high school love. Amor liked him from the first day she saw him in Elementary school. It was the day Ada introduced them. Though her parents sent her out of the peninsula to France for her first three years of high school, their memories of each other were fun and alive. When she got back to the peninsula she made it known to him. She was a big girl and wanted more. She was the first girl who ever sent a love letter. She taught him the French words for kiss and love. She had sent him a poem which she entitled "your shadow." She wrote it the day he left. He kept a copy of it and took it out every often. He read it trying to put the puzzles together. It was morning, he pull it out began to read.

The shadow grew with every bit of the daylight,
Evening came they dwindled.
The next morning I picked a chalk
Made huge traces on the wall.
Every day the walls reflect
What we shared
It was more than love, it was divine
You became part of me.
I close my eyes it's you it's you I see
I walk in the streets,
In the rooms it's you
In the kitchen, on the table it's you
I close my eyes it's you
I open the books it's you
It's you I see
What we shared was divine.

The distance, we created
Yet every force they resist.
These souls found themselves.
The walls speak
Stay don't go away,
You became part of me.
It's your shadow all over
It's your thought all over
Your speech, your whispers.
Stay,
We can make this place home
Like the shadow on the wall.

He called it "escape from Africa." He folded it and puts it back in a book on his book shelves. When he first read it, he was thrilled, he allowed Stan read it. Abii was the first girl that made Stan feel that way. They shared memories, "but she loved another now", he told Ulu. "Man, it will be alright." Ulu told him. Months before when Stan told Ella about Abii, Ella introduced him to Edna, her only female friend. They started dating. She quickly found out, there was no reason to pursue a relationship there. It was a dead end. It was over before it started.

Ulu was eager to hear how things were at the peninsula. It had been a long time. As in the old days, he pulled out a post card and began to write a reply.

Ulu prepared for his appointment to speak with one of his research associates in Europe. She was a nice woman. She was a doctor of letters. He seriously wanted to hear her tell him about the decision of their research committee at the university. The committee was contemplating cutting down their budget. And he threatened quitting the research if they did. He kept dialing without anyone picking the phone. After several attempts, he picked up the receiver. Looked at it as if it was responsible for the lack of response on the other end. He felt like smashing it. But gave up the idea. He would speak with her Monday hopefully. Then he dropped it.

The woman was married now. Dr. Elisa Danah married a man who was once in love with her. He was madly in love with her. But day by day that love metamorphosed as her pride grew. She became something he did not know. Yet he loved her. He could not get her out of his head. Gradually she took the shape of a tree, a wooden image. Still he adored her. Her world, full of her, in her head was images of her growing nails, her nose pointing to the shadow of the vain air.

In his reality he was no longer sure what those noblest of emotions had become. Then in her world, the shadow of dawn began to disappear.

Those hands, once warm were now cold. But he took them in his. Was it his pride, he did not know. In truth his soft and gentle whispers were gone. And so were those smiles that came with his every heartbeat. Time was all they once had. But that was then.

Around, young lovers fell in love, holding hands, smiling, singing and dancing to rhythms of the season's new songs.

CHAPTER
≈40≈

Ulu heard the sound of the water tap in the kitchen running. "She was resurrected." He thought. He wondered how safe it was drinking the water from that tap. The tap seemed as old as the house. When you are out of cash or have an urgent need for a room like he was you could always find this type no matter in what city you are in, all you have to do is, "cheap houses.com." But the funny thing was that you could be getting used to things very fast that you never remember what it was that you hated most when you first moved in. He still had not figured out a thing about that water. He bought the bottled water. You could think of several new things you could do in such place. Often it is crazy and weird ideas that come into your head. You pay low rent and what were the inspirations that you get from that or the neighborhood.

Ulu had an email he needed to send to Thomas. He is a very good friend. At troubled times, he is the kind of friend you need. "He is also quite tricky, but that's all right." He said. Isaiah Thomas was a member of one of Ulu's research teams. He was a dark skinned man in his mid-sixties. He found a lot of pleasure feasting his eyes with the beautiful.

Thomas was guest of Fatima. Ulu was visiting her friend. Thomas had in mind it was a party for two. Fatima had tricked him again. He would give anything to be left alone with her. His time was always limited. Because had a family to go back to. That evening he came with some bottles of beer. The girls had glasses of wine in their hands.

Earlier Fatima had joked about Thomas being versed in the literatures of the world. But one thing he did not know about was his own people. He had little or no memories of his own father.

Ulu was reminded of that joke when Thomas asked him if they drink wine from where he came from. Ulu was amazed. Thomas had seen a glass of wine in his hand.

Ulu cleared his throat before responding. Being reminded of where he came from carried with it a responsibility.

"It is said back where I come from, the place my mother sang about, that when one clears his throat the spirits listened." Ulu had cause to clear his throat.

If men like Thomas would ask that question, then society would have no lessons to leave for coming generations. Though he taught math and biology he was expected to still be able to remember. There was a complete lack of cohesion, Ulu suspected. "The monkey had forgotten not to play its trick on the bush pigeon." Ulu thought.

The girls were skimpily dressed.

Ulu told them of a story his mother told him. It was of a field where the hunters caught the monkeys with their bare hands. The field was a popular one. It had a lot of palm trees. And the peanuts did well there. So the monkeys were there for a lot of reasons. Ngozika told them the monkeys went to get peanuts. And, "while at it they bid the tapper well-done."

The monkeys climbed the tree and drank the jag of wine. The early morning wine had the best taste. And that wine was always the one to get the animal easily intoxicated. Once it did. The hunter had no more use for his weapons. He caught the monkey drunk and sleepy. That was also the case with the chimpanzees that scared the women away from their farms. Once they drank the women could tie them up with ropes.

Fatima and her friend listened as Ulu gave Thomas lesson on wine. He only recounted what he heard from his mother Ngozika.

If his father hadn't take wine to his mother's parents she would have been given to him in marriage. Wine drinking and wine carrying was a big part of their tradition. It was celebrated in every celebration. Where he comes from in Alaukwe a young man who seeks the hand of a woman in marriage does so with wine. There also the beautiful black woman said that the wine is never rejected, even when the wine had been taken to the wrong household. That meant even if the maiden in question is not interested in the suitor. Once the hosts welcomed their visitors with the offer of kola nut, and the suitor makes known his intention, they sat together and did justice to the wine. They made a toast to mother earth. In his people's marriage tradition, it was the custom to accept the asking wine.

Isaiah Thomas was from the border town where they had run to during the war. He was bewildered at his question. Every man or woman worth his or her onus would have at one time or the other had his or her palm tree tapped for wine. And that wine would have played both social and economic roles in the life of the society. His answer to him was simple, "many people from where comes from made their living tapping and selling wine." Either in private or in social gatherings, they used the wine to relax. It played social, economic and cultural roles in their society.

"They drink wine no matter the color, red, white, black or blue"

"My people say no matter how small the bush rat is, it is still entitled to its share of his father's palm wine on Ore market day." Ulu ended.

If Thomas learnt anything that evening, it was Ulu, showing him before the girls, to see the best in his own and in himself. It was only then he would be able to access the best of others. "If you remain floating – you will lose and lose, you will never find your soul."

CHAPTER
≈41≈

Ulu was hearing the sounds of birds and some girls talking outside from his window. He decided to move outside to quit his stay indoors. He got out and stayed in front of the house. He did not see the birds. He heard the birds sing so clearly from inside my room. Rather what he saw was that usual squirrel. It has made the frontage its playground. It was running around unchallenged. He looked further down the street. The girls he saw were far away. They did not look like they possessed those voices either. Even if one would want to argue that it was the position. The three of them were in the parking lot. The first one he saw was huge, heavy that he knew, those were not the sights he wanted to have to contend with.

His presence would have drawn their attention to the place he was standing. He changed position. He went to sit on one of the three seats his cigarette-smoking neighbors kept there. Their next efforts were to attract attention, which he concluded would no longer be necessary.

Shortly after, the trumpet player came in. He packed his car carefully in front of the house. As usual he yells, "Hey Ulu!"

And Ulu responded "hey, you are back!"

Ulu was just coming out to have a feel of the beautiful weather outside. Joel could not tell if the weather was beautiful. He was wearing a jacket. He seemed cold. Ulu was indoors, the atmosphere had a nice feel. He came to one of the seats took out his cigarette lit it. And talked about his day. His professor called him up early that morning. He is an old blind man from Virginia. He would need him to help do some of his household chores. The trumpet player was easy going he never complained. As he smoked remembered how many hours of sleep he needed. Ulu knew he did not mean to say he has not been sleeping. But he did need some sleep.

They talked while Joel puffed on that cancer stick. They talk about their activity for the next day. It was a Sunday. Joel agreed to drive with Ulu to church. He would drop him off and pick him up. He did not really want to bother anybody that much in, matters concerning him and god. Ulu wanted to get him to come with him. He told him he doubted if his cell phone had enough credit to make the call in the morning. They finally agreed there must be a way out. He went inside.

It had occurred to Ulu to find a place of worship around that neighborhood. He went around in search. There were many church buildings. But the question was, if he would understand what they did and if they would understand him too. Apart from that he could walk into any of them and join till the end of their service. When he started the search on the Internet it helped a little. But then he stopped.

Ulu stood outside for a few minutes and decided to take a walk. He was a bit bored. He could not make anything out of staying indoors that long. More so, he had a lot of places he could still familiarize himself with around there. He took the next turn on the street. He was going to walk through the whole of that street until there was nothing more interesting to see.

Some minutes after he crossed the first few traffic lights. He noticed that there were really nice places he could have seen before then. The shops, restaurants and hotels on the Somerset Street made the evening a little lighter on his mind. As he was about to cross the next light, he saw that Latino beauty. She was walking the opposite direction. Then she turned abruptly to cross to the road.

She was coming to his direction. She could have moved on her former course. But there must have been something that he reminded her of. That side of the street had its own magic. Or she was probably bored of staying at home and decided to take a walk as well. After all they were all watching the same shows, listening to the same songs and breathing the same air. He would opt for the latter.

That decision to turn to that part of the street, when she could have continued was a sign. The light was on green on the part that she was formerly on. It was sign of someone worried about the day passing her by just like that. Ulu did not want to think she was a prostitute. But from the look in her eyes, he knew immediately where they would end up, if he asked her how busy she was. He did not ask. He did not speak Spanish, that bothered him a little. She would understand his English if he said anything. But he did not speak. He imagined he should have slowed his pace more in lieu of not saying hello. He had kept his pace once the traffic light was on green.

When he was at a safe distance, he turned to see how far off she was behind. He worried about attracting much attention with a full 180 degrees. But he noticed she was still coming behind. He thought about stopping to wait for her.

Because at that time he noticed she was a companion. He did not stop. At the next turn he could not see her again. "Where would she have walked into?" He did not have an immediate answer.

A few steps ahead he found a church on its corner. On the sign board was written Rc church, daily mass 7.30 am Sunday masses English 8:00 am, Spanish 10: 00 am Polish 12:00 pm. He would have to tell the Trumpet player there was no need to waste gas and pollutes the environment that Sunday. Save the environment and serve God. He noted and walked on.

An angel or a ghost in the form of a Latino woman has led him to that house of God. The next place he passed was Saint Patrick. It was a pub. A woman in her mid-40s asked him, "what's up?" He smiled at her and kept on. There were interesting places around. The numbers of these different enterprises were of equal proportion. He decided to end that walk and turned back. It was a successful evening walk. As he walked, he kept looking out for that beautiful girl. She was either angel or a prostitute yet to enter a category.

CHAPTER
≈42≈

When he got back he felt the impact of the fresh air he got from the walk. It made his mind clearer. It was only then he looked in the mail box. It contained some mails, two for him and one for Ella. He decided to stay there to read his. He tore open the letter. It was from his sister. Things were fine at the peninsula. She went there to visit over the weekend. His mother and stepfather were doing fine.

It was the first time Ada his sister was informing him of her decision to study geography at a college in Cameroun. It was strange, he thought, Nigeria had better universities than Cameroun. His sister was probably no longer interest in their home country. Geography was another thing. He thought she would have made a good medical doctor.

Her grandmother was a healer. She was the one who took after her. She paid close attention to things about health. She gave him leaves to put on his leg when he had any injury. When she had malaria, she got guava and pawpaw leaves boiled them till the pot of water changed color. She took the pot down from the fire. She looked for a blanket covered her head in the steam, inhale it as much as she could. Afterward she turned the water in a bucket in the bathroom. She showered with the water.

Anyone who saw her shivering from fever and sees her after that treatment would not believe it. That was how she treated malaria and encouraged her little brother to. When Ulu had liver inflammation, she went into the middle of their farm took a leave squeezed its juice and puts it in a glass of water. When he drank the mixture he never complained of that pain again. She ate mangoes. "It burnt excess fat which caused discomfort in the stomach." She would tell him. Ada was the one who had fruits, honey and vitamin c tablets for everyone in the house. She said it was good to help Mr. Stone avoid heart attack.

"It heals sour throats, cough or broken lip." She said as she served it.

She prepared them her favorite Okoro soup. She encouraged them to eat the Sour Sop in their backyard. "The fruit, the leaves and bark of the graviola tree is the miracle cancer cell killer. It heals and prevents cancer." She would tell them. She would run into the room and announced to everyone the importance of taking a break to enjoy what nature offered.

"Stop! Take a deep breath!! Enjoy the fresh air!!! It is free."

Tata called Ada "the healer." And they believed she would make something of it in college. How times and places change people, Ulu thought. He was not disappointed by the decisions of her sister or mother. He loved and respected them. He had stopped trying to understand women. Often he told himself, "if you see what they see, you will do what they do." That did it for him. He took his mind off the topic.

He opened the next letter and started to read it. Midway he folded it and puts it back in the envelope. He went inside. He would write his sister the next day. He placed Ella's mail on the kitchen table.

A few days after Ella announced her intention to relocate. She will be moving out of the house. Ulu was not there when she made the announcement. The trumpet player was not there either. She left the message on Joel's voicemail. He was shocked when he relayed the news. UIu did not really know what it was. But his expression shows he was down. He said out loud, that it was bad for him. Then said, it means that he has to look for another person to take the room. He then added if he does not, it means she would forfeit her deposit. That seemed to be some kind of consolation for him.

For him, Ulu would not say he was not prepared for that kind of news. When he said it his first reaction was to shout "what!" It was like his ex-girlfriend telling him that they were no longer lovers not minding they had been over that 100 hundred times before. They practiced quarrels and being separated. Saying it was a shock was natural. He had to say something. And that was what he said.

Ulu found himself feeling guilty without asking what it was about. He had read Ella's last note to him without writing back. They did not have much time to talk. If they did she might not have taken that decision. He was not sure how to dissuade her, especially when the message said she intended to move the next day.

He had to do something at least find out the reason or have her give him a reason whatsoever. He wrote her an email. She wrote back explaining that he does not have to worry so much about her. Her parents wanted her to find a place. "Psychology of the little white girl," he thought to himself. May be she was eventually ready to travel to Tanzania to meet her Masai warrior.

Joel played that morning and the tone sounded worrying. Ulu was trying to think of it in term of the benefits. But he liked her so much even when she comes back by one o' clock every morning and sleeps all day. At least that floor of the house had the special feeling of a place with a woman in it. He maximized those few days. He did not know if that was what worries the trumpet player or something else. But he did not seem to have any answers. Though they had lived there longer, Ulu tended to know her more than Joel. Joel even thought he was privy to the information about her sudden decision more than he did.

The email he sent her was a great therapy. It worked at least to some extent. He had admired the quality and quantity of good neighborliness. But in certain situations one cannot really say with the varieties of spices that there were on this planet. She came back that night he knew she wanted to talk.

But what was there to talk about she tended to have made up her mind. She said that was what you wanted, that worried him. He could have done anything to let her know that he wanted her to stay. If it was not for the guy in gray pullover at breakfast, he was certain to persuade her to stay. He told her that the only good news about the whole thing was that she was not moving in with that guy. That would have been a mistake and would be any day should she decide to spend more time than necessary with him. It may still sound good. She was only moving about two miles from where they lived. He went pass the street every time on his way to the library or the campus.

The next night when she came back from work, he helped with moving her thing into her car. Joel was not aware of that, he was sleeping. He knew the guy in the gray pullover was never a lover. Ulu however expected that, being in the middle of all of the drama, he would have been kind enough to help her move. He did not show up.

Ella had stayed in her previous relationship for two months. When she abandoned the guy, he went crazy. He threatened everything imaginable. Some days he came to the house and dropped another of his threat mails. His threat included whoever it was that she was going out with, so Ella said.

It had been thirteen days since anyone saw her. It was the first time that long, and this morning might be the last time that they would see her for a long time. But it seemed she was leaving her ghost behind.

CHAPTER ≈43≈

The Ella, the Trumpeter and Ulu were in the same cycle of life. It was the unknown above them. They themselves were soul searchers. But there was a mystery they did not understand. However it brought them together. They became roommates. Stan was the house guest.

Where Ella lived there were vacant rooms. She needed to keep some guys away from the house. They decided to live together. They became roommates. It became a heaven of some sort, save for the noise from the second floor at times. Everyone took a bit of everyone else. It was that oneness, they shared. Some nights when the stars were out in the sky, they met in the field and communed with the earth, the moon, the stars and the sky. They dreamed of making it big one day as artists and academics and they bonded more. Departure would create a big void. But it was the way of the world.

On the floor above Serge, sat there listening to 50 cent, lil wayne, NeYo. Snoop Dog and Drake. He was wearing a very tight black jeans and black tee shirt. His tee shirt has different design and patterns on the back it was eye of the iris in front it was the dragon. He loved rap music and he rapped whatever came in to this head.

"It is a long way from home. If I need to run I should be able to run well. If my pants sagged and almost dropped from my waist I may not be able to do this at all." Serge explains.

A few times he has been able to run fast and ran out of trouble. When he got caught he was later released and put on probation. He could still dream of college and medical school. He was from Russia. His American wife Katrina was at the other end of the living room. Her hair colored between red, pink and blue. She had massive and elaborate body art. Her tattoos and piercings were intimidating, if not horrifying. The tattoos made her body looked like the next edition of Harry Potter was started on it, but was discontinued for lack of space.

She sat on the ground on a corner of the room. She had her music plugged to her ears. It was pounding loud Serge could hear it. Mark was on the other end playing his games on his laptop, he called himself the best gamer in the world. He was good at it.

Frankie and Toya shared the floor with Serge, Katrina and Mark. They were a little older than the others. They came now and then to ask for salt or milk or beer. The fridge on the first floor was bigger so it was supposed to hold more. Toya would have the fridge already opened before she would ask for permission to get whatever she wanted.

They were nice and friendly folks. They have both had run-ins with the law. Toya had a full time job which paid at least half of their bills. Frankie either had no job or was a full time drug dealer. If he was, his specialty wouldn't not go beyond crack cocaine and weed.

Their last clash with the law seemed to have left them paralyzed. Toya came out first. She rented the room and above her bed was the sign "gone with the wind." She vowed to have nothing to do with anything that would take her back to jail. Well maybe she did not know Frankie was also coming home soon. But he did. And the first person he went to was her. His love was as fresh as the song he sang to her the first time they made love. "It was fresher," he told her.

Frankie had a musical talent. That talent died before it developed, Toya understood. When he came the second day she took him in. And then she had him to worry about again. It seemed her freedom was again being taking. She was a chubby woman with smooth and beautiful shiny skin. She used any opportunity she had to admire herself. She wanted to show it off whenever she could without offending anyone.

Toya wanted to be able to look at herself in the mirror with the water still dripping. She enjoyed the feel and knew the power of that over any onlooker. Her bedroom and the bathroom were such places to enjoy such freedom. But she began to fear Frankie would complain. She would no longer leave the bathroom door open when she went into the shower.

Frankie always had a story to tell about how bad Toya wanted him gone. He said she was trying to lure other guys. But in truth she was trying hard to keep him. Her family objected to her bringing him in. But she did and there he was singing to her again. There were days he would disturb the entire house with his songs. It was her duty to plea with the neighbors to bear with her. To Serge and Katrina as long as he brought the weed, "homie, it was all good."

CHAPTER ≈44≈

The house was the merging worlds of creeping and crawling reptiles and ants, and those of high tech racing and super gaming, in which they were all champions for as long as the smoke was in the air.

There were days when all they did was just sit outside exploring the world. They told stories of many parts of the world, their city and people. The Ella, the trumpeter, and Ulu understood his business of alcohol sales through Stan. Stan the drunk worked for one.

He was aware how much money the check cashing in the store brought in. He also knew the power and effect of cash on desire. "A little alcohol created more desire. Whatever it was that the people wanted a good Liquor store should be able to provide it." He told them.

Behind the counter, whenever Stan felt important and wanted to impress a stranger whom he knew spoke more than a language, he did his number two, a fake British accent. At times he used it to pass as a Brit on vacation that has to raise money because he is short of cash.

CHAPTER
≈45≈

It was Friday, pay day the drunk came home with a six-pack of Budweiser. He bought it with store discount. As Stan staggered in, he yelled, "Let the party begin." He tried his two steps dance. As bad as those steps were, compared to those of Maroon 5 vocalist, Adam whom Stan loved, Stan would pass for a superstar dancer. Even the dancing with the stars judges would agree.

Earlier in the day he was a bit drunk, but behind the counter. At the sight of the guy in the military uniform he sobered up. His younger brother was in the military. He admitted the younger man was smarter than him. He was not sure why he opted for the marines. He was always thrilled about the navy, about the sexy girl in skimpy dress holding their flag. That was the old flag and the amazon beauty. Their imaginations carried into their adult years through cartoons, books and TV.

The news had come his brother was not coming home. Bad news, they fetched him first, they were going to his sister in law.

His brother was a smart young man, as he was always quick to say. He and his beautiful girlfriend of two years had their one year old son. When the insurance man told him that one day his pay check may not be coming, he said no. It was him who may not be coming. He signed up for life insurance. Looking into the face of his little man he smiled. At twenty six, life was sweet and filled with adventure. Their son was three and his girlfriend had gotten the kind of wedding she always wanted. It was a wedding with all the military honor and fun.

His brother in law did not visit often. Seeing him and the man in military uniform beside him she knew it was not good. That day what she was not expecting was the news of the Iraqi sniper fire. While they grieved he was busy making mental calculations. He felt sad but was not afraid of his nephew's future. Stan had more reason to drown himself in alcohol. The liquor store held hope and comfort for him. If he was ever to invest it was the place.

CHAPTER
≈46≈

Not far away from where they lived there was a liquor store. It was called Joe's Liquor and kegs. It was like any other normal business in that neighborhood. The owners knew about the saying that if you dined with the devil you use a long spoon. It was the way of the city. Someone living miles away from the poor neighborhoods always came on with an idea. People desire to be happy and there is not better business than keeping a poor man happy. It was brilliant. In the projects or close to them there was always a businessman willing to exploit the occupants.

At the store one afternoon a man walked in for lottery tickets. He looked at the man for a long time. It was not a meal ticket. He had none. It was a lottery ticket. When he bought it, he looked at the casher behind the counter. He told her, he has just made his little contribution to education in the state. And to no one in particular he said, "..and I reaffirmed my belief that luck may save the day." The man indulged in a sense of security through false hope. He enjoyed momentary fantasies of lives being changed by those tickets.

Joe's Liquor and kegs was a complete business setup. John Lee Brown was the investor and financier. Joe Brown as many of his friends called him was shrewd. Though he did not drink he always said he knew a good drink when he saw one. In actuality Mr. Brown referred to business investments. On Fridays the people collected the welfare checks. The liquor store had a check cashing in it. For a little percentage you got your cash. If you have the ATM card Joe's was still the place for you. All you did was swiping your card and you got your money. Joe's place offered you liquor, wine, beer, cigarette and many more. A visit to his place and you are ready to party. With seventy-five cents you could get a can of beer. Joe was a smart businessman he had about ten more of such setups in many poor neighborhoods. And hip-hop has helped his business. Some songs put some of those labels on the hottest selling lists. Joe did not drink but he knows where to get those who drank from dawn to dusk. He sold more there than he would in his own neighborhood. To some of his friends he would say some people relied on alcohol to be happy. And to others he would say he is helping the government to keep their money in circulation. He paid taxes and met people's demands. He was a good man. He did not run the stripe club on the street or at least it was not in his name.

Joe came up with the idea of a street picnic one day. He sold it to Stan and he in turn sold it to the house and everyone else bought it. They had street picnics in the park. And it helped reestablish friendships. They enjoyed the time they shared. Even Jay, he was black and the oldest guy on the street. Or maybe he was not, but he lived in a gated old folk's community. He was the only one from there who interacted very well with the rest of the neighborhood. There was a white woman and her family he visited often. He had a huge idea of a servant leader and he flirted with everyone. He thought the new girls at the end of the block did not like him. He was happy they liked his jokes. He maintained a Facebook page. He updated it with jokes and happenings in and around both communities.

Almost everyone on the street and their friends were at the park that Saturday afternoon. Uncle Tony was there. He was Italian and had a good heritage. Mama Tarri Lavic. She loves younger men. Her husband was in the military. Leslie she was half Portuguese and half African. Jen was a student at the university originally she was from India. Her friend Eva was German. Antonio and Diana were Mexicans. Their dad was sent back to Mexico. Their mom was in a new relationship. The two were in high school and did not know what they want to do afterwards. But Antonio was in the Jackson Jaguar Marching Band, Jackson Memorial high school. Their friend Ali was also Mexican, a sweet little kid, always got books from Uncle Tony. And they joked a lot. She did not know why he bought her more books than her parents did. Her parents and their extended family crowded a tiny apartment. They wake up every morning before everyone on the street. Natasha was the girls from across the street. She was on vacation. Occasionally she came over to hang out with Uncle Tony. A friend of hers whom she met in Germany lived nearby. She was extremely gorgeous. She was the girl with a million dollar boobs. That was what they called her. Natasha had a breast enhancement surgery.

A few years ago she met and married her rich old oil man. Her husband was a Russian billionaire. He only spoke Russian. Already vast in three languages, she was bent on bettering her English. Natasha saw a world beyond the old rich man. "Not even their son was going to hold her back," she had vowed. Her vacation was almost over and the old man was waiting. She was having fun, enough of it.

Freda was the nurse. She worked at a hospital not far from the street. She and boyfriend would break their flat if one stopped them. Alice lived in a flat not far from Freda's. To Alice - happiness meant everything. It was no longer love. She has been beaten by a marriage and a few men. Out of it, she has chosen. Happiness came first before any other. It meant everything. Happiness was love- love without it was nothing. And she sought it wherever she found it. It came with the alcohol. It came with the parties. It came with the men. It came with the sex. Sometimes it was a revenge mission. No one not even Alice was sure how it would end. She was just back from Las Vegas. Ask her, in Vegas you can get everything. Get drunk and get married. Get impregnated by a stranger, if he looks good. If you're lucky, in the same night you can win too. She was a sweet love song searching for a voice she never found. Tonight was another night. She searched the faces in the crowd while scrolling through her phone.

Charlie was an occupational hazard specialist. It was not that it was any use to his people. They had more immediate worries. They were far removed from those thoughts. He dated Alice in the past. Their hearts were in the same place but their heads were not.

When he got tired of constant fights and break ups he sold his business. He went back to his home country Equatorial Guinea.

There he started a new business. But a group of foreigners were arriving in their numbers. They were running from a natural disaster, they claimed. The bad news was that they were likely to displace the natives. It was not always a favorite destination in the region. Nkwoeke had lived in Fernando Po. His people had to undergo great pain to get a visa to go out to other places. But there had been changes. The nation of under 800.000 people exported more crude oil than her neighbors. Their fears were great. But he was back to party. He has quite a taste in women. No one was sure of where he met the beauty in his arms.

There were two cats and a dog in the park. The dog was chewing on a bone and the cats were playing. They came from a house at the end of the street. They lived alone there. The owner of the house was a fragile old woman was back in the nursing house. The cats and dogs maybe other cats looked after the house. And a friend of the old woman, Tina from Meals on Wheel, came once in a while with help to clean up the place. The dog from there fought a lot with Jim and Kate's German shepherd. Jim and Kate were a middle age white couple. They just got another dog. It made their dogs two. Kate's mother gave it to her. Mama Tarri said like the dogs, the couples were trying to get pregnant. One of the cats ran after a giant fly. He stood on both hind legs using the fore legs to catch the fly. The green grass was not making it easy. He was having fun. The cat caused a stare, people were laughing and clapping.

It caught Reverend's attention. He was a big time soccer scout. He used little soccer pitch at the park. Sometimes Ulu played with him there. He has successfully placed many stars with big football clubs in Europe and elsewhere around the globe. In the USA he was learning the ropes. Soccer wasn't that big yet in America. He had big plans there though, after all most of his boys came from places where no one else was searching. He broke new grounds. Reverend was sipping a glass of wine while chatting with two Hispanic guys. He was enjoying the conversation.

Craig was in a corner smoking. Someone had dropped a cigar. It was the Executive Branch, a fine cigar and he was making the best of it. He is Serge and Katrina's friend and responsible for Katrina's body art. He was a tattoo artist. He did most of Katrina's tattoos and piercings. He suggested Katrina become an adult movie star or a pole dancer. He was apolitical and a free spirit. She had asked for advice. He was sincere, that was all he could offer. The park was filled. Everyone had fun.

At the end of the night it was important Jay updated his profile. And he did. To his friends on Facebook, he wrote.

"My dear friends you have been great. In my own book of the most wonderful people in the world, you shine brighter than the stars in the sky. May you never lack those who bring laughter, joy and sunshine in your lives. I am no longer a candidate for favor, I am God's favor. -Update. Thank you."

No one was sure he was writing any book. If he was, it was probably the tiny notebook he kept beside the old bible on his night stand.

Old Jay, when he finished. He turned to a lady friend sitting on the edge of his bed. He smiled and said.

"All we know and believe about ourselves over the years are what we have read, heard and seen from people who have bettered themselves telling our own stories. What has been our lot? Well we are laughed at. And sometimes we share in the laughter. That at least eases the burden. It takes our minds off the worries momentarily."

He updated his profile that way and blogged tirelessly every day. If he didn't there were those who would update theirs by announcing his obituary. He was proud he did that whenever he did. If he did nothing else for himself, it had the feel of an achievement.

CHAPTER
≈47≈

Several months after Ella moved to a new apartment on another street. She still came from time to time to pick up her mails. Or maybe that was the pretense. But she came to relive the memories she left behind.

The last she came before her long break was that last visit was one early morning in February. She said something it would take months before she came again. Ulu did not take her serious it was her usual joke. Weeks and Months past she did not show up though she foretold it he knew something was the problem. UIu did his best to make contact with Ella. It was then that he realized she might have checked into the rehab. It was actually time that she went in there and spent some time for her mental and overall health. On that last visit she all of a sudden started to complain and blame her younger sibling of being greatly responsible for her abuse of drugs. Ulu could not understand her excuse or even her reason for sudden outspokenness about her use of substance. And because though she knew that he was aware of her use of drugs it was not an area that he discussed often. She did not like to discuss her private life as social affair. It was private and they respected it. She seemed to have gotten disturbed about the last time, that she felt the need to talk about it.

She talked about rehab, which as it came to be, she had not been to yet, when she eventually resurfaced a few days later. She had wished her doctor had recommended that. But she did not. It was evident she wanted so much to get out to any place. She hated her job environment more so the social atmosphere. She was not always a very sociable person but socializing at work should not be that difficult. Ulu thought of that in the contrary as she mentioned that as a problem. He did not consider that as a reason to consider leaving a good paying job. It was a nice job and good paying. Ulu did not want to think of her leaving that job. But it appeared to him she might need some time to herself the way she spoke about it. Ulu suggested a sick leave rather than quitting.

That boyfriend of hers was still there. Why quit. Why relocate, why considering another part of the town. A place that was conducive for all the quay guys. Able to give her the relief she was seeking. She was mad at her supervisor. She pestered her and her boyfriend. They refused to take the STD test. She was not sure if she cared about them. She was not sure if it was just part of the employment blood work protocol. It pained her. She probably just wanted to be a bitch with her.

Thinking, Ulu grabbed his crotch. He felt a sharp itch on his balls. He had partied with a girl the night before at the frat house. In the past he refused opportunity of such invitations. He was invited to join the fraternity. He turned it down.

But curiosity leads men to places they want to go to and to places they don't need to be. He was a member of the world's largest and richest confraternities. But the invitation of a German girl took him to the frat party. Maybe he got something from the girl. Not sure what. Easy on the eyes, she was such a beauty. He removed his mind from such thoughts. Those thoughts themselves got one sick.

They hadn't really done anything serious. It was such thoughts. It took him to the hospital. After a couple of the checks all came back negative. He hissed a sigh of relief. He posted the result on his nightstand. Reminded himself it was, "the working of the human mind." It was the way the doctor had put it. He had to affirm it. In truth they had done anything unsafe. They only lay in bed and watched "Stranger Bed Fellows." She never stopped complaining about his being too careful about life.

He would have taken advantage of company provided health care screening. He came back to where he was before his mind wandered off. If it ended up that she left that job. She would be creating an opportunity for another who needed it.

They talked about her leaving her job. He imagined that as the reason for why she came. She wanted to make a sound decision about it. She said if she left he could apply there for a part time job. Well that is if that blue eye, gray hair old guy is eventually considering letting one not of his race to join that group of his. If she left that would mean he would call that guy more often. He would equally know that he knows there is a vacant position. This race thing sometimes is like the madman at the market square in the village. He runs free and wild. He brandishes his machete. He runs free in the isolated communities. In the bigger cities he is constrained. And he is lost in it. His force is overshadowed by other forces. He was hopeful.

A colleague of hers from work had left the job, some weeks after, she started having insomnia. One day she walked into a clinic. She requested to see the physician and was asked to sit in the waiting room. When she eventually entered the consulting room the man asked her what her problem was. She had sleepless nights. The doctor asked if she had any special symptoms. When she finished, he was convinced, it was insomnia. He wrote her a prescription and instructed her to pick it up at the pharmacy on her way out. The rest will be delivered to her within the next 24 hours, some 8 hours later the woman got an email. It was a friend request from Facebook by the doctor. With it was a message, confirm receipt please. From then on she was not really sure how she spent her nights. When she was not in her room groaning she was seen driving out of her parking lot in the middle of the night or men dropped by on short notices.

They went on cleaning the kitchen. She commented on the way the kitchen looked when she came out of the basement. For Ulu the basement usually took him back to their escape from death during the civil war. He told her about the war.

"The war was fought and lost on both sides that, was what they said. At the last count the young nation had not only lost a war. They lost over two million women and children. Where the gun didn't do them in, hunger did."

Emeka Ojukwu went into exile. "You live to fight another day." He said.

Years later he came back home. Enyimba was agog the hero was back and has entered the city of champions.

Ndubisi- was what mattered. Ojukwu enjoyed the warm embrace of his people. The women, children, men, young and old wanted to touch and hug him. On the faces of those survivors he saw warmth and pain. In his heart felt their hearts and their pains.

In private tears filled his eyes. He wept for his people. Politics was like murky water. But his people needed a true leader. Numbers on the streets were not always the same when ballots were counted. "My heart bleeds every night when I think of those military boys who would fail even as administrators of daycare centers running a country."

What he did not win in vote counts he won in hearts. One of such hearts was the heart of a queen. Ojukwu knew the beauty spots in the jungle. But the love of young beautiful queen was over powering. He was her lion. She was a well-protected and jealously guarded jewel. Then their bodies, hearts and soul merged. They stood tall, Lion and the jewel of the nation. They breed peace, joy, progress, beauty and unity. Their blessings were known to the world."

Ella had gone in the basement straight as she came into the house. She picked up that bubble gum machine. It was a gift from a psycho friend of her. Ulu could not tell why she needed it now after avoiding that guy so much. If she was going to sale it, he did not know who would want to buy it.

As she cleaned the kitchen, part of it was sparkly than they saw it in a long time. He could not stop wondering why she did not clean it that much while she lived there. Ulu took out an empty coffee container, missing the fresh aroma of real good coffee beans. He dropped it in the trash can. "I want Starbucks taste without breaking the bank."

"Coffee?" Ella asked.

"Yes. real good one. I gave my Starbucks card away."

It should make it simpler.

"Yes, sensible."

"Hmm, nice tasting coffee. When did the search start?"

"Kinda like searching for that nice tasting palm kernel."

"I know you don't drink instant coffee."

"No, not looking for the quickie, home processed, um, those taste good too. Please don't say Mcaffee."

"Gone to the Tea leaves and coffee bean place?"

"Some fresh coffee beans? Something real, like Kernel straight from the under the palm tree."

"Yeah, but the birds and the squirrels had their share." Allusion to something they shared in the house. She laughed.

"But you don't get enough of it, do you? Seriously where do you find it?"

When they finished cleaning they talked about their friends and other things. When Stan left his friends the last they heard from him was from a 90210 mailing address. They knew he has rented a virtual office space.

And Ella asked of where she could get some food, before she left.

Outside two kids are playing soccer in the street. One is Palestinian and the other is Israeli. They will be friends till the day when one becomes a victim.

She had offered him that machine as a gift but he did not find any use for it. He did not accept it. But it must have meant something to the guy who gave it to her. He considered it hers that she ought to keep. As she left she shouted he should consider it. That was a form of greeting. She said something about should he change his mind. He replied, "About what?" She drove off.

It was her first visit in a long time and in the daytime. She seemed really different. She would be back soon as she said, she hopes to come before she moves, which he thinks she means before she finally decides on whether or not to move. He smiled at the work we were able to do, and sent her a thank you text, which he knew she would read as soon as she had the opportunity. The world remained one patch of scotched earth in need of constant moist. It was an end of a season. It went with her and she left.

Ulu got up and out of bed. It was cold on Christmas day he went to drop off a card for his neighbor. The sign at the door stopped him. It read "the house of the wicked will be overthrown but the tent of the upright will flourish." For the first time in many years, his mind went back to where they had crawled out from after the destructions of the war. He did not understand God's rules of engagement in wars. He did not understand why God allowed wars. But he remembered what Mr. Stone had told him about wars as a little boy. "The tent shall flourish", he said. Ulu dropped the Christmas card in the mail box and went away.

CHAPTER
≈48≈

Ulu finished his post doctorate research, and planned on moving to Europe for some months. Before then he went to the peninsula to see his folks. They were happy to see him. And he was very happy to see that they were doing very well. His sister was working with the Nigerian National Aviation Authority. On the weekends she taught geography at the University of Yaoundé. She was happy with her job and dating a medical director at the national hospital. His brother Azuogu was done with his degree studies in political science and administration. He lectured part time at Nsukka, and was still up and down touring many parts of the world with his many pet projects. A trip to southern Africa was an eye opener. "There were newer realities and opportunities," he told them.

It was a happy family reunion. His mother and stepfather were happy together. Their family dogs Fido and Tiger were happy and excited too. It was Sunday and the two women went into the kitchen. They were preparing their favorite delicacies. In her kitchen she always remembered what an old woman told a group at a dance "Acquired taste is not bad. But if you can't grow it, watch what does to your pocket, the economy and your body. And watch you don't lose that which you can grow." It was a lesson she passed on long ago.

In the living room were the three men, they chatted over whiskey and beer. They caught up on what everyone was up to. They discussed their personal lives, politics in the country and current events worldwide. Ulu inquired if his brother was seeing any girl. He informed him he was. She was sweet, he said, "if she was a bottle of wine, I will sip her forever." His father was delighted. He smiled. He knew he had the son he always dreamt of having. Mr. Stone said to his boys, "Any man who found a woman that gave his heart joy would live and die a happy man." Every now and then the two boys went into the kitchen to see how the women were doing.

The phone rings. It was for Ada. Ulu takes it to the Kitchen for her. It was Tom her boyfriend. He was calling from work. A few minutes into the call, Hauwa enters his office. Hauwa was Tom's best friend at the hospital. Ada had spoken to her on a few occasions. The night before he went on and on about her, "nothing stopped her being human. Amongst competitors she had an edge. If it was a race, a little raised chest gave her the win. If it came to looks, she had grace. That which made every other thing seems like nothing. The smile on her face was magical. It was a gift. Even in the rush of time she still had a smile for a stranger. In the most difficult of times to be friend, in her big heart was space for honesty, humor and forgiveness. She said her prayers fives a day."

The way he talked about Hauwa got to her. She was a little envious.

Ada confided in her mom, "I don't doubt he is faithful. But he gets on my nerves when he goes on and on about her."

"Adanne, men are like kids. He idolizes you through her. It is his best effort in telling you that, and besides she keeps him in check for you. I wouldn't worry about her my daughter"

When the meal was ready they sat around the dining table. Ngozika joined her hands with that of her husband and children followed suit. They bowed their heads in prayer. Mr. Stone asked Ulu to lead in saying the grace. He did and they started eating. They were delighted to be eating together as a family again. They joked about their first meal of antelope on the peninsula and everyone laughed. "Goodness and kindness are forever good." Their mother quipped and squeezed her husband's hands gently.

In the few days he was staying in the country, he would be visiting friends in Owerri, Alaukwe, Abuja and Lagos. He would meet a friend at Okigwe Road in Owerri for a drink. His friend was a graduate of that place where they gathered every Saturday evening and made joke of everything under the sun.

He would be a guest lecturer at University of Nigeria Nsukka at the same time that his brother would be lecturing there. Another guest Lecturer from the University of Nairobi was on a panel discussion he would be appearing in. Mark Njororge was a philosophy professor, one of the best from his country. He was very well known. The students called him mad Mark. But the truth was that if he was not teaching he would be homeless. And the world would still seem normal. The lecture for Ulu was a sort of stock taking. He wanted to reflect on where the country has been, where it was and where it was going with the students. He was eager to learn, the country needed answers.

In Lagos Ulu went to visit an old friend. He walked to the Kpako Bridge. Everyone crossed the creek to get to the other part of town. He was already in the middle of the wooden bridge. He discovered that it was not the kind of journey he bargained for. It was the only way to get to where he was going to. The wooden bridge has almost collapsed in the middle. It was only a wood that still held it in the middle. He was terrified. The flow of traffic on the bridge didn't indicate condition. There was no way he could have imagined what he had come into. He had followed the undisturbed faces streaming in and out. Now in the middle, he either had to go back or try what the others were doing. They cross bridge. He stood there for a while. He shakes his head and decides to proceed. He places his legs carefully on one the end of the bridge, it slid into the water. The wood was supported by a stump inside the muddy water. He almost slipped. He caught himself. But the dirty water and a decaying leave splashed on him. It stank of compost. A few steps further he was prepared to swim the rest of the way, it was the option. He could not imagine those people were able to continue using the route that way. They paid their taxes to the state. But that is the bridge where hopes, dreams and tears mixed.

Eventually on the other part of town houses were being searched. Things were being destroyed and residents were harassed by supposed authorities. In the house of his lady friend he watched the scenes reenacted. He felt violated.

In his hotel room, he had a glass of gin, pen in his hand. The paper on his desk had the word Lagos underlined. Then he began to write. "....Lagos walking on the sandy beaches of Lagos, barefoot for the quest for fun or power, there we leave our footprints. We all are Lagos. What it has become from those before, when the coconut trees were fresh and beautiful-when the breeze was fresh. From here we have moved to the rock. But in this melting pot lies our heart. Do not destroy it, build it."

When he was done, he picked the telephone. He called New York.

CHAPTER
≈49≈

Joel was in New York that weekend. The trumpeter got constant gigs in the big apple. In New Jersey he was also done with his Masters study in Music. It was time to go back home, he had told him over the phone. They talked for a while before Ulu wished him a happy birthday again. Joel walked slowly back to his friends in the living room.

There were a few questions he always found hard to find answers to. He didn't like it when on Sundays the pastors say love conquers all. On Mondays it turns out money acquires everything and always solved all problems. As a kid he loved to eavesdrop when his mother and father talked about what gifts were necessary to get him for his birthdays. Then he always hoped to repay them with big gifts and birthday parties too. But today he didn't want to wait forever to give that perfect party.

"I called you here," he began.

"I didn't want to be alone on my birthday. I am not yet able to throw a party to the whole world. But as friends you know, the fears we fear. We may be shy to admit it."

Everyone liked friends they can whisper to. And friends they can trust. He wanted his friends to remember this day.

He was not sure his friends were in the mood for too much talk. He knew some of his friends would have loved to be left alone. But he also knew everyone needed encouragement. And he needed it too.

Joel opened a bottle of wine and poured everyone a drink. As they drank, he took his trumpet and began to play. More friends joined them. He played his heart out and hoped his friends would understand. He was neither rich nor poor. He was always something in between. He was a man who had hope. They partied into the night.

For every dream there is a waking moment. But New York and Los Angeles were the places where the world came to when they dreamed. It was there they prayed to wake up with better dreams. But Joel woke up one morning announced he had a calling. His Calling was not for his present location. Some days later he went home to Columbia. He would teach music to children there. He would use it as a healing art. He was sure somewhere in those green fields and gardens he would find his dream girl.

CHAPTER
≈50≈

In Alaukwe the rain finally came. Tata was a woman who never ceased to marvel at the ironies and wonders of life. She saw the flood. She also waited for the rain for many seasons. The rain washed away dry dusty earth. It fell on the trees. It fell on the spot where the naked black woman and her daughter stood and bathed on a stone tablet before the marauders deflowered the forest. It left droplets of water. It washed away the blood stain on the earth. It washed away the hymen dropped through a forced entry. It fell on the spot where the earth held within its belly wealth and beauty, before she was raped and killed by the greedy ones. They burnt the green and polluted the life sustaining substance in the waters. On that spot the water was pure, and fountains fresh and the spring was life. It was life's sustaining force before the spill thrust into the river swelled the belly of the water and the fish.

Tata woke up in the morning. She looks into the sky and on the ground. And she offers her prayers. "These are the words of life, the words of a new day" Tata sang. It is the voice of the woman who rejoices for the gift of sight to the eyes. Her words were as fresh as the dawn of a new day. The words of the singer of hymns flowed through her mouth, "You who make the outgoings of the morning and evening rejoices, you who visits the earth and waters it. You who greatly enriches the rivers. The river of god is full of water. Your path drips with abundance. Your daughter greets you, mighty one."

"This rain will bring life," Tata says. "I have managed to live three thousand years into the past and a thousand into the future. I have seen it"

The cloud moved and the earth was in accord. And so was Igwe; the heavens.

"May the souls of the departed converge at the shrine of Nri at the ends time." It was the Ofo Nri.

It never failed to rain, if the cloud got to Isenri. It was a fact, from the oracle of Nri. Tata looked up, lifted her walking stick and pointed it to the sky.

"We are all heading there." She said.

Most of her short frames were now supported by the walking stick. She still had the smile of an old woman who has seen several seasons of war and peace, rain and drought.

Tata when on a journey walked carefully. She placed her walking stick at the right places. If her left foot hit a stone on the ground, she carefully retraced her steps. It was no good luck. She left it as a journey for another day.

"The earth has a relationship with the feet of the walking one. Only those who have listening ears understood."

Every journey ends at Isenri the spot where the creator began it. Souls converged there after their earthly journeys. The stick in her hand bore the tales of many generations who had been there.

CHAPTER
≈51≈

After wars have been declared over, men who carried bazookas and armored tanks drop them. They now walk on their feet and would feel tiny drops of blood on green grasses. They will feel the scratch of a sharp lemon grass when they walk pass one. They inhale the scent. "Peace may come at last," the people hoped. The night usually seemed peaceful after days of mourning and celebrations. But peace is not easy to come by, not as easy as it was to send men to war battlefields.

Growing poverty became the war the government would never win. Not that they had won any. In fact since the end of the civil war, government after government situations got worst. Year after year more complex and systematic apparatus of state were used to defraud the people. Corruption and corrupt individuals grew. And so did the quest for riches through the occult, violent crimes, kidnapping and armed robbery.

Year after year, the survivors celebrated the departed. Ahamefula- the Remembers recounted, the years of suffering and deaths. For a whole month they prayed and replayed their lives. They prayed their land for forgiveness where they wronged her. The spirits of the dead fared well. Their ghosts sent away. They prayed for peace. They prayed for justice.

Men and woman still tried to put the pieces of their shattered lives together. But they needed a revolution and a miracle. "Unless by the revolution of the minds, generations after, those defeated in wars were always the enemy. No matter, on what terms peace was reached. They were always treated as the suspect, if not the enemy." It was the silent voice of reason, the voice of Biafra before her exile. It was the voice of a leader saying the war was fought for a good cause.

As was the case then, many feared. "What shall we call normal. Is this war ended?" It was the post war weeks, months and years. The folks faced greater agony. Many would not dare to dream of leaving places that offered them shelter, food and protection. Some dared what they called, "Return to the land. The earth would feed its people." Cassava, cocoyam yam and many other corps were a life force. The people with crops were to be lured to cultivate the land. But the earth was dotted with bones of loved ones who never reached the battle fields. The cries did not stop. Their tears were fresh. They chanted, "...awoh, the stopper of wars. Our pots are dry and empty, your weapon of war. Oh prophet of the republic, whom have we offended. Why do you block the manna? Why did you hold god's hands? Mothers and children die, not from the fire of your guns. But the pots you have burnt. Oh you giver of grace, how is it millions die chanting awwwoh, awoh, awoh, while their empty, protruding and kwashiorkored bellies become food for your vultures. We're healing. We will heal."

Some returned with the herds and mats on their heads walking back. To places they were no longer sure of what they would find. Still they expected they would see a house, a store, a shed, a sibling or a tree standing with a ripe fruit on it.

CHAPTER
≈52≈

It was under that atmosphere that people remembered the lives they led in the past. Men, women and children planted flowers, cleared graves and headstones of their loved ones. Many left the cities to go back to the places that were truly home. Places they left many years before. A woman was cutting the rose bush around her husband's grave. A little piece that secured whatever remained of the man she once loved

Peter Madu; the Rock and his wife went home from the camp after the war. As they remembered not much seem to have changed. They were one of first who went to his hometown. He was one of the first to witness the shock of the scenes of destruction and the desert that their home had been reduced to. Though there were still a few houses standing. The enemy soldiers had them used as their own houses. They stayed in them to rape the town's women and children. The town was a ghost town. In the next days, weeks and months the great Peter would move from place to place searching for food and fruits. They would go back to the city. It seemed that life was returning to normal there. They were back to see what was left of their houses and stores. He and his wife were big people in the city before the war. The banks and the bankers knew them by their first names. In the past they hosted parties in which everyone that mattered in the city were present. They will go back and start life afresh there. Their money would be safe there, they thought. The city was still there so also will their stocks and money in the bank. The houses, the stores, were all there. Port Harcourt was calling.

Back in the city the human traffic was greatly reduced. But things had changed. The properties belonged to no man. It was a government order. Peter would stand in front of the building and could not get into them. The run to safety has become an automatic change of ownership. They had become abandoned properties. To their shock and bewilderment they had no place to spend the night at. Unknown to them the greater shock was in the news they were yet to hear. Their wealth was not used up in prosecuting the war. But they happened to have gone back to the place where they would find safety. They happened to be the defeated folks. They happened to be alive. And as a result they had a penalty to pay. It would last generation after generation, phase after phase and season after season. The oil wells will be drilled in their backyards. It would be taken in pipes to be refined. Their shares for the few cars and roads were to be a few gallons scooped from leaking pipes. Their roads would be overgrown with bushes. Their water taps would run dry. It was for them to learn the lesson of being on the losing team. They were sentenced to stunted growth. It was a national decision.

The new law required that every man and woman with a bank account in their name be paid a fixed amount. That amount was to be twenty pound. The fiscal regime required that it be so. Peter was not a man to be told tales about his money. But those in control of the economy and in charge of economic policy decide what happens with wealth of the defeated. So it came to pass that every man or woman who had any money in the bank before the war was to receive twenty pounds. That was for them restart their lives and their businesses. It was due to the generosity of the government of the day. It was the same men who over saw the blockade of food and medicines. It was their good will.

It would take some twenty years to get back to what they once were, and that was only if they were not completely paralyzed. It was the kindness of the generous new managers of the economy, men who days before the war had nothing to their names. They redistributed the wealth of the defeated. They gave themselves shares in every company in the land

and overseas. Their gold and treasures they took, even the best of their women.

That economic policy dealt a deathblow to Biafra. Men whom the bullets, mortars, rockets shell and hunger could not kill during the war had their obituaries written and kept with relief officers and their bankers. Peter was one of those men. When he received his, he could not imagine it. His heart was broken. He went home and had a heart attack. His wife was stronger. Being from the family of moneylenders, she could understand the nature of money. It went from one hand to the other, from the lender to the borrower and verse versa. It was men who put value on the paper currency whatever name it was call, naira, dollar or pounds. She has learnt from starting life afresh as a war survivor, she would survive anything. That was what she told herself. She told herself that the beauty of life lies in understanding of one's inner strengths. That was one thing her husband did not completely understand. He saw folks fighting at the slightest provocation. But for many years he lived with a woman who took in everything and came out on the top. Peter could not be revived. A few days later he passed away in his sleep. She buried her husband. He was a great man. The world mourned at his death and the cruelty of a nation to her people.

She had lost the four most important men in her life. Her younger brother was the only one of them living. She went back to the city. She had learnt to laugh at life and herself. Walking in the city one day she stopped. She stopped and had a good laugh. She had just remembered the great women with whom her mother-in-law was friends. They called each other by the nicknames that amazed her. "Honey-well" was one of such names. The two women loved each other. They were very old women. As a younger lady she couldn't understand them at times. She knew those two had time on their hands and made the best they could with it. "Honeywell, Oil-well, Manu-well" she came to understand the reference. The women saw themselves, the holders of the invaluable treasure and wealth of the land. Even after the area was bare and those wells declared empty. They were still there.

The grave held that which many once loved and valued. Trimming the plants and flowers around one brought back those feelings and their stories.

CHAPTER
≈53≈

Her mother in law and her friend enjoyed life and tales of days when they were young girls. The two women grew up together. They both acted as single girls though they were married. They married very early in life. They found themselves married to their husbands who encouraged them to enjoy what young girls their age did. It was rare. But their husbands were young and understanding. They did not prevent them from spending time with their single friends.

Their friendship became tighter when they both knew there were married. This set them apart from the other girls. Gradually they began to form a separate group from the bigger whole. Their recollection of Ofege dance, a dance they danced as newlyweds was so exciting. They would not cease to discuss it when they were to together. The story has been that one night they got to the dance which was a maiden dance, joined the group without incidence, but as the night went on young men came in to watch the maidens dance and play around under the light from the moon. The young men who came around were often unmarried or a few married men who helped the women play the musical instruments.

That particular night Manu-well and her friend had gone out of the enclosure for breath of fresh air after the group ended a dance session. The moment they came out and walked to a corner of the arena, two men followed them. They professed their love and secret admiration for the two beautiful dancing queens. The women went on to flirt and enjoy the evening. Before the next dance session words have gotten to their husbands about the evening. But the young men excited about the evening went back to the scene again. That night a big fight broke out. They never went back to the dance. And words spread about the fight. The young men were not allowed to come back to the town to watch the maiden dance. They were marked for the misbehaviors for a long time, men watched out for them. People in the town did not want to see them near their wives or their sisters.

The two women did not forget. Each time they remembered they laughed like young girls. They were old but the follies of their young days remained lively memories.

CHAPTER ≈54≈

She remembered the woman who was her mother in law with a lot of love. There were days when both women sat and told their sons and daughter in laws about things they did as girls. They had Tata the woman who watched the lake. Tata had special gifts. She recalled her telling her.

As little girls they went to her, because she always had something to tell them. She was their guide. She guided them through the lake. Sometimes she held them by the hands, guided them by her words through the dark. The woman took them from one place to another. At certain nights when it was only the sound of the whistling of the cricket and the sound of her walking stick heard. She took them to places they have never been to without losing or abandoning them. Tata delivered many great men and women on plantain leaves in the back of their parents' homes. On those walks that she taught them the use of herbal tea, kernel oil, long walks, spicy foods and sex to a pregnant woman or ones about to induce labor.

Walking with the women once, hearing to the sound of the music from the flute coming from afar, Tata stops and exhales, looks at the women, then up in the heavens and says, "One of god's greatest gifts to man is the breath of life, yet greater is the power to call into being out of that thin air. It is only given those who know how to attain it."

"A story is like a fire. It illuminates the path, it warms the room, it cooks the meal, and it also burns the place." Tata told them.

When her mother in law passed away she recalled the incidents that took place. Her mother in law's friend came and asked to be given a room to stay till her friend was buried. She was obliged. She was given a room close to her friend's room. The next morning she woke up and dressed up. She sat in the front of the entrance to where her friend was lying in state. "Manu-well! Manu-well has left her!" she yelled. "Manu well, has left me alone to face the insolence of years of inexperience from the hands of kids." Looking around she started crying, "how could oil-well, honey-well do that to her." In between she stopped, responded to greetings and greeted faces that she recognized. Then Peter was coming crying as the emotion over took him.

The old woman would have a special performance for her friend's son. He was from the city after all. And would have a lot of money to bury his mother with, she concluded.

As the emotion filled Peter approached, the old woman started crying. His eyes were red from crying. She increased her wailing to draw more attention. But the crying and all the noise only worsen the man's emotional state. He was not looking at any faces. He walked pass his mother's friend. As he did to the old woman was surprised. She stopped crying and yelled his name.

"Peter! Peter!! Did you not see me here? Why have you passed me by? Will you spread money at me?" The old woman queried.

The young man could not but stop. He was already on the cross like the Christ, but he was continually tugged on both arms by those he loved.

All the tears on his face cleared and he started smiling. He laughed along with the crowd. Amazed, others asked what caused the laughter. Peter knew the old woman. He knew his mother's friend well enough. Though he was taken by surprise, he could predict her under certain conditions. The friendship has been on before he was born. He knew with those two there was never a dull moment. The two women had always said to themselves that they never had any regrets. They loved life. Though the memories of the friends they have lost over the years caused sober moments. They still had a lot to be thankful to life for.

She said the death of her friend Manu-well has uttered the unutterable, but was short of cursing life or the day she came into the world. The world was a lonely place. The world was a wicked place. And there was no one in it who could understand the loss of a true friend. Her performance was both genuine and to amaze. But she was able to confuse those who listened to her to believe most of what she said.

After her friend's burial, she told people that her only son was not wealthy enough to give her that kind of burial she deserved. A few years later at a very ripe old age she died in the hands of a motorist. The motorist was not sure if he was responsible for the death.

He however took the responsibility. He gave her a befitting burial. The type she would have liked.

When Peter's wife thought of those women she smiled. "Life was worth living." Her mother in law had told her once. "It took less energy to smile or laugh than it took to frown or cry."

CHAPTER
≈55≈

Her husband has been buried. She proceeded. There was a lot to live for in life. In the city she met some of their trading partners. Some were still in business and others have folded up. There was no longer space they could identify as the store. When asked some pointed to ashes and heaps of destruction. It was what was left of there one time booming business. No one was happy there. But they had to continue living. She approached a few of those who still had the stores standing. Some were barely managing to come out. Others were open and doing fine again. She made a mental calculation. She was checking, what it would take to bring her back to business. She concluded that with the state of things there was no way she could do it on her own. She would need the support of their former partners. She narrated the story of her misfortune to them. But everyone seemed to have their own tales.

They all had tales of how bad things had become and did not also spear any opportunity to tell them. People sat around and there was a lot of time and not much activity in the city so stories took the place of most activities. She would tell of how there were no stores, no goods in her name or in her husband's name.

A few of the men who were in a position to help her were not just going to do that. They wanted much more from her. It was not just the money. They were of the belief if they were to help her she should also help them. But the help they want was not something she was willing to offer. She hated the idea of men taking advantage of young women because of monetary favors not to mention a woman her age. She simply told them she does not sleep with men. She had in the past said the advantage of being a woman was that you could start a trade with anything. But that was not what she meant, she told herself. As a younger woman she had the reputation of being tough. But the moment she hit thirty she realized she had to quit intellectualizing romance. She learnt her intellect should complement her husband's. There was no way, she was going to trade her body with those fools. She had respect for her husband and wanted them to respect the dead and her misfortune.

It took months before she was able to find someone willing to trade with her in those simple trading patterns. She started again from the scratch. The life of a woman after the war was nothing than a continuing war. Every day she struggled to survive and build back her business. She was living with a friend and using space in another's store for her business. She however kept hope alive, believing that one day her property that had been tagged abandoned property, would once again be given back to her. But that was a wild dream. The hatred that runners of the economic system had was too much. They secretly loathed the earlier dominance in the economic life of the country. "They had to be put in check," was the secret phrase behind the action. And the geniuses in power were applying more deadly measures to control the people who had lost the war.

She never got back any of her properties nor any other money from the money they had in their accounts in the banks, than her twenty pounds and the one Peter had on him when he died.

She left the city for a bigger one when she saw that things were not getting any better. She moved with her daughter. In Lagos she started a flower shop. She lived with her daughter and their cat. The flower store and the cat were memorials of her past life. The life they enjoyed with her husband. On the wall was a picture of her husband, beside it was one of his favorite paintings of Da Vinci, "The River," another was his "Dreaming on canvas" and his Nsibidi paintings on textile. They were all original paintings. Though she enjoyed looking at that part of the store, the memories never gave her the time to think of the worth of those paintings in the market. They were almost always covered by dust and cobwebs. Every day she went to the store repeating her regular rituals, to keep hope alive as she called it.

Through the shop, she hoped her husband was smiling down on them from wherever he was. And he would send them the right people. Every day as she watered the flowers and plants she made the same wish. She called on the sun and the daylight and spoke to the reflections on the flowers.

CHAPTER
≈56≈

For many there were men and women who were walking memories of the war. The tall man and his short wife lived close to the flower shop. They were another couple that was affected by the post war economic strategy. It seemed to have left them with some level of lunacy.

The man was already a veteran of the Second World War and several peacekeeping efforts in the West African region. He felt there was nothing more to live for when he lost his wife. He left home one day to end the war, he was a man of war. He could no longer bear sitting at home while men came in and took all he loved. He left a son and a mother in law. But the war was not something to be ended by one man alone. Deep into the war the way home had become too far. It was the madman, who said, since he did his house warming at the market square, it had become too easy to go pass his father's compound without recognizing it. But, that he keeps walking, was not why people called him mad, they called him mad, because he keeps saying a different thing and while doing another.

After the war the tall man received his twenty pounds, it did not seem strange to him. He was the strange one himself. The war might not have taken everything from him but it took what was the most important. But he was still thankful. He thanked the heavens, for the sky, the sun light and the air. If the air he breaths, was by subscription then he knew, his account would have long be suspended and cut off. People who knew him did not call him mad. They called him "artillery." The war had damaged his hearing capacity. His mental alertness was affected by brain nerves damage. He suffered severe post war trauma. His condition got worst seasonally. He was always in deep thought and never bothered anybody.

No one knew where or how the tall man met the short woman. Their lives seemed to suit each other. They lived together and seemed to be very happy. Some prankster had called them jihadists, when they sought for other words to substitute for artillery. He never responded. When he did, he would simply tell them he was neither a jihadist nor a crusader. He fought for king and country once. But he no longer fought. The book of the law had been rewritten in the language of faith, grace, peace and hope. Heaven had become his country and the laws were God's. No. He was not one given to Ghilman's poetry, its beauty of eternal youth nor its promise of sparkling wine- sex in paradise. Sweet lines in the mouth of the masters, yet more dangerous than the wines of paradise. He wouldn't die for that kind of promise.

The law was "thou shall not kill." God fights his wars. He was simply not always accessible to everyone. He had his views. Sometimes he gave lengthy lectures. If push came to shelve, he would simply yell "I am not a soldier of this world." The tall man was a used man.

The pranksters would have heard what they want to hear. They would then leave him alone, unless they were interested in taking lessons on world war two, the Biafra war and his new conscience. Major was always enthused to listen to Artillery. He would pull his old bicycle to the side of the narrow path. He stamps his feet on the ground to maintain balance. People considered that one of the things he did out of habit. Though he made them laugh and smile, to them he was still a non-entity. But he knew that even when your opinion doesn't count, that you have one, is a gift that shouldn't be taken for granted. Whatever news there was in the area Major got it around. And as an important opinion leader in his own right, had come to consider himself a friend of the couple.

Looking at them walk pass the neighborhood, two times a day, at times laughing, at other times talking or making no sound at all, other than their footfall, the neighbors knew that, that was all it could do to them. Neither the war nor poverty could do more to them than it already had. He lost his first wife to the war. And the short woman was another reason to live. He was probably in his late fifties and she was in her forties. He wore his trousers and shirt tucked in. His belt though brown had already lost all its color, if it had any to lose. His shoes were no different. He wore them in a pattern that looked as though they were forced on him. He had gotten used to the routine. Seeing him that way for the first time, you would think he was uneasy in them, but no. He was comfortable. Her own was simple; blue jeans, a sweatshirt and a scarf that even in the heat of the sun, she felt cool and looked comfortable in them. She was either laughing or smiling most of the times when they were on that street. But something had kept them going for years. Maybe it was because they had each other and knew they had each other.

It had been weeks since they were last sited on that street, most neighbors began to think they were gone for good. But where would they have gone to? One of the neighbors had no answer for this, even when he curiously missed them. Had they disappeared? Had someone in that community anything against those two? He kept wondering. Except for the area boys, Lagos seemed pretty calm. It was the safest part of the country to do business for many of the traders who ran from the north. Though the neighbor had not really bothered to talk with them, he was deeply worried and concerned about them. It was an indifferent neighborhood. He did not really consider himself indifferent, but it had all of a sudden dawned on him that he had been for that long. It was a society he did not completely understand. But he felt sense of community would not hurt in any way. They were only victims of circumstances.

Though they were seen drunk occasionally, it did not seem to bother anyone. They had a way about them. It undoubtedly seemed they had some respect for them, if the poor had any in that society.

The couple made the neighbor more curious. He often compared them to his onetime very good friend. She had always come to his mind when they walked by. He was probably happy she eventually found a man. She had a persistent question which to him became rhetorical one. She would always ask,

"Don't you think that I am a wasted beauty?"

He knew there was no need talking about it. Even when it seemed she was not expecting any answers. About being beautiful, it was a known fact. But why would she want to know what he felt about her. It was about hundredth time of Q and A on the same issue.

Well maybe that was her only way to appease the spirit within her. She was a lesbian. He had been attracted to her as beautiful woman. Weeks after he met her for the first time. He knew he would have her. What he did not know at the time was that she would not stay. When he approached her it was smooth. He never really considered getting a woman a big problem. Once he was convinced of attraction he made his move. Before they started dating he had seen her beauty as a worthy trophy for someone like him. But before long he felt different. Being with her was different from other girls he had been with in the past. She was different in many ways. Their sex life struck him as unusual. She did her best to be good in bed. But somehow it was not coming. He would not lose interest then. There were other things to think about the relationship than to be worried about sex. "It would come with time." He concluded.

Seasons come and go. It was her turn. She could not hold what she felt any more. She was disappointed in herself.

She did not know she would give in that soon. She had counted that relationship as her last escape. She was not going back to that part of her that she was both ashamed of and tried hard to conceal. He was handsome strong and black. She was not looking any further. She had come to the conclusion. Being attracted to girls was the fault of the boys she had been with as a little girl. It was her chance to better, normal and happy life. From him she had somehow come to forgive those who had hurt her in the past. She led a new life. But all he could tell was that they were happy, till that morning when she woke him up with tears in her eyes. And she announced that liked girls. A cold sweat ran through his body. It sucked the bed cover in which they had slept. He was speechless. He did not anticipate the relationship would end, not even in that way. She wanted him to say something. But he could not form any words as hard as he tried. Making her feel bad at all was the last thing he wanted to anticipate. But no words came as he sat up in the bed. He looked up and counted the ceilings, tears filled his eyes. He could not hold himself. Lowering his face tears rolled down. In her confusion she could not understand. Like her he had thought of the two of them growing old together and possibly seeing the grandchildren someday. Her being a lover of girls that did not occur to his mind, no, not his queen for whom he had given up the girls. Though he was afraid of being committed, she was the woman who changed him.

It took them several months to get over it. He urged her to stay. But she felt she was betraying such a wonderful and trustworthy man. She wanted to leave. She wanted to go out of that city. He would not agree. He loved her. Even if it was a habit, somehow some people never got to quit smoking, once they were hooked, no matter how hard they try. He didn't want to claim to know or understand the science of it, if there was any. But he has seen the great agonies and depression - hiding from what they were or who they have become. It simply didn't look like great pleasure or fun at all.

That love had grown. He could no longer understand, what had taken possession of him. He wanted to protect her even with his own life. He had come to associate being with her as the meaning of happiness. But she was bent on leaving.

Years later when he heard from her that she was married. He was happy for a while, though he thought that they belonged together. He was happy she found happiness or was she still protecting him hiding away somewhere in that relationship. Whatever it was he knew that they shared more than she could share with any other man. And there she stuck to that guy she described to him. They were married and happy, anyone who saw them assumed.

There were some answers to his curiosity. The tall man and his short wife must have something they shared that was known only to the couple. It was something that had brought and kept them together. "But was it poverty, their drunkenness or the society, whose victim they were? It kept them walking hand in hand in that neighborhood. It was one or the other or all," the neighbor concluded.

Months later they were back again. Dressed as always, holding hands and walking on the street. A neighbor doing his one stop shopping at Christie's Place; the neighborhood mall, with a filling station, a restaurant and a grocery store sighted them pass the flower store. He walked across, grabbed the hands of his neighbors and said hello for the very first time.

It never worried the tall man's wife, their neighbors did not think highly of them. From where she was, she knew some things they did not know. "The future they talk about with puffed up air, yet making or raising the children doesn't even get half the status of their part time job." She told the man. She did not have any child of her own. But Nwa was a happy woman. She felt complete in the hands of the tall man.

CHAPTER
≈57≈

Some birds dread water ducks sleep in it. Ukah was Peter, the rock's good friend and age mate. Though he called the East his home his heart belonged to the North. When wars take men by surprise, sometimes they are able to retreat till they are ready to attack. When the war broke out Ukah ran home to the east. He came home in one of those trucks that had more dead bodies and wounded than those who were alive in them. Ever since, he has become the first to take his family out and first to take them back, whenever the attackers called for their attacks.

When Ukah first heard that his friend's wife was living in the city of Lagos, he made effort to visit her there. He was delighted he did. Their families shared a great friendship. He would have failed his late friend if he allowed the relationship to die.

Now Ukah and his clergyman friend, who had a drivable Honda car, were on their second missionary journey. They were on their way again fulfilling the terms of that undying friendship. The Clergyman had agreed to go with him to the city. Before they set out for their trip the clergy opened his scripture to book of the palmist and read out loud.

"The clouds poured out water, the skies sent out sounds, your arrows also flashed about."

It was a simple prayer, his friend thought. His friend should have said a prayer about the ditches and potholes they were about to encounter. He did not understand. There were no major natural disasters in the land. It was gully erosion. They built up over years. They have become ready-made burial grounds for armed robber and kidnappers. Those made it necessary for a prayer.

The clergyman has heard rumors his Friend had converted to Islam. He has never heard it from him. Driving for while there was a cloud of silence, the men were in deep thought. Both men seemed uncertain how much religion had taken away from other. The Clergyman broke the silence. He told him a story.

"It happened the night before. I spilled a glass of wine. It touched my books- my bible and copies of the others. I began to pray. I didn't want it wasted. I had to convert to something. I prayed till I was sure it turned into the blood of Christ."

His friend giggled. But they were quiet again.

The Clergyman wanted Ukah to take the conversation from there. He wanted it to flow the way Ukah wanted it.

The Northi-fication had gotten his friend, a fear entertained. The enterprise of his people, they must be kept down at all cost. Politics, religion or economics fair was foul, foul was fair. For those same reasons, no matter how shallow or deep the blood of innocence flows on the streets.

They talked about friends, places and things - the war and the intermittent peace. There were many things the situation in the land would never let them see or do again. They talked about the good old days.

The clergyman outlined his plans for the future. He asked Ukah what his plans were. Ukah was taken aback, when he eventually answered, Ukah did not have other plans other than to wait till things returned to normal. "There are wars and there is peace. These situations people created." He said.

The clergyman wanted to hear him talk about family. When he did, he seized upon that.

"Do you plan taking your wife and six children back to the north?"

In his response, Ukah spoke about his shop and cows, before speaking about his children. As they talked Ukah looked at his friend and smiled. Years later he would describe his friend the clergyman in black, as the man whose blood relative- a black man, almost became the head of the Catholic Church. To him they were men who pursued faith, its work and the promise. His shop and cows were his means of livelihood. He doesn't know any other place in the land where he could do his business, than in Kaduna. His friend did not understand the magic of that land.

The town was a hot spot for trade and violence, especially religious violence. The city still attracted large business from many parts of the Sub-Saharan Africa. So many southerners met their ends there. After each violent episode some people left never to go back. There were those who vowed never go to any other place. That was life, another man's food, and another's poison.

Ukah and his friend the clergyman drove another long distance without talking. Ukah had a flash back. It seemed he was reliving a moment from the past. He had seen someone pass them. He was not sure if his friend saw what he saw.

"It is Brother Sule."

"Who?"

The Clergyman was not sure who Ukah said hello to. But he heard him.

"He is now called Paul," he said.

Sule was a high ranking member of a sect whose members had put fear in everyone in the land with their plot, to convert. After long trainings and career he too was stroke on their way to Damascus. He only made it to Damatru. It was a never ending plot, he later confessed. His group held and forced people to recite the Quran. Many lost their lives and loved ones in the process. Men, women and children who could not remember the national anthems were forced to recite from a book they neither understood its language or logic.

Paul's past had not been peaceful. He wasted no time letting people know that now. Bro Sule himself had encountered Mark the friend of Jesus from Egypt, who later followed him, Philip from Ethiopia and Constantine-nople the man with, "the sign on his shield set to conquer." At Saint Sophia he had prayed, now he also stood on the rock transformed.

For a moment Ukah was disoriented. Alhaji Ukah knew him very well, or he was sure he did.

CHAPTER
≈58≈

There was always violence in the old city. In the days of Queen Amina before the trade changed. It was that way, the old slave route. When she had seven cities under her, it was always that way. From Asia and Arabia they came. Men from kingdoms far and near brought her gifts there as wars were being fought. She was a woman who made wars and peace.

"She too loved the River Niger." Tata told stories and sang her songs. She said men changed the story. They changed the story of who she and the empire she ruled were. They called her a woman and refused to honor the treaties she made. They made her actions of little significance and turned people she called friends into enemies. Tata described her as a ruler who flourished early. "History left her out," she said. It was men's world.

They traded as kingdoms were being conquered. Had Ukah's ancestors not traded through the same trade routes,-haggled with men from Mecca, Medina and Jeddah. He would know what to tell those calling him greedy for his love of the hills of the Northern country.

Even the prince of Baghdad, the brotherhood of the snakes, under the pretense of killing a snake came to the same land. "Why would men like Ukah who listened to Tata, run away forever? For whom would he leave the money to be made there to? Was it not only a war led by men?" Ukah queried.

"Aminatu's great deeds put her in the ranks of great African women like Nzinga, Sheba, Nwanyaka, Fomilayo and others." Centuries later those great women and deeds were only memories to guardians of the past. Their spirit would rouse those of women in Aba who harbored anger and hate for those who wanted to control their lives from afar. Those were women whose blood flows in Ukah's veins.

They were women who drove the greedy tax collectors away. And reminded them when their land was ruled by dynast of queens. They were the women who got tired of men who could not hold their fronts. They got tired of debates, useless and pointless arguments, and use of words between men, who could not be trusted to watch the back of their friends in battle. They broke out into protest. The mother of the earth went into protest with her bare breasts. They launched their own spiritual drones to hunt down all who attacked peace in the land.

The women's anger was on the male tax collectors and their female name givers. That year words that the women had put in the air hit the heart of one of the name givers. And she passed away in her sleep faraway in her home on a cold winter day. She had dreamed up a name better for business in their land, a name better than their pagan names on the bed of her lover. The women had taken enough. They waved their brooms in the air. The dust went thousands of miles away. It was time for revenge, the women had said. A woman came to their land, a land which travelers before her saw the unity in the flow of its waters and nature and changed nothing, but described as the Center of the Sudan. She was the changer, who did not want to offend the neighbors, but not the indigenes.

The neighbors were equally dividers and tax collectors. They did not see the beautiful flow of the lower and upper Niger, they did not see that Nile was her sweet heart and the Congo her lover. All they saw were pagans and Mohomedans who ought to be taxed. Those women gathered in Aba. It was time for thorough housekeeping. It was time to undo the companies formed in 1897.

The leader of the women was Ukah's grandmother. They were all women like the ones he has in his house. Ukah kept a collection of portraits of famous women. The women who conquered and some he conquered. Fortunately for him, Ukah's love for women was protected by an Islamic code which allowed a man to marry up to four wives.

For hours Ukah spoke and the Clergyman listened.

Ukah he was showing him his own pact with the north. He was in love with Aminatu the beautiful, ruler or of the ruling house of the northern hills. It was not a surprise.

CHAPTER
≈59≈

Alhaji Ukah was one of those men who would not leave the town. He had every reason not to leave, if you listened to him enumerate. He has gone to the city to live in his mid-thirties. He arrived there during the Harmattan season one year in the month of November. His arrival was a bit out of place. November and December were months that almost every Igbo man trading in the north and other places went home to the east for end of year's celebration. But he was a man just arriving in the city. He was the center of attention. The young girls flirted with him and the women behind the veils made eye contact.

He had a plan of starting a home in the town. A few months later he had settled into a life of a trader. He had a bigger plan. He would travel to the east at the right time. He knew whom to speak with. He wanted to be a major player in that ancient city. The rope maker was his woman.

She made the finest ropes of raffia palm. She would spin every fiber into beautiful weaves. She carefully crisscrossed every line of the fine raffia. When she has her desired length she begins to carefully trim. She would check for the texture of the rope she has made. She did not stop till she was sure that every rope was smooth, devoid of spikes. She would then cut off every end of any line without cutting the fiber of the rope. She made fine knots on both ends of the rope one couldn't tell the difference between both ends.

She was a woman given to her trade, early in the morning each morning, before the sun was out, she set up her post. She brought out her chair, a chair which she could relax her back on. Place the finely made raffia fibers on the ground, arranged properly for easy pick. Then she began. She worked till the shadow from the roof showing the progression of the day, signaled that it was 2.00pm. Then she would stop.

She made the best ropes in that part of the world. But she was just a simple woman, making a simple living. She did not glory in her ability to make those ropes that controlled both men and beasts. Yet she did not underestimate her own powers. And the proof was always there in the market place. Before she would finish displaying her wares traders from different parts of the country would cycle her.

They were waiting to buy what she made the week before. Every man was ready to outbid the other. But she traded fairly. She made sure everyone got something. They were her old customer, or that the other man, already placed an order, she would tell them. She always puts a smile on everyone's face. She had that power to silently manipulate and maneuver the market, but did not. From hundreds of miles the traders came. The rope maker was Ukah's woman. She was his hope.

One day Ukah came home from the North. He had a scheme that had to work. He applied every trick known in the trading business. He would pay for the ropes before she made them. The rope maker would not budge.

Then next time he came with his daughter. The rope maker was the little girl's godmother. She was happy to see her goddaughter. They stayed for a long time. When they were ready to leave, he presented his business proposal again. He told her he was only trying to feed his children. Looking at the face of the little girl, the rope maker saw the girl's mother in the tiny frames. She remembered the friendship they shared as young women.

That was how Ukah became her sole distributor. He came from the north to her house and picked up every raffia ropes she made. Opened a store in the ancient city, went round town telling the people, there was no need for them to be travelling the long distance. He had all they needed in his store. For some weeks the traders did not pay him any mind, but after two trips to the market without seeing the rope maker. They decided to do business with Ukah.

One of them told him, "na now, I know say you be chief."

The whole traders who travelled hundreds of miles no longer did. The cattle farmers came into his store on their way to graze their cattle and so also did the butcher on the way to the slaughter house.

CHAPTER
≈60≈

Ukah found his wife in the town and married her according to Christian rites. Their six children were all born there. The clergyman adjusted the collar of shirt as he listened. When his first child turned six and was about to begin school, Ukah learnt to adjust to fit in more in the society he found himself. Names and titles will do him a lot of good. Learning the language and practicing the religion of his host community will bring about the desired goals.

He found a friend with whom he went to the mosque every Friday. He practiced the Hausa language and gradually his wardrobe changed. He was fitting in with the disapproval of his wife. She fought with him for weeks and accused him of deceiving her. One morning she was making breakfast in the kitchen. Ukah walks in.

"Good morning darling"

She warned him to stay away.

"You say greetings of peace. But in actual fact you mean prepare for war."

Most times it is the absence of peace or the fear of its absence. It was never love in the first place. They had had a big fight the night before.

But over the years they found ways to cohabit. She stuck to her guns and he stuck to his. Wining each other over depended on the occasion.

At the mosque, when other worshippers sought for the direction of the sun to bow their heads, Ukah struggled with his newly bought attires. It took him long before he finally understood the echo of the call to prayer. And to follow the union of the brotherhood and the rhythm of the day, as they went at various times to pray. He gradually became used to the rituals of prayer and Muslim worship.

One day he went to Mecca. It was a dream, comes true. Those who knew him, his brother and sister in the religion, customers and friends will now address him as, "Alhaji." It was a title, he wished for even on the day he was being wedded to his wife in the church.

When he came back he became fond of writing letters. He wrote even to friends he never wrote to before. At the end of his letters, he sent the greetings of peace and signed his name.

"Alhaji Salmanu Ukah Udeh."

Soon after, people caught on with the title, which he advertised greatly. His friends and neighbors began to address him as Alhaji. He was very pleased. It meant another level of acceptance in society. But his wife vowed never to utter it or to have it mentioned in the house.

The sky was his limit. And he knew it when he looked at the moon and the star. He began to dream more dreams. Once he had a dream in which he was worshipping in a mosque on a tower. The mosque was overlooking the whole earth. He kept his dream to himself. Whenever he remembers that dream he told himself;

"Dreams connect the future and the past, insha Allah."

A consolation in a wish he had no one to share with.

The clergyman saw the passion, emotion and reason, and the fate of a man pursuing those passions. As he listened to Ukah, he wondered why he has chosen the religious life. But those were moments he was both proud and worried. He examined his role in society and what ought to be. He wondered if he had a greater calling. He certainly did not want to meddle in problems he had no total control over. But he was a man who once said all his mass in Latin. But now did in English and his local dialect. He knew a few things about life, faith, change, language and the power of the state.

In the past Ukah had a friend Wale. It was with him he shared such inner feelings. But that was before Wale followed his true calling. They were friends for a long time.

Wale was for a while married to a Fulani woman. It was not entirely strange for a Yoruba man to fall in love with a Fulani. What was strange was that a Fulani woman would fall completely in love with Wale.

But the last woman Wale dated had left a hole in his heart. They were from the same state. After the breakup, the man said he was done with love. But, then along came Tilatu.

Tilatu did not have much but her pot of fura de nunu. She carried her pot on head, as she carries her beautiful figure gracefully. They had little or nothing in common. Months before, their conversation did not go beyond, "here fura, pay money," and then a bright smile. He was not able to take it beyond a minute. Obviously she cared nothing about him. He was just one of the guys who stood outside the bank during lunch for a stick of cigarette, fura or cup of kunu. Wale did not see beyond her covered face and painted hands.

If she lusted after any man it was not one of those. Among her friends, if any man would show the proof of manhood for her, it was undoubtedly her brother's friend Tango. He was thought to be the man who would receive the lashes for her. Pay her dowry and in turn be able to whip her. He already had three Cattle of his own. When she went to get milk for her Fura, she had an eye for his cattle. Tango like any man trying to win the heart of a woman, he found reasons to give her special discounts.

Wale was the man in an air conditioned room. He was not thinking of putting her pot down, unveiling her or any other strange display of affection. As much as love was concerned he had nothing more to prove. For Tilatu untying any man tie was not part of her deal. It would be easier to strangle a dying cow with those ropes, than have to pretend to handle it in any show of affection.

Wale's heart had been shattered. He opened his office windows more. He went out more and stood longer in the sun. That was how he began to see the things wrapped up in the Fura de nunu woman. "Even if it is not love, if I can get her to come out with me…" he found himself saying many times. Wale would be healed. He would be a happy man again.

In reality he had no idea of what he would do to her or how. Wale however got ready each day. He did. He took extended lunch breaks. Then his office refrigerator broke down. He had added reason to take his Fura de Nunu home to refrigerate. Tilatu sold more Nunu. Gradually she paid more attention to Wale's Nunu. She made it in the way he liked it. Soon she even started selling frozen Fura de nunu.

Tilatu had two beautiful kids for him. Then they could no longer live in the same house. Her friends wanted her to take him to the divorce hut. But she followed the sound of shepherd boy's flute in the forest. It was all Wale ever wanted.

CHAPTER
≈61≈

Interreligious dialogue was an area of interest to the clergyman. But it was not a comfort zone when it came to such issues as marriage within the religions. To him marriage was a burden to the experienced and amateur. Dealing with an angry wife, all he had was superficial knowledge. He had overheard his bishop once admonish his colleague. The guy was dealing with his midlife issues. The bishop had told him, "You would serve society better if you only had a wife. She will keep you in check." Free and unchecked as he was, meant the bishop was not spared the complaints of angry parishioners with loose wives.

Alhaji Salmanu Ukah Udeh went on and on about his family, his wife and would be wives. The man he was with was lost in thought.

The two friends had picked up Musa Ali and Joe along the way. Both were soaked to the skin when they picked them up. The vehicle they traveling in had broken down. It was due to a heavy down pour. The roads are terrible.

They were caught in the crossfire of madness.

People in countries they have heard of or visited drove on wide and well maintained high ways. Up to seven well paved lanes on opposite sides of the road.

There they were dodging potholes and drunk drivers on tiny narrow roads. The drivers coming from the opposite directions try hard not to bump into one another. Both the clear eyed driver and the ones whose thinking ability leads to believe the eyes are clearer when drunk. Even the police who set up his make shift road blocks, where he collects his toll from every driver. The human blood is sacred. But it's wasted a lot on those roads. And those who cause such waste do not take responsibility for it. The government officials were the least to recognize it.

The man who is charged with the building of roads and houses, he doesn't think so. He is not responsible for the lives lost to road accidents. If he ever gets Aso Rock to award road construction contracts, then it is pay time. He looks for his friends. So contracts are given to contractors who once they claim the money, he gets his cut in several private accounts and investments offshore. He takes government media and plays the people, the less you look the more you see. What the citizens see are pictures of foreign contractors and government workers smiling ahead of the funerals of the unknown. It is the unknown. Because when government functionaries use the same roads, they go with vehicles blaring with sirens. They push everyone else to the edges and corners of the roads, because the gods of the land decided to make appearances. When they're done the human sacrifices on the roads continued.

If the flow of traffic on the roads was an economic indicator, many times no one was paying attention. Alongside the potholes on major roads, the express roads were jammed. Here was the country's growth rate. There it showed where the country was heading and how fast it was going to get there. Unfortunately it was a stampede.

Since they got aboard the car Musa and Joe hadn't said much other than, "thank you."

They listened. As their bodies dried, the car seats got drenched. Both men were on their way to a conference. They seemed to be in a deep thought.

While they were waiting on the road, a luxury bus sped pass without stopping to pick up anyone. It was unusual. Drivers and their conductors made extra money with the attachment seats. They packed people till there was not a single space left on the aisle. It was the norm with the operators of the luxury buses for the few old men who dominated the transportation business on that route. "Why didn't they pick them?" Joe's mind raced. But it was a new company. The owner of the buses saw something the old men did not see. He knew it was the edge he had over them. And he was going to change the face of transportation business in the country. He eliminated time wasted on frequent stops either for passengers to stop to eat, go to toilet, pee or even to pick up extra passengers. He provided alternatives. Comfort, relaxation and safety in his buses were top on his list. People were happy to pay for the services. Then it became a class thing. People talked about it to their friends. People watched movies and listened to music in the buses as they travelled. Travel time was shorter. He left and arrived on schedule. With foresight, focus and calculation, he became the king of the road despite the terrible roads. Joe continued to ponder about it. The two friends in the front of the car continued to talk.

The talk about marriage excited Musa. He turned and looked at Joe. Though they made each other laugh occasionally. They were neither friends nor enemies. Both were men who knew they would get whatever they wanted. However one knew he had to earn it. The other worked with an air of one entitled to a place on the job. They were both good.

"God," he thought. It was a huge structure along the road, a place of worship. "The structures being built for Him on earth, while the hearts of men were in embroiled in the lusts of the flesh." The priest began a mental calculation of the money expended in the country. He wanted to change the topic.

He thought of where taxpayers' money and revenue from natural resources were going into. He compared the church and the mosque, the roads and the schools in the different part of the country before the war. He worried about what they had become. He worried about the Alhaji taking his family back to the north after they had seen the work of hate in the land.

To the clergyman the entire trip was like an exercise in stretching the mind. The next that came to his mind was resources and their distribution in the country.

The distribution of the resources according to the clergymen was like sharing spoils of war before and after the war. He worried about what the outcomes of the economic policies that have continued to be the guiding principle in the land.

In what appeared to be a prophetic insight the clergyman addressed the occupants of the car.

"Corruption would breed corruption. The air would be hard to breath. A search for where the deliverer would come from would be hard if not impossible."

It was a message well received. The car's occupants nodded in agreement. Musa felt the urge to say something he had in mind all along. Then he did- "Talking about what was being done in God's name. You either did not see the presidential spiritualists' contracts and contractors or did not want to talk about them. To a great percentage, they too worked the country to the ground and many to their untimely death. The Abacha Marabous from Kano, Borno, Mali and Senegal followed presidential stars hovering over Aso Rock. They saw coup plots before they were hatched. And sentences were handed down to the plotters before they would dream of a coup."

The groundnut pyramids were flattened. The streams were flowing towards a different direction. It did not flow where it used to flow. The Niger was no longer the River of live, which it once was. The palm nuts and kernels dry up and rot away in the bushes. The cocoa farms are infected with incurable land diseases.

Already in the city center the passengers were ready to get off. Musa offers them money Ukah makes a sign for him not to bother.

The potholes and death traps were a trade mark of the roads to the markets and cities. The paved roads lead to nowhere. And the Honda they were in was a witness.

Ukah seemed contented with his achievement. But he regretted the incessant riots in the North. That was his only concern. He made it known to the priest.

They finally arrived at the flower shop. They were both happy to be seeing each other after all the troubles and things that happened in the land. Ukah introduced his friend the priest. She called her daughter to come and say hi to her dad's friend. She did and went back to the room. The three talked for hours. There were solemn moments and moments of great joy and laughter. Their reunion was heartwarming.

CHAPTER
≈62≈

For some years no one heard or knew who Sylvester Stone senior or junior was. The senior has continued to lead his quiet life in the peninsula. Junior got into far bigger and mightier concerns. He left the peninsula went to the city's university, graduating from law and public administration. He traveled overseas went to business school. From Columbia to Harvard he went pursuing graduate studies. He was bright and he did not hide it. He got involved with many groups where he contributed in several ways. In Los Angeles he interned with security and defense companies and partnered with internet giants. He helped tutoring kids, hosting seminars and giving lectures. He studied the country's civil and industrial disobediences. He studied attempted revolts and coup d'état. He entered into negotiations with counties and states. He got involved in international liberations and student politics.

From what his father had told him, he sought to find out for himself who he truly was. What he was capable of and what he was not capable. He wanted to know his limitations as Stone Jr. when he sat alone at home the image of his father dogged him. He had a future he saw its promises. He had a father whose past made him dread the word family.

He secretly met with a group of investigators and an old and trusted friend of his father. His father's old friend was shocked to see what his friend has made of himself when he saw Stone Jr. He was pleased and wanted to do anything he could to help his young friend. He promised to handle the investigations and to provide answers to any questions he might have. That way the younger Stone would go about his normal business without having to deal directly with the investigators. He would meet with his father's friend once a week and they will discuss the findings. There were money, in banks accounts, bonds and stocks that his father ran with names that were still redeemable. S.A Stone Jr. was curious, and wanted to know how safe it was to get involved in those businesses. They were legitimate businesses that Stone Sr. ran for a future day and that future had arrived. He knew that there would come a day when his own seed will look into the future and question what their flesh and blood left for posterity. He was no fool. He was not always greedy nor was he always a bad man. He was simply a businessman.

Growing up in Europe had taught him to pray and go to church. He did till his mother died of a preventable disease.

When she died they thought the plague was back. But she was a keeper and lover of all things black. And she kept a Black cat. Her ancestors passed that down in lore "keep the cats and keep the rats away. Keep the black cat and the black death away." Her death was not due to any plague. But it was not natural as a young doctor from the church had hurried proclaimed.

Sylvester went to the old rustic church building where he ate once a day. One day he met a man who took him in, fed him and taught him to read and write. He taught him principles. But the man was a criminal. He was the man who encouraged him to go to school. He was the man who taught him the value of education. And what he could do with it in any situation he found himself in life. He told him he could do more stealing with education, than with a gun on the streets. When Mr. Stone Sr. started his first charity he dedicated it to that man, his mother and the church. Some of those foundations and charities were still in operation when his son arrived.

"Those would pay for sins and debts" Stone Sr. once told a friend.

That friend happened to be the man his son met with the investigators. The friend took that to heart. He was a catholic, he understood. When his own father was dying, one of his dying wishes was that a particular amount of money in his bank account be used to say mass for him for two years. He was the friend, the younger Stone, had the fortune of meeting once a week.

CHAPTER
≈63≈

Stone Jr. had vowed to himself. He would have nothing to do with his father's wealth. However those vows were shattered. Business school had changed those. In the school he has learnt how nations built empires. Many were with stolen wealth and oppression of the weak in the names of higher powers. His father was no more of a demon than those men. Whoever they served kings, queens or emperors. His crime was that he did not build a national empire. He was like those other men in palaces around the world, controlling the lives of millions of men and women. He however had his principle and his limitations.

Stone Jr. had a lot of good things he could do with his wealth, he was bound to recover from his father's past life. Back home his people were fighting over nothing. Conflicts erupted over mere space to graze cattle. Malaria was killing people left and right.

"Stealing for these folks I have in mind, would not even be a crime,"

He told his father's friend. He was not about to steal, he was only on a quest of recovering lost treasure from his father's loathes.

His father's friend and the investigators were working very hard. The last time he met with them he had documents to a few onshore and off shore accounts. He thanked the men and paid for their services. He told the old man he would leave some money in an account, should he need prayers after his death. But the man was not a believer. He told him to give the money to the people his father had already marked it for. The younger Stone was full of appreciation as he left the old man's presence.

A week after leaving business school Sylvester Stone Jr. flew to the peninsula. He met with his father, a very sick old man. He was receiving the best of attention and asked not to be taken out of the peninsula. The younger man wanted him flown out to better medical facilities. But the peninsula had been a haven to him from the day he arrived on that part of the world. That was the way he wanted it to remain. He was not going to be moved to trouble. He told his son.

On Stone Jr.'s, second day on the peninsula, his old man felt a little stronger. He was ready to discuss whatever business brought him to his bedside. They spoke for a long period of time. The old man was happy at what progress his son had made in a short time. He was happy he came to that part of the world. He was happy he was pursuing the antelopes the day he met his mother. He was not sure if he should be happy there was the war on the other side of the border. But whatever it was that led him to the women, who gave him that son was destined. He told his son that there was no woman in the world like her mother.

"No one so loving and caring."

"I know dad, mum is a blessed woman."

Ngozika was blessed. The men in her life love and appreciated her to a fault.

CHAPTER
≈64≈

Days later Stone Jr. was back in the west. He had appointments with banks in the Caribbean, Europe and other remote tax havens. He was busy moving, businesses and money to where they were needed. After two months he wasted no time, traveling back home. He built schools in the east, west, north and south. If the country was to move forward education was a vital tool.

If the country was to produce men and women who would be developed in mind and character, education should be the key. He was tired of a place whose guiding philosophies were those of the age of basic needs of man.

"The stone age was a need for food, shelter and clothing," he said.

His people were no more in that age. But they needed to prove it. They needed to put men and women in position of authority that would treat them as people with values. He was tired of wars caused by people politicking hunger and religion. "If there were to be change, a new breed of leaders needed to be raised." He told teacher and principals of the schools he commissioned.

Mr. Stone Jr. invested greatly in the future of the country. While others saw him as the future they were waiting for.

Party men and women lured him to get involved in political leadership. They told him they needed him to lead. He was on a mission, some said. He told them he was an international businessman. Some took offense at his response. He was being careful. He would tell close confidants. He wanted to be sure who to trust.

They spoke to his mother to convince him, to run for public office.

His mother spent time with his father in the peninsula when she was not with her daughter in the big city. She like his father was pleased with him and encouraged him to follow his heart. Those two were not the kind of people to force their opinion on their children. And they were not about to start politics at their waning years. They avoided politics at all level over the years. They knew their son had a great future and blessed him. And they told him to pursue it wherever it was leading him.

Sylvester Azuogu Stone Jr. was still studying the political landscape. He was studying the war after which he was named. He was about to make a decision after several prominent citizens contacted him and vowed to back him, should he consider running for elective office. He valued true friendship. He had great respect for those who told him and themselves the hard truth. It is easier to reach forgiveness where it is hidden away in the heart, than dealing with the lingering self-doubt and distrust. He had little regard for men who committed the double crime of making him and themselves liars. He knew it was time. The voices that could be trusted had gotten involved. And he saw it as a duty.

But there were a few things that needed to be put in place. The structure of a formidable politician included a family. For him that meant a woman. One he could trust with the lives of the people, if important decisions needed to be made while lying down in bed.

He had the backing of powerful politicians from the east, the west, the north and the south. Men who had played the power game in the country and had become tired of it. They were those that were considered kingmakers and thought to have the apparatus of the state secret service in the palm of their hands. People who when they said go you could trust. That yes, they mean go. That it was safe. It was due to the turn of events and the coincidences that led to him to meet with some of the men. But once he met them, he knew it was meant to be.

CHAPTER
≈65≈

At first he met with groups who showed themselves as men from powerful political forces. Their deals were simple. They were set for a trade by batter. When he paid little attention to them, they went on to bring the faces they represented. The younger Stone was not one to trade the future of his people for political power. And these men noticed it. The men felt threatened, men who feared neither God nor the devil, but willingly offered sacrifices to both because they were never in short supply of anything.

Whatever interest they were protecting may no longer be protected, should he be elected without their sincere help. He agreed to a series of other meetings. The meetings did not produce the desired goals either for him or those who convened it. He began to understand.

"The true nature of the politics of shareholding… That was not his politics." He told one of them.

He went on to meet with one of the former military rulers and a top secret service chief in the country. That meeting with the two Generals disturbed him a great deal. But he learnt a lot from it. He realized that there were a lot of mysteries in the political life of his country.

"It will take years to fix this nation". S.A Stone Jr. said. The two nodded in agreement. Like they did not have the answer.

They spoke sincerely and openly to one another. As the meeting went on, after absorbing all that the Generals had to say. Mr. Stone Jr. felt there was no better time to point out to them what he has seen as their false sense of security and inapt corruption veiled in a sense of duty.

"Let me tell you Generals, tell them, I would have worried about a coup. But you and I know this country has no place for military take over."

"Nobody was suggesting that." The two replied in unison.

"I mean the people will in fact laugh at any attempt to force another military rule on them." Stone Jr. continued.

The generals were quiet. They had spoken and it was also proper they listened.

"If anyone is planning on taking over, then they should prepare for war. And you may as well prepare for the hawks."

"They will prey life out this generation and those to come." He continued.

The two men whose combined experiences of dealing with enemies and friends have come to agree nothing beats dialogue sensed anger in his voice. The soft spoken former ruler, looked him in the eyes and said, "We know these things. That is why we came to you."

"Dr. Stone, someone must end these anomalies. But we have to work together." It was the security service chief.

"This nation cannot continue to reward crime and incompetence." Stone replied.

"That is what we are saying. We have a constitution. But you can't change these things overnight." The former head of state added.

Stone sensed they were tolling the same line of argument they tried earlier. And he attacked

"The idea of royalties to former heads of state and other office holders was not in anticipation of the magnitude of crimes committed or the astounding levels of incompetence in the office."

The two generals maintained their cool. They understood the game they were in for. It was no longer the military era. If it was that small boy would not be talking to them.

"With all respect General, I know beside your little education outside of the military you understand neither history nor economics nor law. Our people neither want to be shackled in chains nor to be led in just one direction. The poverty in the land is hurting" Mr. Stone Jr. was addressing the man who spoke last.

He turned towards the secret service chief.

"The states will secede. We have suffered and endured years of backwardness. And we waited patiently for your boys to get tired. I respect leadership and constituted authorities. But each and every passing day, I see that these men have devalued the black man more than any other has in recent times."

The man nodded again and Stone continued, making sure he got the movement of the eyes of both men in front of him.

"Our past has been riddled with legacies of shame, unemployment, poverty, disease, and death. This country needs to move forward and you are welcome to move along. It is the people who make the government. It is neither the government house nor the seat nor your gun. The house, the seat and the guns are just a few amongst many in this country."

Stone exhaled. He took the bottle of water on his table and drank from it.

The generals knew the meeting was over. They tried some little talk and pleasantries.

Like the snail if it finds splinter in its shell it looks for a new one. It was democracy. And the people can decide which to call their own, at any time they deem fit, who to vote for and what party to join.

"We can work together in one country where every citizen's right is respected."

The three men laughed as they exited the meeting.

Mr. Stone Jr. looked like a man with a broken heart, but still sees love in beauty and happiness in hope.

Those direct meetings were very useful and convincing. They were better than those who claimed to represent interest groups, when actually they represented none but themselves. They were negotiators dealing in power bargain. They sold power deals once they were able to broker. The direct meeting was the only thing that could have brought him to that realization. It equally assured him that the country was ready for a transition. And he got the facts clear. He was truly seen as a transitional figure by majority in the political sphere.

He weighed the odds, at times he thought of himself as an outsider. It was not the circumstance of his birth or his skin color but the history of the country. He weighed who his major opponents would be. He took weeks analyzing those who would come up to challenge him. Friends in the secret service helped him with his study of those characters. He was satisfied with the situation, should he decide to go back and tell his constituency that he was ready.

He decided it was time to work on the one area that was his weak point. He was not seeing any girl at the time, though many admired him. He has never felt the need to commit to a single woman. He feared it would take away his freedom. It was not something he wanted to happen, but now it seems urgent. But still he was never in a hurry over anything. He believed things would sort themselves out at their own time.

CHAPTER
≈66≈

So it happened that day, that he was in Lagos, and all of a sudden, he felt the need to pick up a flower for his mother who was visiting his sister in the city. In the flower shop he saw a certain beauty. He was never able to remove from his eyes even after he left the city. His mind went back several times to the shop, before he could even reach his mother. On getting to his sister's house, he was told his mother had left to see his father. It was urgent and she left on a short notice. S.A Stone Jr. caught the next plane to the peninsula. He still clutched the flowers in his hands.

His mother had been attending to his father when she saw him. She stood up, took the flowers. And told him they were beautiful. He understood what she meant. He was happy.

For Ada when her brother left her place with all the excitements, she decided to fly to Abuja. She was going to drop in on her fiancé. He was in the hospital wards. Hauwa must have been in on it. The night before, the two were on enjoying the 11:30 gossip.

"We will find cure for that one too

That is why we are here" Hauwa was eavesdropping.

It was Dr. Lucas in the room close to the reception area. He was on the phone with a satisfied customer. It was a patient whom another hospital had given an expiration date. His encounter with the dandy old man changed things. He was happy, healthy and back in his home. He just informed the Dr. Lucas of his bequest to the hospital especially to his cancer research project. It was a substantial part of the man's estate, the doctor was really excited.

Hauwa was still giggling when Ada came through the main entrance.

She meets her.

She leads her through a crowded emergency waiting room. The seats were all filled with sick and injured people. A man was lying on a bench. He has been waiting for more than three hours like most of the others. His wound was fresh. But the blood was caking. He was one of the minor injuries from a bomb blast that claimed many lives. He was lucky to be alive and lying on the emergency room bench. An off duty nurse part of the team that brought him was sitting on plastic chair beside him. She was tired of standing. And went into one of the rooms and grabbed the plastic seat.

Hauwa and Ada walked pass them. The expression on Ada's face was that of shock and sadness. Though she might have prepared for such a sight, she was still shocked. "Kpele," Hauwa said. They continued walking toward the wards. Tom- out from a room, surprised, "look who is here." He was in his scrub. He looked different from the last time she came to see him there. The hospital was really busy. Ada- pleased, "busy hmm?" She hugged him, "Happy birthday."

It was his birthday. But that was the least thing on his mind.

Hauwa had a smile on her face. She giggled as she watched the expression of surprise on his face as they hug. She was also a little worried. She planned a party that looked like it was not going to happen. It felt like one of those nights spent at the hospital. The hospital staff was increasingly exhausted. Those on vacation had been called back to work, even when the threat of a strike was on. The ER and other wards had remained constantly overcrowded in the past week. The three of them went into the break room and chatted a little. Before Tom went back to help in the wards. He turned toward her.

"You know I would like to wake up and see a missed call on my phone, but not from debt collectors." He told her as he walked out.

He came back but very late, did not want to disturb her. But she was waiting for him.

Like the reflection of his body on the water so was their shadow on the wall. It was mutual and unspoken, like in the beginning. Then it became regular.

He was just out of the shower, wet and the water dripping from his body. She was on fire, hungry for his body.

First it was the sound from the midnight cricket. Then a slow continuous squeaking sounds of other insects of the night. The chirping becomes louder and faster. Somehow, it was not only the cricket happy with the night. It may rain in the morning, in a few days a new life may begin. She tried to go back to sleep.

CHAPTER
≈67≈

A few weeks later Stone Jr. was back to the flower store. Peter's wife was just completing her morning rituals in the shop. The cat was on the couch. He asked about the girl who sold him flowers the week before. The woman smiled. She had a feeling. It was a special feeling. That morning when she decided that her daughter takes over the chores in the house while she went to shop. She felt something important was about to happen. Whatever it was she was not sure, but the presence of the young man in the store seeking to know where her daughter was, was making that clearer. Looking at the man standing there, she was sure she was not the one he wanted to speak to, it was her daughter.

She asked him to sit down. The young girl in question was her only daughter she told him. They looked very much alike, he thought. For him, as they spoke, he began to understand, what had brought him to the city and to the flower shop. The woman was beautiful at her age. He was glad her daughter would also look like her at the same age.

Ihuoma had finished her chores at home and coming to check if her mother needed her at the store. When she stepped in she was surprised at the man sitting there. He sat and talked to her mother as if he was a regular at the store. But if her memory was not failing her she had only seen him there once. When she said hello and he responded, she tried to place the face with the voice. She immediately remembered that first time and their exact words to each other. She was filled with joy, though she had no idea why he was sitting down there.

For a moment they would not speak. Her mother stepped in to break the silence.

"This young man came in inquiring about you. And I offered him a seat.

"Thank you mother"

Stone Jr. interjected immediately.

"I was in town and wanted to pay a visit."

He smiled and introduced himself again. They chatted for a while and exchanged phone numbers. He gave her the address of where he was staying in town. She was delighted he came to town and wanted to pay her a visit. The next day he gave her a call. They spoke for a long time. She was happy and so also was he. The next few days were different. She seemed to have changed her mind all of a sudden. His calls were neither answered nor returned. He had no explanation for that action. He was a bright and promising young man. He had the power to hold the world in the palm of his hands. He did not understand why the only girl he was devoted to would not return his call. He went out of town without being able to see her. He was disappointed.

Their phone calls became an on and off habit. It continued that ways for weeks and months. He was not at all happy about it. But he had to play too.

He was in one of his rented apartments in the capital city. He felt the need to talk to her. He has not been able to take his mind off her since they last sang to each other over the phone. She played a tune on her piano with which she held his heart captive. Because of the off and on relationship, they called it "basic and advanced progression in falling in love." He wanted to speak with her, but he was not sure what to expect. He picked up the phone and dropped it again.

The next evening, he was relaxed, like an entrepreneur on an early retirement. He sat in the bathtub, glass of wine in his hand, inhaling the exotic fragrance of the candle on the top of a marble slab in the bathroom.

He gradually picked up his cell phone with his right hand, transferring the glass of wine momentarily to the left and back. He dialed the number and listened. The sound of the warm water dropping from the left tap and the music from the Bose speakers in the bathroom seemed the only sound in the whole house for what seemed like eternity. Finally the phone was picked up, and her voice back from the other end.

"That is all women want,"

He sighed when he finally dropped the phone. "They all want wealthy and comfortable man."

But somehow, his naked body in that bathtub and the red candle light had always managed to evoke that feeling. Whatever it was whenever he rang her from the bathroom. He did not know why. But somehow it worked. The walls of that bathroom seemed to hold the magic that worked with her subconscious self.

Unknown to her, he was ready to offer her the world, if only she would be his. He wanted to wake up in the morning beside a girl whose face told him it's a beautiful day. Not one who would remind him of past night's nightmares. And she was that girl. She was the girl. He saw the future of the world on her face.

He would be in town soon. He had told her on that last phone call. She was excited about meeting him again. A few days later, he called from the same hotel he had given her the address in the past.

CHAPTER
≈68≈

After a few minutes, Dr. Stone was in the store. Their next meeting, things seemed like they never stopped communication from their meeting the previous day. Things seemed smooth and her mother had customers in the store. She asked her if they wanted to go the room, which they used for private meetings. They both excused her went and sat there. Her mother was pleased with the giggles heard from the inner room now and then. Though his intention was to ask her to go to the nearby restaurant with him, the conversation seemed to move quite nice that they both forgot how fast time was moving.

The cat came out from the store, into the inner room, then ran to the door fast enough to see her owner move into the street. She was going to the store across from theirs. Inside where the cat came out from, it was quiet and the silence spoke a lot. The two smiled at each other, not speaking a word for lengthy period of time. The sound the cat made was the only thing that revived their conversation to a verbal one.

It was time for lunch, her mother announced as she came back to the store. She would watch the store while she went home for her lunch. And she would do the same when she got back. Going to eat out meant she may not be back on time for her mother to take her turn. She insisted on the lunched she had ready at home. He obliged.

They walked to her house and ate. She explained it was the first time she went home to lunch with a perfect stranger. But she was not worried at all about that. She promised to eat with him at the restaurant of his choice, the next day before he left town. She was proud of their home cooking, and enjoyed the opportunity that afternoon afforded her to eat with a man, by whom she had been enchanted by the first time she saw him. Eating on that table he seemed like sibling she never had. Though other relatives sat there and eaten with her there in the past, this was a special feeling. After they finished eating she went in and did the dishes, before they left the house and back to the store. They got back to the store and thanked her mother for the meal. She walked him to his car.

They had a date for the next afternoon, which was Sunday. That Sunday date proved what they both felt earlier on. They knew they were in love from that first day. The day he came to buy the flower for his mother, what neither knew was how they would ever meet again. But they always believed in fate. And that, what will be, will be. That evening she watched him take the flight for the peninsula. When they said bye she was sure he would be coming back earlier than he said he would.

CHAPTER
≈69≈

Their parents approved of the relationship without really knowing or spending time with their choices. The families looked forward to when they would meet. What none knew was what the other was going to become in the months ahead. Even when they considered each other with the level of importance and seriousness, there were still thing they still kept from each other. She was the woman who would be mother of his kids, he told her several times. But he did not mention his political ambition to her. Nor did she mention her preparation to represent Lagos state in the Miss Nigeria beauty pageant. Though she loved to make him repeat those lines about the flower he had picked up. He had written a note attached to the flowers. It read, "These flowers are for the woman clothed with the sun, and the moon under her feet. And I am a crown on her head."

The next time she made him repeat those words, she was in his arms, in a tight and warm embrace. It was the Hilton in Lagos. It was the year's music award, a night that brought together the best in music and entertainment in the country. She was at the airport to pick him up when he arrived in Lagos. They went straight to the Hilton. The show was still hours away. They went for their dinner. Back in the room there was a bottle of Champaign. It was romantic, the music was soothing. He took her in his arms and they started dancing. She asked about the note. The night went on and on. Nothing else in the world was more important. Thirty minutes into the show they were still in the room, lying in the bed naked. Then she reminded him what time. "It is 11.00pm" she said, looking into his eyes. He changed his position. Moved closer, kissed on the breast, then on the lips. Then he whispered into her ears,

"Even if the hosts of choirs of heaven were to be singing tonight,

I will still prefer your soft and gentle whispers
here beside me,
If I had to walk a thousand miles to get to you, I would.
If I had to swim across the ocean I would
But here we're
There is no place to run to, there is no place to hide
Let's make this moment last forever,
Let's make this union remembered for a thousand years and more
Let's make this kiss last."

Though they eventually got up and went to the show, that response meant more to her than the rest of the night.

The next day Stone Jr. got up early in the morning. He had promised Ihuoma, he would drive her mom to the British high commission to pick up her visa. It was an Am appointment. His plan was to avoid the traffic. But he didn't. He found himself spending hours in the badly jammed road. He eventually made it out of there. He drove pass the crowds waiting in fronts of embassies and high commissions on the Island. He dreaded who and what he saw, schoolmates and friends from the past. He was not sure what that was; all of a sudden getting a visa to get out of the country seems like a profession.

Walking towards the end of the line, Iyke was the first person that recognized him.

"Hey Iyke." He shouted.

Iyke was frustrated. "It is not easy being a Nigerian." He said.

"I know, right."

"Look at the roads, bad infrastructures, bad health care, crimes, armed robbery, kidnapping, corporate theft, government corruption, greed and incompetence." Iyke continued.

Iyke could not think straight for a minute without hitting road bumps. Everywhere there was fast declining value system. He looked different from when he was in school.

"I think of these every day myself." Stone Jr. added in a consolatory manner.

The anger on Iyke's face and voice was infectious. He was tired of it all, a growing crowd living in filthy and growing poverty. He had camped outside the Embassy for a week waiting for a visa. Like the others there a visa seemed like a ticket out of hell.

Andy was still his usual happy self, the life of the party. But he was tired, most of all of being governed by a group of selfish and power drunk rulers.

"People in power in this country, they have no interest of the nation or its people at heart."

"It is obvious." Stone Jr. added.

"I find it hard to imagine the fates of millions of bright men and women in hands of men who could hardly tell their left from their rights." Andy said with a half-smile on his face.

"I was just talking with Iyke over there." S.A Stone Jr. said shaking his head.

The weekend before, he attended a party thrown by a friend of his friend, Ahmed. The guy had just got a mobilization check for a contract he won from the government. That afternoon he bought himself an Aston Martin, completely paid for. Executing the contract was the last thing on his mind. He invited friends to celebrate.

It was his share of national cake. God baked it the night before.

CHAPTER
≈70≈

At the flower shop Ihuoma was listening to the radio. The music that was playing from the radio drew her attention. It was music from East Africa. The announcer was fond of calling it music from the home of the sunrise of Africa. The announcer's name was Kola Bari. He called himself, "Alusi." He said the music was from the Congo, Zaire, and Tanzania. Those countries when unable to provide material support to their brethren being eaten away by hunger and the civil war, found a way to say we are with you. They provided emotional support. It made gari Gabon have more meaning. Tanzania was a country that saw the suffering and did their best to alleviate it. They saw the humanitarian conditions and knew before anyone else that it was genocide.

"They saw death at birth and cried foul." The announcer intoned,

It was the bight of Biafra. They too are of the earth. "They signed treaties and recognized us."

They delivered support and their music. This music replaced the war drum. This music replaced all that was lacking. They were a people fighting with their brothers, though they were not present in the battlefield. Radio and music kept the war going. It was all our men had when they had nothing. It was all our people had when food would not arrive. It was the medicine when our bushes had no more leave that could cure. It was the second soldier beside that lone soldier. It was the second bullet when the order was one-man one bullet. It was the hope that sometimes milled out hope.

Ihuoma liked the voice and its subtlety. She was listening to it for the first time. She was sure the announcer was a daring man. When she later explained the program to her mom, she compared it to the holy books. She told her of how, despite wars and tales of wars in the scriptures, they remain one of humanity's most sought after.

"Daily there's a seemingly childhood lust to encage, memorize and exalt them. It is a dream of knowledge and pleasure enclosed in the peace follower seek. We lust after its otherness and treasure how distinct we become- through association. Yet we let our own lights burn out. Let your own light shine." She told her mother.

"Ihuoma, I know how much you like those songs. We went days and nights hunger, those voices became known to us. It is not the Igbo-Jew who brought the Israeli. They understood our pain. They did the little they could, not because of your friends who thought they were Jews, or those who though there were sounds connections between Hebrew and Igbo. But because they too have known these threats and experiences, Lisbon did and so did Paris. They have heard those voices." Her mother too has been listening to the radio.

It was on that show that Ihuoma heard of the death of the former leader of Biafra. Kola was devastated at the news himself. He was in the middle of a text and call in. He was reading the last one that came in from a friend on air.

"It sounds like music to my ears"

Reading that out loud, then his cell phone beeped again. It was not what he was expecting. It was the news of the death. He interrupted the show. When Kola came back he came up with the news of the death.

Ihuoma was shocked. Ojukwu has died. The news of his death was everywhere instantly, on the radio, TV, newspapers and social media.

Stone Jr. had called Ihuoma to cancel some of their planned engagements. His was very busy he hardly could make it to see her. They went back to the phone as usually. But this time every single minute he found between his schedules he was on the phone with her.

Kola had become a household name after the war. When he was on the airwave people listened to radio. He was a young nice handsome radio reporter and announcer. He covered the war as a hide and seek reporter.

Days after the war, he woke up in the middle of the night. He announced to no one in particular. He had an idea. He dreamed up a program. As a man of ideas and a dreamer, he knew some ideas would surely make it to the mountain top. And others would fall by the way side. However it never meant that those that fell by the way side were not as good.

"The gods have crowned every idea in its place and time." He said.

The program started as a memorial. Soon it became the only program in the land that taught the history of the country. The history books would not have it. The teachers did not know it. In every front people were helped to collectively destroy their own dreams and memories. They became a people trying hard to live without their past, without history, trying to run away from the things that have conditioned them as a people. He would be announcing names of people who were yet to make it home since after the war. He would start with his big brothers. He had two brothers who did not make it back from the war. He started with them. Nobody has heard from them since the night they joined the armored division.

When the military government eventually allowed the ownership of private broadcast station he got a license. Some years after he started his own radio station with the help of his friend Agueyi; the importer and exporter international. Kola got more help. But he still ran his own show.

Each time Kola was on air, he started the program with his favorite music, music from the East of Africa. He described his feelings and journeys as those of a young cattle herder. He was in the bush, grazing his herds and feeling the pores of the earth. He tended to his cattle, goats and sheep knowing that at season's end he would return. As the music played, he drifted to the life of a shepherd boy and so did his listeners. He would be home when he hears the voice of a baby, in the hands of his bride. His voice came alive and loud.

"I'm a walking man
I don't look back
I'm lost,
But I know the joy of the past
And of destiny,
I know the joy of a walking man.
I know the Fulani, the Masai, the Ejeje

and the Gypsy spirits
I close my eyes,
When I wake if the pastures are greener
I smile for the joy of tomorrow,
If I wake under a tree with the dews dropping
Over me
If I wake in a hut and a roof over my head
I make a step, another and another step
Three steps to the door.
If I see the intercity of sunrise
If I hear the voice of a simple queen
and the cry of a baby
I know it is the season of my return
The calf will find a new home
The cattle will be returning
They will be returning with me
I'm only a Shepherd boy
Following the direction of light
I have seen fairies
But I know the voice that calls me home."

His people were yet to come home. The struggles were yet to produce results. The people continued celebrating their dead. The death was a renewal of those lives and memories. Nki di na iru ka; the future is greater, he believed.

The station started receiving several letters and phone calls from many people. His listeners glued to their radio with the hope they would hear their letters read out on air. And above all, they listened with the hope that they would hear from the people still in the forest. Somewhere in the world someone was listening who knew where they were. They hoped that prayers would be answered one day. Everyone listening hoped to be able to hear a name that they recognized. People hoped upon hope. People called or mailed in stories that made others cry. The stories reminded them of their loss. Some brought back vivid memories of what others have lived through during the war. They were stories of when the rain began to beat them as a people, as Achebe the old Wiseman puts it.

Once a boy wrote describing how he became an orphan.

"His was an example of what many went through," the announcer said with cracked voice.

It gave graphic details of events. It told how his mother was raped and shot. The same afternoon was the last he saw of his father. His father who hid in the bush when they entered the house only came back to inform him he was leaving to join their men fighting. He cried. But his father's mind was made up.

"His father was mad he could see, if he was not there was no way he would leave him to fate", the boy wrote.

He was hoping someone would have a way to help him find his father. His story though similar to others drew a lot of sympathy. The announcer kept it in his breast pocket. He pulled it out of his pocket after his wife had almost destroyed it in an attempt to wash his clothes. He made a copy of the letter after it survived that first attack, he was making sure it does not happen. The boy's story would be read again. He wanted more people to hear that story. People heard it because every week he went in to the studio with a copy already in the studio and one in his breast pocket.

CHAPTER
≈71≈

The name kola was increasingly more popular year after year. When he was not playing music from the East he played local reggae. Alhaji Ukah Udeh, was listening to the radio one morning when he heard his son on radio. He drew the radio closer to be sure he was hearing correctly.

"This boy never stops pulling up surprises" he said.

The oldest of his children, the music lover has gone to become a musician. He was playing reggae a music that was not popular in the north, compared to other parts of the country. It was a time when the music was doing well in the country. Many young artists went and became reggae artists. The country was brimming with support for the fight against apartheid in South Africa.

The songs of the freedom fighters were popular in Nigeria. The country had more artists than the other parts of the continents. They made and sold more songs. Every little child on the street corner was singing freedom songs. They were all calling on Margaret Thatcher to free Nelson Mandela. Kids woke up and went to bed singing the songs that never stopped calling those names, and places they did not know. So

Alhaji's son, Abu made a hit song. His song became known everywhere. Radio stations played his songs, the streetcars blasted and the airwave was filled with his songs.

Alhaji son's dream became going to South Africa one day. He would go there and show his support in person.

Some years later the apartheid regime became tired, they decided to set the Madiba chief free. The world was aglow with hope. Blacks and whites hugged themselves in the streets. They were all happy. The chief after several years behind bars, thinking thoughts that made the hairs of head gray, came out on top. He was elected leader. He called on the world to join his transformation. The transformation would mean men and women of good will making journeys and sacrifices, looking inwards and discovering themselves and outwards with the dreams.

The trade and production of reggae were on decline. Freedom has been born. His people were looking for new means. The world was one big global station. The dance of the time and tunes were fading. The tone was what it seemed like when radio stations played them. And that which holds the stars holds the sky.

Abu was interested in whatever the south was going to offer. He longed for a hand shake with the chief and an embrace with Mama Afrika. She was the angel she sang about, she was Malaika. He hoped to meet her there. It was June when he arrived in Cape Town. He settled down in a friends place at first. Days went by and he got himself an apartment in a neighborhood called the little Mexico. It was filled with criminal gangs, drug dealers and petty criminals. In the actual Mexico fear, secrecy and guns unleashed a different sound of the Mariachi.

There he did menial jobs. He met a white girl with whom he smoked weed. They were both stoned day and night waiting and hoping for the day to come when he will sing again. Sometimes he practiced all day, at night before all the stores in their neighborhood closed he ran out of the room to get food. Once he ran and bought cat food, they finished it before realizing it. Some weeks later he proposed to her, he asked her to marry him. He told her he wanted her to bear him a daughter. She called him poor. He was a poor African boy. That night the picture became clearer to him. The next morning he dropped a note on the mirror for her, "if you don't become a part of me, I'll still make you mine. One day you be carrying a piece of me in your arms, you will smile and I will tell you this is me." He packed his things and left her house. Two days later she moved into his apartment and promised to be a good girl from then on. She did not want the sisters to get to him before she did.

For one moment Alhaji was proud of his son. He did not know where he was or what he was doing. But it was an honor to him, that his son made a recognizable contribution in the country. His music was that contribution to nation building. He was a proud father.

For years Ihuoma was convinced there has never been another radio program like that in the land. It was the holy bible of radio programs.

CHAPTER
≈72≈

Kola was a history and communication graduate. He could tell what was missing in the history of his country. People lacked the knowledge of what has manipulated their lives. Like the boy whose letter he has in his breast pocket, "what does he know about his people, country and the war that his father has failed to return from? What future was there for him?" He queried.

He had a father, who though he still believed was alive, did not care or has lost the ability to care. The situation destroyed those it destroyed. Somewhere in a corner of that country that boy's father was removed from reality. And all he was, a comic relief, for those who sought cheap laughter, who called him "Artillery." The sentiments before the war were returning again. The cry of marginalization was louder, the riot and the fight over the oil wealth and the pollution of the environment. The traders in the north still ran back to the east three or six times within a year. There was constant fear in the air. Politics and religion have become topics to be avoided for the sake of peace. Yet there was no peace. How can men who hated, consider themselves worthy of the kingdom of peace.

Kola decided to explore the past so that listeners could have their say. He wanted them to send letters and to call in. He has been doing that, but as the conflict returned, he thought more needed to be done. He was skeptical, there seemed to be no panacea for the countries myriad of problems. The constant out breaks of conflicts in many parts of the continents bothered him.

The next morning when he got into the studio, he started his program with a signature tune "I love the land and people." He was taking the second burial, through memory lane. He spoke of the blessings of land and natural resources. Before he continued the phone rang. It was a caller searching for a long lost love. He was not necessarily calling because he was hoping for a reunion. He was calling to keep memories alive.

He kept a memorial fire, he said on the phone. Kola was going to divide his program into segments. He wanted to accommodate the history topics. He was going to discuss the basics. He wanted to go back to a time, when a man called Beast Mark, had called a conference legitimize the criminal holds, that was going on in Africa. It was a time he was referring to as the partitioning of Africa by Europe, the Berlin conference of 1885. He called it legitimizing crime. He said though, most of the countries were scrambbling for a hold on land in the continent, to support their economic growth, they nonetheless, called themselves by phony names, such as protectors and protectorates. He said Europe at the time was struggling with internal rife. A caller called to ask if the convener of the conference had marks of the beast. When he answered "no", he asked why he is called the name. The announcer called it a name trying to make it clearer. The man who called, had already made his conclusions. He said it had spiritual implications. He added that, that was the reason that he committed such evil. The announcer gave in. He said something, that the caller did not understand, and he thanked him for calling.

The next caller was furious. He wanted to know if the announcer was out of his mind. He asked him and the last caller, how the events of 1885 could be responsible for the war of the 1960's. The announcer answered politely. He told him that they were trying to explore history, if there were any connections. The man, who was a veteran of the war, went on to tell the announcer the country's civil war was the single most deadly war in human history. "It was two million people, women, children that died not in the hands of Nigerian Army, the Russian 122 fighter plane flown by the Britons and the Egyptian, but by the blockade of aids." He said.

After the war had stopped, the federal authorities still declared, she would control all medicines, food and clothes going into the refugee centers. The slow process added to more deaths. The announcer agreed with him. The voice of the caller came up again.

"It was a slow death. Starvation was a war strategy that should never happen again. Umuigbo, when our tears dried, images and memories, of the past, lurk in our heads. We feel pain. But it was no longer in our stomachs, we survived. In our minds, we see the faces and hands that gave us food. We ask again, as many did then, are you God or his mailman? Men like Rev. Huessler of the Caritas, others of the Red Cross and the World Council of Churches, the American public, who though their man in Lagos looked the other way, looked at us. We still ask, and thank you."

The announcers thanked him for his call and insight.

For many years, the future of many great men, women and children continued to be lost to the war. Some retired to national memory. In death, some awakened the entire nation to the truth. It was the truth, they feared to face, when he was alive. Everywhere in small groups or large gatherings people paid tribute. Kola was there all those years for his people.

When the next call came in the caller cleared his throat. He thanked the radio station for such a program. He was not a regular listener, but had the opportunity, as citizens to listen to his candid discussion as a heartwarming one. He went on to agree with the second caller, before him. He said history was a guide to the future. "Before I go to me point, let me address the man that calls these old wounds." The callers paused, and then continued. "If all you call the history of the killing of millions of innocents is a wound, and you want them forgotten, may you be forgotten before your demise. Would there be enough memorials for those innocent lives? If we are to be a people who value our worth or the worth of those who came before, let every family remember their loss and their wounds. That way, we may curtail fresh wounds, happening every day before us. If not, one day this generation, shall equally be referred to, as old wound, because now these butchers are mobilizing to kill another million."

Then he spoke, about the formation of the Oil River Protectorate. The National African Company Police Force, about the Royal Navy Fernando Po, he said there were put together by a group of men, involved in organized crime. He asked without expecting an answer, "how was it that the same vessel that was used in shipping men and women out of Africa, into the new world, were the same ones to guard its coasts? The same privateers, what was being protected?" The announcer wanted to make a correction, but he probably was not listening. He went on to speak. He asked, if that was not the same ship, that the king of Benin was captured, and was taken away in 1897. In 1895 it was our palm oil, today it's crude oil we die for. Who knows, what it will be tomorrow. He stopped, as if he was expecting somebody to answer, his charges. The announcer had decided to give him a free run, knowing the moment he opened his mouth, the man had something to say. The man took advantage of the airtime, and continued his lecture, which the announcer later called,

"Berlin conference 101."

He informed the listeners, he was putting together a group of lawyers to seek redress. The caller summarized by calling a conference by proxy. He was the last caller, the announcer had for the day, though the phone lines kept ringing. Fela's music was in the air, when the announcer said to expect and interesting addition the coming week. The new segment, he just added had drawn more attention, he noted.

He was going home to his wife. His people still dug the ground for yam and cocoyam to feed themselves. But in their backyards, the multi-nationals have started drilling oil and mined for precious stones. Like their neighbors, they were the next in line to be dispossessed of the means of livelihood.

"In this place, those who know, pay direly, for knowing" he said.

In some places, people get killed for having good ideas. Those ideas could be for the good of all. In these places, politicians and pro-reformers are hundred times, more likely to get killed, than a day light armed robber.

CHAPTER
≈73≈

When the announcer got to the house that day, he was tired. He took off his shirt and sat on the couch. His wife came and took the shirt into the room. He was fond of that especially when he has had an exhausting day. When she came out, he told her, he needed to do more research. She was listening to the program, so she agreed. She went to the study and pulled out a note she made for him. He read it and agreed with her. Those were, some things, he would need to pay more attention to. With the turn his show had taken, a degree in history and communication was no longer, what was needed, he needed to be ready for the man in the street. Radio listenership was huge in the country, and men and women in their cars, in their farms; in the market place and the cattle herd's men, everyone was hugging their transistor radio, wherever they went. More and more radio stations were being built.

Ihuoma though in her final year at the university, where she studied medicine, has not heard so much about the country from any other source. She had the radio at shop tuned to her station, each time kola was on air.

Many segments of the society were listening. For some, it's the idea of something new, that made sense, to others, to them was the voice and its magic that kept them glued.

The program, to some, had the possibility, to strain relationship in the country that was the concern of a caller. He or she was not particular about what type of relationship. He or she was equally anonymous.

At his death the nation mourned. Ojukwu was made immortal in the hearts of men. The world witnessed the peak of memorials. They relived those lives sacrificed, and failed efforts to preserve peace, justice and equity. The grandeur of the exit of Eze Igbo Guruguru, caught the attention of the low and the mighty. He took the message of the living to their departed. Peace, he took to them. It was what the world wished them. The green, white, green of the nation draped his coffin. It flies half masked. The nation defiled that, which was his, and forced him out to the battlefield. Like it was from the book of old, the president announced.

"A prince has died."

A new beginning and peace, those guns and armory once pointed toward him, and his men where pointed to the sky. Men in the national army, fired shots of salute to the man. It was the exit of a man loved, feared, hated, respected and yet celebrated by all. He fought on the side of truth. Men who opposed, the core of that truth, spoke up in the open. They wished his soul and the millions of souls lost peace. Those who oppressed them were powerful. And they had no comforter. Their death in the fight for justice, peace and equity was a message of courage to generations yet unborn. It was a message to the continent. It was message of peace and respectful handshakes across the tributaries of the Niger.

There is time for everything. Time to love and time to hate, time to comfort and time to be comforted, time for war and time for peace.

In the eyes of his jewel, the beauty he beheld, her hero was going. It was an end of a chapter. She celebrated in songs and poetry. From her heart, her highness the beautiful, her soul poured out. It was a pleasure she treasured. A live with him, he was her dreams come true.

"Ojukwu lives on in the hearts of this nation and this great people."

Listening to her speak, tears rolled down Ihuoma's eyes. "A people whose heroes and tales of are swept under the carpet, will suffer their defeat hundred times over." She sobbed openly.

CHAPTER
≈74≈

When the announcer, sought through those mails, he could not use all of them on air. As much as he would have wanted to use them, he could not. He had to select them based on geographical zone and their contents. He would use the next segment of his show, to address the issues that will be first on the show. He was applying the result of the research by his wife. He found out that what his wife had spoken about concerning addressing, the concerns of the man in the street was very real. He was working on accommodating all sectors of the society.

His show being on Fridays gave him time to address issues and sought things out as they arose. On his next show, he got on air with the signature tune. He spoke about the great response from the past week. And thanked the people who called or wrote. He informed his listeners, he would be reading some of the letters, but would not be able to read all. He also informed them, he would not take calls on the issues that were discussed the past week. He wanted them to be on point. He would dwell on the issues of the 1960's.

He wanted to hear from informed listeners. He wanted balanced debate. He continued to read out the new guideline to the show. He was sure there would be people who wanted to be heard on radio, those who had nothing to do, and those who simply are unable to stay on a topic. He had plus or minus three minutes from his calculation that will take care of those stray calls. As he read the rules, he secretly hoped that the numbers that present week would surpass those of the previous week. What, the past week, did was wake them up, he hoped. They had not responded that much in writing before. He was going to do his best to keep them on their feet. He was beginning to engage them. The issue of a national dialogue has been a long overdue one. Many sections of the country have called for it, after several failed talks. It was time to revive the talk again, for the good of every one. The court of public option may be able to do, what those assemblymen and women have failed to do. Their job it was no news, has always been left on done, while they ran after contracts.

After all the struggles, nationalist fights and noise about indepedence1960 came and went, the ugly got uglier in the land. They gap keeps getting wider. The suffering continued, as did their differences. The differences over the census figures, had not and did not seem to be solved. It has been advanced by many, as the single most problematic issue in the land, then aside that, from the religions, and the difference in the language. If the people were at least able to have a reliable census figure, their management would not have been such a problem. Both counting the men and women of that country meant trouble. The first head count only took two years, before it brought the strange kind of ill feeling. The numbers were put at about fifty five point six million men and women. The other parts of the country accused the north of inability to differentiate the human and animal populations. The four point eight million that gave the north advantage over half of the rest of the country's population was blamed on the counting of cows. It has always had the ability to start a bitter contest. When Northerners were with their friends from other parts of the country, they usually joked that cows ate more than men. That alone gave the animals the right to be counted. Twenty-nine point eight in a statistical record of a country was no joke. The bitterness continued. Some people began to blame the miss counts on the ingenuity of the British. However, the northern was more likely to have more wives and have many children, even from early marriage. Others argued the north was sparely populated despite the landmass.

CHAPTER
≈75≈

The radio announcer played the "everything dey for Nigeria" call tune. He continued with another sound, which took people by surprise. He normally would introduce himself and his show, but this time he continued with Fela's song instead. His colleagues thought it was a mistake. Many thought someone else was standing in for him. One of the senior studio managers ran in, he was thinking the mistake was from his people. The manager discovered it was deliberate. He went out of the studio and asked if he came in late. He was told no, he just wanted to change his style. "Wars and war tales could bring the best and worst out of people", the manager said as he walked out of the station.

Many listeners were still speculating when they heard kola narrating the events that led up to the situation in the country in the sixties. From the war to the post war conditions, the country and its people were estranged from themselves. The radioman was of the opinion that the country had little in common. Though his call tune was aimed at the praise of the land, but there was little or nothing that actually spoke of nationhood. Unlike his usual self, he sounded removed from the program that day. As he finished he introduced himself and his program. He said, the phone lines were open, and that mailman has got the back, of the letter writers. He announced the phone number and the mailing address. The lines started ringing. It was ringing off the hook. He let them have their go at it. Callers were calling from all parts of the country. Many argued for the census and many countered it. A man called and said it was the formation of political parties along tribal line that was the start of the problems. He blamed the chaos on the leaders of the four major parties. A man who, sounded like a trader from Onitsha main market, said it was simply, that wherever the Igbo were doing business, the rest of the country moved there in anticipation of a time to loath their goods. The man spoke for his constituency. He said this was rampant in the north. He added,

"It was not hate, it was greed."

More people called to support him with facts and figures. As usual, a dispute ensued over that. But it seemed like the kind of thing, that the announcer was prepared for that day. He kept intoning, that they were having a debate. The debate got more and more heated. It was in the course of that, that a caller called to inform the listeners of the situation in the delta. He said the nation may yet be seeing bigger crises there. The wealth of the nation according to the caller continued to move from where it was being produced, to faraway, to the hilly countries of north, to be refined. And at the end of the day, the south saw little or nothing of it. If the north was not in power, some there would cast a terrible religious shadow over the nation. Boko Haram was the tool, it was political. It was religious. It wreaked havoc on the lives of innocent people. As he spoke, he hoped that, that was not prophetic.

The program was a changed one. It was no longer a long list of names and addresses from unknown hideouts. It was men who sounded as if they had the solution to the problems in the land. Yet they were the very causes of those problems. The announcer patted himself on the back "this is going somewhere."

After the program a man who called earlier, called again. He wanted a name from the announcer. He was inquiring about a beloved journalist. The name of the man he was asking about was Forsyth.

The journalist like another man whom he called, "the Swedish Count," was loved in the east of the land. Some said the count was still grateful for the miracle of his grandparent's escape from Nazi Germany. The man wanted to know what the journalist was doing and where he was.

He knew he became an author. He was not aware of his recent works. He wanted to know those. Mr. Frederick Forsyth, who the announcer happened to be a big fan of, was a reporter that reported for the BBC during the civil war. Throughout the career of the journalist and during his short stay reporting the war, the man was a fellow who cared for the truth. He made himself a name telling stories no other reporter was able to tell from the war front. He did not report from tanks, for the federal troops. He reported as a man covering a war.

The announcer liked dropping the name of the journalist who he had come to love as a colleague. He was a great admirer. The caller was grateful he was able to get the information he wanted. The announcer had a picture of him, the Swedish Count, John Lennon, Jean Paul Sartre and few others in his library at home.

That evening when he gets home, he was going to dust those pictures and light a candle for each one of them. They were men who understood that the blood in every vein was red. They were men who could not understand the madness of the world watching as spectators while a people were being massacred. For that same cause Mr. Lennon had given up his Membership of the Order of the British Empire (MBE). Though Mr. John Lennon did not understand the Igbo language, he knew their members were truly "mbe", the turtles and the trickster. He no longer wanted to be a member of an order of protectors, who watched those they were supposed to protect die, while they amused themselves. Jean-Paul Sartre, himself had seen it coming and warned, though he did not believe it would happen, but it did.

CHAPTER
≈76≈

As the announcer drove off the studio complex, he was held up in a traffic jam. A passenger on his side of the road in a red Nissan car shouted a few words to him. Though he did not reply, he knew they were people who admired his show. There were days when the show seemed more like reporting from the battle field. He would be exhausted and wished he did not start the show. Kola was loved and hated.

People had divergent views and were entitled to their opinion about his program. Kola was probably, the only disciple of his professor at school, who believed radio to be democratic. He preached that it was a tool which spreads ideas fast, and its reach unmatched.

Kola tried to avoid the traffic, unpleasant faces and comments. He headed to the toward the market street.

The traffic on the street was a bit fair. Kola made it to the market. There the market looked very different. It wore a festive look, which he did not understand. The decoration made him curious. As a radio man he felt he should know. He got down from his car, walked to a man who was putting up a sign. The preparation was for the next day, he learnt. That

Saturday the legendry masquerade was coming out. The union of the living and the dead was about to take place. And he was almost not aware of it. It was said the living brought back the spirits of the dead back to celebrate them. The dead were also believed to do the same for the living. It was a time of settlement and understanding. They came out from the ground and from the air. They were in male and female forms.

The last time the announcer had experienced the masquerade it was pomp and pageantry. That was several years ago at the burial of a great man. The living and the dead celebrated his last rite of passage, it was said. The announcer was in attendance.

CHAPTER
≈77≈

The dance, the maneuvers in the air and enthusiasm of the spectators convinced any new comer to the town that there was an interaction between the living and the dead, the masquerades and those behind them. Some people believed, the masquerades, were spirits that emerged from the ground and went back to the ground, at the end of the day. When the radioman was a kid, that was at least, the story he grew up with, over the years the phenomenon has not ceased to amaze him. Mere representations by the people or any other things, he had come to see that those times, brought joy and excitements to the people. The experience and memories, he has had of the ceremonies, made him decide not to miss it, though he was just hearing of it. It was a spectacle that everyone ought to witness once, he noted in his writing pad. The list of possible appearances could be seen, on the banner placed, by the guy he spoke with. The different groups, placed, their signs and posters, at different corners in market square. He walked round and noted spots where the towns were likely to display their masquerades.

Looking at the eager dancers, the announcer was convinced, there was a true exchange of information between the masque and those behind them. He wanted so much to be part of it. Recalling and replaying those experiences in his head, he promised himself to be back the next day, and the day after and the coming year. He did not want to miss any bit of the spectacle.

The least of the groups appearing, pasted posters everywhere in the market square and all over the town. He knew which group would be where and when. In their struggle, for particular spots, the masquerade spilled blood. They fought over spots, and who was more powerful. Many like the announcer, sometimes, wondered if their spirits were bloodthirsty.

The festivity was usually on a Saturday. On the eight market day of the Igbo calendar, made up of the big and small Eke, Ore, Afor and Nwko. It was always decided by the hosting community to schedule it, on the day that coincided with the Saturday, when it was not an entire week of celebrations. People prepared to look their best. Single men and women, were excited, it was time to meet their counterparts from participating towns. They were ready to explore the fun. The towns displayed their beauty, as the groups came out with their displays. The groups claimed all forms of magically power. One group never came out, till they found the cat, to be tied to the head of their masquerade. When they did they came out. Some spilled the blood of goats, cow and chicken before they crossed.

They said it was to avoid spilling human blood. One year, it was speculated that the group with the masquerade and the cat on it, would not come out. The cat had disappeared. It was a bad omen. Eke who wore that mask, was believed to have defied the mask or himself. They feared another group may find out and capitalized on that weakness. In that Market Square, there had been news of groups that came and were made unable to display by others. They were said, to have been charmed and transfixed. Pinned to the ground, and made motionless for hours. Every group feared the thought of such an experience. The incapacitation of a masquerade by another was never taken lightly. It was a great defeat, a tragedy.

People saw it that way that the groups, took many months and years to prepare, before coming out. The market square, was not a place for armatures, it was regarded. The groups guarded their secrets and those who prepared their little charms. When those were known, the groups became an easy target. One of them was said, to have the power to hold water in a hand woven basket. Another had the power to make their staff into snakes. They speculated, some appeared and disappeared at will, during an outbreak of violence. The tales seem, like listening to those of Pharaoh and Moses, and their serpents.

Amor reconnected with her schoolmates and high school besties on facebook. Her relationship status was already, "In a relationship." She occasionally sent messages reminiscent of those years of girlish excitements and escapades. But the fear of the new image and ownership of the social network was the beginning of wisdom.

She had gotten invited to the festivities.

Amor was married to a young successful French film director. What she had jokingly called, her little cross cultural experiment, had become the life she was leading. And together they continued to conquer the world anew. Her husband, directed movies that portrayed the exquisite palaces of Europe, the magnificence of the great Zimbabwe, the beauties of the Zuma Rock, and the pinnacle of Kilimanjaro. His first project was financed with stolen money. It was a forged check for a million Euros, cleared from her brother's account, with the help of a banker.

His dream was to oversee the marriage of Bollywood, Nollywood and Hollywood. Amor was a midwife, who has found a way, to make and bring special babies into the world. And she has two of her own. While in town, she would meet with some friend's recommendations. She was there to make it happen again, for someone.

Somewhere, a Nollywood Star, an actor who has conquered the local market, and has a lot to show for it, was sitting by his laptop and watching his cell phone. He wanted to sit at the Taj Mahal. He wanted to do the cycle of fire. He wanted to dance his own dance in a different land.

"Tomorrow, tomorrow" he consoled himself, "The sun lingers, and beauty will meet bravery."

"Africa will meet the world in that which is, was and will be. Some things are understood better when left unsaid. Today, I let the music guide your soul." He continued.

"Listen to your inner voice" he recalled his father had told him, as a young man. And he was a man used to doing simply that. It had always told him that the right time would come. It would. And he would spread his tentacles beyond his wildest imagination.

He continued waiting. Then the telephone rang. It was loud and noisy from where the call was coming from.

CHAPTER
≈78≈

Very early the next morning, the people started trooping to the market place. The Ikoro sound was heard. And after a few minutes, loud drumming followed it. The sound of the flute drowned voices, invoking millions of years of ancestral past. A cheering crowd turned solemn, transported to the distant past, when men were gods. It was healing and soothing sound of the past. It healed men of their heartbreaks. It was a distant time, before the violence of the violin interrupted. A time before the screaming voice of the dancer screamed murder. It was the sound that was heard after the flood was over. The masquerades came out, some in very colorful costumes and in terrifying and horrifying make-ups.

All the displays, the magic, the dance, were a direct communion between the dead and the living. The connections between the masques, the masquerades, the ancestors and their tales attracted men from far and wide year after year. The announcer was in the crowd. There was one thing that he was eager to see, the masquerade with the mark of the scorpion and bearers of the arrow. He wanted to see the men from the group that climbed the palm tree with their bare hands. And went into the top, making sure, all the leaves pointing upwards pointed to the earth. After that, they took the palm from the newest of all the leaves in their hands and brought it down with them. They never allowed it to touch the ground. The palm frond it was said possess so much power. It had a lot of contradictions too. It was a symbol of peace, yet the groups fought over it a lot. Many of the groups targeted any one they saw climb the tree. They made effort to see, they deterred any group or person, from successfully bringing down the palm frond without dropping it.

It was a symbol of triumph, that anyone, who succeeded either way, is seen as possessing special powers. Ochaku children of the archers wonderfully topped the performance each year, with new or strange displays. The Archers were men skilled in the art of bows and arrows. Men whose forbears survived the hard times, because of their shooting skills. Times and survival made them take the image of the scorpion for their masquerade.

Climbing the tree required skills. Stepping on the sharp ends of the base of the tree, without piercing and bleeding one's feet required luck. It was the skill and the luck that others sought to disprove. It was always a silent wish to know how much power those up there possessed. Most times their opponents stood underneath the tree invoking their powers to incapacitate the one on top.

In the afternoon the whole square was full of activities. There was music in the air. There was sound of triumph in the air and spectacle in every corner. Cameras were flashing their lights, everywhere in every corner video cameras were rolling and enthusiastic crowd cheering. Some people were there for the very first time, others were regulars. Cameras were capturing more and the different perspectives. There was no end to the spectacle or what to expect. The sound of music filled the air. On an elevated stage at the square, the distinctive voice of the Ahamefula Igbo Opera celebrated victories, sorrows, defeats and survivals. The voices brought a different soul of the memorial to the market square. The people could not get enough of them.

On one corner the Nkelebe played. Ichie Onyenwe a man of great title and art, brought to life rhythms from those have gone centuries before, and voicing the dreams of the future. On another corner the drum beat of the Abigbo, its call and response opened a window into the hearts of men and women in love. Dee Vita the honey merchant, a patron and a member of the Abigbo was applauding. The honey merchant traded in the good product. He traded in that which for many thousands years his ancestors, their counterparts from where the Niger flows to, those from Egypt, China, India and their Mayan friends certified as good for the mind, body and spirit. He performed a sacred duty. "Buy your special honey here" the special was sacred and its healing power true. Men sought for him from faraway. There with his tone and moves, there he was lending weight to the day.

CHAPTER
≈79≈

The announcer at that point had seen many of the displays and was waiting for another particular group. He wanted to see the men from the clan of warriors. The Izuogu, the men said to possess the wisdom, knowledge and act of war. He was interested in seeing the communication between the spirits of men who have paid the ultimate price for their nation in the display. It was a terrible past that he hoped to see a re-enactment. He was looking for a connection from the display. In what he saw there was history, future and above all sense of purpose. The men were said to communicate with the past national heroes. Though it was daylight it was equally claimed only the initiates understood their communication. This was known to be possible to many in the dark of the night. People initiated into special cults, were known to be able to communicate with their dead especially the night before their burial. The fact that it was broad daylight and the sun was up in the sky made it more intriguing for people. Expectations were high and people wanted to confirm the rumors they have heard.

The announcer was eager to learn more. He was going to ask questions. Kola was not an initiate of any cults. He waited for the opportunity the daytime show was offering. Well before that day he had told himself several times. The sky, was not his limit, it was rather, his landing and takeoff pad. He had worked for so much, and there before him, was all what he sought so long. He was happy. He made notes, took photos and gathered all he could gather.

Jonan, Onye foto; the photographer, took a nice picture of the radioman. He is one of the best in the town. He captured the past and the future. The present was his duty, he was known to say. Onye foto was said have taken picture of spirits and he had the copies and negative to show it. A painting "Nne- nke – Chukwu" Mother of God, an image of Mother and Child adorned his stand with its magnificence. It was in many places, on big structures of worship. He laid claim to its origin, though it's revered the world over. "Man is always a complicated being, death never stops that." He told the radio man as he handed him his wait and take.

He knew a girl, who when she came back; she came back as a tree. She grew in the front of her enemies, in the gardens of her follies. Her seed sprouts all over town.

The future was there before him and he saw it. Jonan Onye foto, marveled at the beauty of the sky that was turning thick blue.

"Men had so much power within them, yet often the accomplished so little." He said to himself.

Kola Bari was thinking of the many ways, through which the manifestation of the things, he had seen that day, could be put into use.

For him there was no doubt, he knew where the duty starts for a radioman. Information was the key to changing a people and a society. He had that information.

Kola has heard men speak from the nation past. There, time and place had been made to merge. The future, the past and the present converged. It was the market square. It was not the hills of Idanre or the Emenike cave. He was hearing the voices of men, he had only known by their names. Their actions, he has replayed and made their names into heroes and legends. There he gave a part of him to their world. He was a believer in the many dimensions of life. The world that the humans interacted with every day and the one that they were not privy to were his entire playground. He believed in the here and now and the hereafter. He did not limit himself. The one eyed man saw what the blind fly sees. He was the man that had made a ring with white chalk around his eyes. Kola had been given to superior sight. It was reward for men who dared to dream. He has come to see himself constantly dream for the good of land and people, for the world, which he had come to see.

The voices and the notes he took made him alive to new truths about family, nations and peoples. The voices kept him from sleeping that night as he got home. They mixed with the songs and dance steps. He did bother about the sleep that did not come. He was a man working on the cause of change. He was first working to change himself. And that was the duty he has started.

CHAPTER
≈80≈

As Kola Bari reviewed his notes, he saw that a hidden secret about the nation's past had been revealed. It was a revelation. He was guided back, years long before the country's was independent of the colonial rulers. Those days were young. There were three young men fresh from the homes. One was from the west of the country another two from the north. They had one thing in common, they who fancied the rulers of the day. They had been shipped from their homes to the military academy. When they were not wearing their starched khaki, they were in their regular white shorts and tee shirts, which they were obsessed about. They wore them to sleep and woke up in them. They wear them to games and at all times they were in them. They were men the British were training to take over the rule of the country. They were the chosen.

Their choice was not clear to any one and no one cared. To some, they fooled around, to others it was, a source of concern. A trader from the east of the country worried so much about the development. He woke up one morning and told his wife, his son was leaving the country. He was going to school. That was all he told her. He was not a priest of any god. But he wanted an eye in the things that transpired in the affairs of the nation. According to the book of records, that son studied and excelled. One thing however, was that he did not have the pleasure the other three had. Those three at their spare-time, which they had often, sat on tables and chairs, playing games, allotting themselves time-tables of how they will govern the country. They sat over draught boards in their white tee shirts. Played checkers, deciding who would loot the most wealth and power. It was the beginning of a dream they believed in, that a few years later, turned into the people's nightmare.

CHAPTER
≈81≈

It happened in the country a few years after independence.

The country fresh from the grips of greedy men who went from land to land administrating as it pleased them. Their young enthusiasts secretly encouraged unrests. Before long it brought them into power. The military school, rather than train men to protect, trained men to rule. Many realized it and cried foul, but it was too late. The harm had been done. It was the game of the masters. They went on to rule.

At several intervals in the nation's history, they ruled. They inserted themselves, still in their heavily starched khaki uniforms and their badges. They had won on the draft table. They made themselves into generals and made false promises to the people. Power went around them, till it got the dullest amongst them. Then the country was bleed red and desperate. People were dying and being killed for the least of reasons. The game plan was always of change and change of strategy. The three ruled, their new game was to come back in muftis. Forty years later their return was from their farms. It was no longer from the barracks. They wore camouflages that made them look like the people.

They called themselves new names, joined groups and political parties. They learnt new vocabularies. They wanted to lead, they said. Men who were neither good shepherd of their flocks, wanted to lead other men. They walk the dark paths of their farmhouses. They were always able to trick their car wash and shoeshine boys who were always available. One was only a wolf in a sheep's clothing, they thought. They could handle him. But he was more dangerous than a wolf.

As years went by Nigeria was still ruled by a succession of chop I chop leaders. Corruption turned out to be the only way that worked for majority of workers. Honest men found it hard to maintain respect, even in their own homes. Food price had gone up. The target of every man was to be able to put food on the table for his family. What was there to live for, when a man could not keep that part of the deal? Many devoted lesser time to job that could not pay the bills. The love and passion for hard work was gradually affected. Politicians came up with diversionary technics. They increased fraud and tricked the people. The military takes over power, the population cheered. The country turned into a circus. They introduced worst forms of rules. They turned the country into one man dictatorial rule. In a country with the history like that of Nigeria, the decrees replaced the constitution. The suspensions were strange and laughable. There was another coup. It was quick to follow. Still there was none better than the one it succeeded. Infrastructures were also quick to collapse. No new roads or bridges. The export of crude oil equaled the import of refined fuel and petroleum products. The leadership did not see the shame in that. It created new brigades of rich friends of those in power. It seemed normal. The population continued to grow. There was nothing to feed them with. Frustrations forced labor union leaders to demand pay increase.

Demands led to arrests and detentions. The inflation went to shameful rates. But that too seemed normal. Another group, a tiny one, was happy they were making money. The bureau de change increased. At every corner there sprang up new Ama Awusa. They traded in money, knew or cared nothing about the economy. Banks were forced to fold. Many joined in on the corruption. The lot of the Nigerian people got worst day in day out. The air, the water all tasted of hardship and corruption. One did not have to be smart to dupe anyone. The languages created new words that accommodated the situation. New born babies soon learned them, they seemed natural. The nation sank deep and deeper. The ethnic, religious and economic struggle took new turns. Unprovoked riots and conflicts broke out on short notices. It was also the same reason for which a young military officer suspended parts of the country from the country. The young man wake up one day, realized the nation rather than move forward was on a reverse course. He came up with a new map. His reign, his revolt was short lived, as was his life. Another wasted blood, in a place where history has no lessons. As was foretold by that young man and those termed rebels before him, the disease and its symptoms continued.

The revolts came and went. And so did war. The spring came and went. And the showers of blessings remained a dying promise. The Ogonis and Niger Delta cries continued. The Igbos still pushed in all fronts. The Odouwa calls continued. A cry is heard everywhere. In the North a heightened theatre of zealousness casts a shadow. The country still held at ransom in the name of the most merciful and beneficent, while the big boys tightened their economic and political sway in a system that nibbled at the nipples of democracy. Everyone wanted answers.

"As long as men lived, their aspirations never end," was the last sentence kola read from the note. He covered it and exhaled. Placed his left arm on his chin, he contemplated. The market place was the oldest theater and the masquerades the longest performer in the history of the land. And he was the observer.

He began to think about the Ekpe dance, the masquerades and the sheep, the wolf and the lion that were portrayed in the display he had witnessed. It was a raw display of power and the bloody political history it revealed.

CHAPTER
≈82≈

Many walked out of the market with different things. Some took away the enjoyment from the music and dance. For weeks many would not forget what they have heard or seen. Most of the children were singing and dancing as they went home. The future was in the mind of others. They looked forward to the next festival. Some went away saying their future had been opened up to them. To some the state of their businesses and families has been revealed to them. One year a man walked away, saying he has been given number for the lottery. No one believed him. A week later the news everywhere was that he won the lottery. He became a millionaire. He said it was a gift from his ancestors, the men who guarded the market for decades. He called a feast. He gave thanks and they celebrated with a big cow. First he discovered that whenever he went to the vendors of the lottery scratch card and asked for a card that would win they always gave him one that was able to cover his initial investment. His ancestors were bound to be more generous.

An announcer had many stories from such events. The ones he saw and the one that he was told. Kola was fascinated by many of what he had discovered. The tourism potential was not maximized he noted. More could be done with that part of the country. There were countries around the world that lived solely on such strengths. Why was there such a waste in a richly blessed land and people?

A young clergy once attended the festival. He was said to have been inspired by the activities and tales he had heard of the place. Within the loud drumbeats, shouts and noise he was said, to be ringing his bell loud and dancing round the square. He was yelling out. He was the sole representative of the God of Elijah. Those close enough to hear him said he shouted the last words of the Christ on the cross.

He was not against the spirit of the day. He brought his own talent as enjoined by the scriptures. He told the people that the God of Elijah was alive in that town and was part and particle of the activities. He took out his Moses' tablets, rumored to have been stolen from mount Taboo and placed it close to books he was calling people to buy. On display were the books of the bishops, Gevena, Tyndale and his secrets. He had brought salvation and the secret of old to his people. He rang the bell almost every minute.

Nwaopara and others with him were in the colorfully decorated corner. He was in his green kaftan. The kwanzaa candles were burning. And he proclaimed the joys of Nguzu Saba.

Under a tree at a corner of the market square was Atuma. She was performing and a group of spectators were watching her. Atuma was probably more familiar with that space, than anyone else. Since she left her home after they declared her mad, Atuma has spent nights and days there. She often told people, she has a busy schedule. Several errands to run, pulse the dance, she has to do at the market square. That day she actually did the dance and the people watched.

As the celebrations drew to an end she did her last dance for the spectators. And she kept looking around the corners and the exits in hope. She was hoping the dogcatcher her lover would be somewhere waiting. She did not see him and his group of dancers that day. She did not see him, that meant she was to reserve some dance for the night for him.

The celebration was like putting the life of a nation, its people and history on a theater in one day. The society was in fragments and various representations. People with many stories of who the area and what they have to be. There were stories of isolation; destruction and loneliness all of which could be seem in a day display. The people who traveled from nearby town to the old towns had their tales. They showed signs and tales of the home before they or their ancestors were displaced. Some of them followed the footpaths that had turned into roads. There were those displaced by the flood they tended to relate to the tracks of the canal. The pond was a fixed presence, many first time visitors to the town were visiting. Many paid homage to it. And so were the children going home from the festivities.

CHAPTER
≈83≈

A small stagnant moldy rusty colored looking body of water. Somehow year after year it has remained there. Even in the heat of the driest season of the year. It has always had a calabash to spear each family in the village, even the neighboring ones. It was a source of life for their livestock, their gardens from the midyear heat through the harsh dry harmattan season. It was an oasis. They developed ways of purifying it. They removed the moldy color which made it look more like table water. The villagers cooked and bathed with it but its smell lingered. Somehow over the years they have become proud of everything about the pond.

It was said the masquerades and the other performers from that part of town before and after going to the market square paid it homage. Some amongst them took water to wash their faces for protection. They inherited it from their ancestors. There was something about it that has kept it preserved. It was not the trees that provided shed for it in the dry season. It was not the bamboo plants which did not absorb the moisture that the heat evaporated. Its bamboo was not the selfish type. It was not the dog that ate what was given to it to keep.

Though they all guarded it like the life sustaining force it was. It was before the village and they believe it would be there after them. It knew their ancestors before their ancestors. It was rumored they settled there because of the water. It was a natural body of water, season after season their ancestors' devised means of making it serve their every need. They made sure it did not run out, they dredged it once in three years. They believed ever life sustaining force was prone to the inevitability of destruction and regeneration, but if the pond was not protected they themselves would go before it. They protected it. Tata said water was a universal force for good and each people needed to protect theirs.

It was the pond that Ngozika went to when she missed her grandmother. She had gone there to weep when she was lonely. It was also the only place where Ngozika responded to people who picked fights with her. It was there that she went one morning when the water was still clear there she sang if Ngozika was a weed. She told the woman who wanted a fight with her many times if she Ngozika was a weed that woman would have wasted no time in uprooting her. She thanked god she was not. There she told her that she was not ready for her. But reminded her, that it was because of what the mouth says, that make man smell from it, even before he was dead.

Ihuoma did not know much about the masquerades or the festivities of her people. But through the radio show she was able to discuss some of the life her people led. She was always happy when she discussed kola's radio program with her fiancé. He liked it the first time he listened. But S.A Stone Jr. was a very busy man. He listened only when he was able to.

A week after the event, a package arrived at the doorstep of the announcers. It was a suspicious package. He did not recognize the name on the label of the package. He bent down, picked it up. His name was written on it in a way that he held it for a few second, before making it out. It was slightly heavy, but not fragile, as it seemed to look in his hands. He placed it on the table in his study room. He would ask his wife if she knew the name on the sender's label. When she came back, she was clueless as to whom it might have come from. If it was a fan, he did not know why the fan had not addressed it to the office. When she went out of the study, he gently and carefully tore it open. He smiled after he opened it. At least there was no explosion. The content of the package was a set of DVDs.

The most current date on the DVD was the date of the festival masquerades. There were some with old dates from previous years. His face brightened up and he heaved a sigh of relief. He immediately read the noted attached to the content and began test to see the contents. He must have someone who was thinking like him. The present was a package he would have spent a lot of time and money to acquire. The sender had been magnanimous enough to tape several hours of the pervious festivals from many years back. And there it was in his study and a note that said he could keep them. The sender's note likened the festivities to the regalia and floats at the annual Rose Parade on San Gabriel Mountains, in Pasadena California. The market square came alive in his study. He called himself happy. He had the great tales. His people past were not all lost, as he had imagined several times when he woke up and wept silently. Their past was not a huge void. He looked up from his window. His eyes in the sky and he relived a pageantry of power, the shadows of pleasure, in still and tiny bits of knowledge revealed.

CHAPTER
≈84≈

In Tripoli that weekend the priest had gone to see a movie. The movie central character was a priest. It was on the eve of the anniversary of the death of Gaddafi. The priest had been posted there to help. The country was rebuilding after the war. He accepted with little resistance.

"It's my life's calling", he said when he accepted. The priest like many before him, saw it as a duty to keep the little light from the little hut shinning. He was only carrying the old cross and rolling the ancient boat the only way he knows best.

He was doing a good job of it. He was even an admirer of the man when he was alive.

Since he stepped foot on the ground. A sheik in the city and two other Arab business men followed his every move. The sheik was Sunni. Somehow the other two were Shias. Pretense was their game. Both were neither men of faith nor religion. But they bore the burden of old. When they felt he had gotten close. They decided to the make their move. Their mission was simply kidnap or kill. But they too were being watched.

"He is an important man." The sheik told his group as they negotiated a busy street. He had a target. There were things he wanted to do before the priest did.

He moved fast and into a busy crowd. Removes the clergy collar on his neck, rolls up the sleeves of his shirt and disappeared into the night. Before he became a man of the cloth he had known the streets of AJ. Answering the ancient call of the fisher man was not an easy one and he knew it. But he was just one of the 2.2 billion Christians amongst 3800 denominations propagating, projecting and protecting the story of the Christ. Some before him faced far more farce enemies. Among friends he told them, "look, what we have become, from God's sole seed. I am a happy sower and a reaper in this garden."

Returning to life of mission was always part of his plan. His experiences from the war in his own country and missions to some conflict zones around the globe had made him a respected resource person. He was equally a doctor of the law. Well respected in the religious cycles.

Back in the comfort of his room at the hotel, he made the sign of the cross and exhaled. He stared at a picture on the wall of the room. "How words and thoughts once draped in fear, blood and terror make it into everyday causal vocabulary." He thought. "Time is a wonderful thing. This too will pass." He said out loud, and made the sign of the cross, again.

He was needed. He was a man who did not see religion as a foundation built on cruel hatred that consumed the children of peace. He was a bearer of the light that he saw in everyone.

Despite his vast amount of wealth and reach the sheik felt threatened. The priest knew something he didn't know. He did not understand his simple logic. None, how he sailed away from the same torrents, storms and waives.

The next day the clergyman, called the local police. He did not want to dial the emergency. If he did he would be drawing unnecessary attention to himself.

He reported an attempted forceful entry into his hotel room. The voice of the female dispatcher was soothing. He did not always feel at ease with the male ones. He was not also sure who the guys after him were nor who they worked for.

The lady told him they would send an officer over. When the officer got there after a couple of hours later, he wanted to know if the officer could take prints from the door knob. The officer explained why that would be difficult get. The officer took a quick look around the room. He took in much info as he could. It was then time to talk about what he had seen.

A book on the desk. The officer had read the book in three different languages seven times. Impressive, the clergy man he speaks one of the languages. They were both good in the language. The book had been banned in a few religious extremist places. The clergy had a message. He had a feeling something was about to happen. It was not just the ones trying to on his door or the ones after him the day before. That book was a symbol of that thing. He did not know how to tell him that. He was not sure he would believe him.

They talked about the other things he read or was reading. The ones he read because of his faith and the ones for interest. It was a day to 9/11memorial. The clergyman blogged from his mobile office, it was supposed to be a furtherance of his warning for folks to be on alert. He ended the line with gratitude to the male and female first responders around the globe. When they save a life, it gave humanity reason to live, he said. He placed emergence numbers for different cities around the world.

That night the attackers did not come to his room. If they did he did not know, because he moved the moment the police officer left. He was out of the country the way he had come in. But the world would be shocked and shaken by what happened a few miles from the hotel. Causalities numbered more than six. The American consulate there had taken a huge hit.

CHAPTER
≈85≈

Ulu was working on a research for the Modern Language Association conference when realized he had a treasure stocked away somewhere. On one of his trips back to the peninsula his mother had informed him of a bunker that survived the war. That bunker was named after his grandfather. Though he did not know him or know such a figured existed he was thrilled when his mother showed much interest in going with him to visit the bunker. He was delighted at the things he found at the bunker. Though inside spoke and reflected the war. It was like the war never reached there. His grandfather had constructed the family compound in the same manner in which the bunker was made. It was in anticipation of a day like the one in which their hut sank into the ground. But when the house sank in due to heavy shelling no one understood what had happened, it was fate his mother had explained.

The bunker gave him a vivid example of what his people were capable of, their creativity and ingenuity. But of all the findings it was scripts that were neatly rolled and put in a box that he could not stop marveling at. The script shined a light beyond the wars and the people who fought it. He took the paper untied it and began to reading it. He did not see much need for the paper in that abandoned bunker so he decided to take the papers with him after he read a paragraph to his mother. It changed the course of his study in what he had termed the African Origins of Christian Rituals.

Now as he edited the final draft his paper for that conference. He got to where he had mentioned some things about living and dead languages. He stopped. He pulled out a script from the box he retrieved from the bunker. It looked a bit dusty but actually was not. He began to read, it was a story that had chronicled land mark changes in the life of his people, their neighbors and their language.

CHAPTER
≈86≈

The lost script read: Ω

"The Obong had taken five wives. Amongst the wives was the promiscuous daughter of the Eze of Umuoba. She was the youngest of the Obong's wives. The Obong was a handsome man and had a reputation as a man capable of pleasing his women. In fact he was notorious.

The Eze's daughter heard news of notoriety and vowed to have him. She was considered wayward by many but she was the princess. She got away with many unheard of adventures. One morning she went to the River with her maids to take her bath. On the other side of the River was a bear chested muscular man. His chest was like that of a lion. He had just gotten down from his canoe. When he sighted the young beautiful dazzling princess it was mutual lust. Her dark nipples triggered a volcanic eruption through his span to hairs of his head. He had a terrifying desire, like those of his infant years when he longed to suckle on his mother's breast. He sent his men after a treasure with words and greetings from his kingdom to a beautiful lady.

That instant lust started an affair that would set two kingdoms against each other for decades. At first the two played hide and sick. They met at the River at the same time every day. The Eze was not aware of what was taking place and so also were the wives of the Obong. The princess was following her heart and the Obong was following the desires of his flesh.

After several adventures he was beginning to think of what that relationship could mean beyond the instant gratifications. Theirs were the tributaries of the River Niger. The princess could be a peaceful channel through the two rivers that divided their people. The next day as the Obong mounted her he swore under his breath to have her produce his seeds.

Those seeds were not for him. They would be for the good of his people. He had explained to his wives. The seeds would share the features and future of both heritages and kingdoms. The future of the world would be in their hands. His kingdom would be loved and respected. The Eze's daughter was the means to build an alliance and equality between their kingdoms and their neighbors. The European and Arab traders would respect him and deal straight with him. The women accepted the king's excuses but harbored deep hatred for the young girl who had deprived them the king's affection and the pleasure of warming his bed.

When the Eze got wind of the news he became sick. He summoned an immediate meeting in his palace. The Eze of Umuoba sued the Obong before the council of Ndi-ichie. Kola nuts were taken to them on his behalf. It was the Oji Ugo, the best of kola nuts. The case was before them. He would not have his young beautiful daughter become a concubine of another man, not minding his social standing. It was his duty to protect that which was dear to his heart. It was his honor and those of his people that were being contested.

The Ndi-ichie were the wise men, philosophers and men of the secret cult, they were the men who were consulted when others were tired of thinking. Ndi-ichie came with their secretaries to hear and decide the case. Their secretaries were men who wrote down the words of wisdom and secrets of the kingdoms. They inscribed the thoughts and words of kings. They held the secrets of the past and of the future. They were men whose omissions and commissions were capable of causing kingdoms their places. The men unfolded the scroll, the book of the old on mats and began to paint patterns on them.

For days the Ndi-ichie worked on the case from dawn to dusk. Both kings and kingdoms were called to give testimonies. As the Obong testified his left eye ball rolled from the left to the center and steadied at the right and he swore nothing would make him leave his lover. And the secretaries wrote down the deliberations and decisions. When they all became tired and the council announced "Nchebidi," it had been reached. Men from far and wide ached to hear what decisions had be reached and written.

The Nchebidi read, "That the young woman was following the desires of her heart which she was entitled to, and the Obong though was following the desires of his flesh when he first encountered her has claimed like the young lady he was following his heart. But he was a king. A king ought to be granted concession in issues like that. Though they were both drunk of a wine of unquenchable taste, they also drank of the water of the river of life. The Obong should go into the kingdom of which he has found that which delighted his heart to pay homage to the king and his people. And properly seek the hands of the woman who delights in him in marriage."

The kingdoms were to put their hands in the nchebidi to avoid further conflicts. The Eze vowed that would not happen during his reign. The Obong can keep his daughter whom he had kidnapped. But a marriage may be after his reign. For years what followed was the reign of series of kidnappings in both kingdoms. Men were caught and sold into slavery. Expansionist policies were put in place, kingdoms like Obong Okon Itata were acquired and their lands were offered as gifts to friends of the Eze.

The Eze denounced Adaeze as his daughter, rejected her upspring and revoked the blessings he had once pronounced on her.

In that same water years later, another beautiful daughter of that part of the land fell in love with a stranger. He was a man roaming the body of waters in many lands. He was an ordinary pirate, but he carried the seal of a queen with him. The daughter was the first girl child of the Obong and Adaeze his beautiful wife. When the pirate left, he left with her. He took her to a foreign land.

CHAPTER
≈87≈

The enmity continued. Generations would never know the genesis of the hatred their peoples shared, as the keepers of the words passed away one after another. Ibini Ukpba became a partial judge ending cases before they would reach the shrine of Nri and sending men into slavery. Men went and never came back, they were declared to have lost their cases before they reached. It was the greed of men who patronized the masked gods of hate and failed to listen to the voice from the kingdom from the sky, the kingdom before other kingdoms, the one sent from the sky into the River. Unity from the source of creation was destroyed. People who Nri had freed from Bondage were classified in caste systems. Those who over 7000 years before once boasted of the best ceramics and metal works from the lower Niger to the Nile and Congo Rivers were now only to talk of hilly farmlands and bread baskets as their achievements."

When Ulu rolled back the script he began to think of what wars and natural disasters that could have been avoided had caused his people. It caused them their memories and who they were. Scripts which recorded the unified speech and tongues of his people were destroyed and five thousand years later men were to gather in Ezinihitte the heart land to adapt a central Igbo language from only a few dialects of their own tongues with letters from foreign lands. The river does not become a sea though it flows in one. The idea of central Igbo only came after young enthusiastic Dennis of the Christian Missionary Society acting on behalf his superiors who themselves were acting on behalf of the bishop in England failed in his bid to put together a union Ibo. If the source of the inspiration of such men whose ancestors answered names such as Luther, William, and Tyndale was not divine, it would be the love of disobedience. Mister Dennis sailed the same currents as did John H Newton but different tide.

"He succeeded like a blacksmith would." Old Achebe would say. The tongue of a people had never been engineered into being that way. A representative language would be anything but artificial. The dam in the middle of the river can generate electricity but it is still water not fire.

CHAPTER
≈88≈

Mr. Stone Sr.'s conditions were not as strong as it used to be. But he refused to leave the peninsula. He has found love there. He has built himself a home there. What more could he ask for. He surrounded himself with those who loved him and those who were indebted to him. "Health is not always what the body says. It's a question of what one felt in the mind." He would tell his son when he worried about him.

Mr. Stone had a few friends who greatly believed in him. They were friends who kept their promises. The trust was mutual. And they consulted with him when they needed. Those were time tested relationships. He encouraged them to come closer. That kept his mind in check. "The continent was still a virgin earth." He saw from the inside. His friends trusted his wise counsel and counted themselves as privileged.

"Nick, if control is the ultimate expression of power, here is airspace without controllers." Mr. Stone was one of the few people that called him by the name. A few weeks later Mr. Branston was bidding to take over the national airline. When he closed the deal, he paid his friend a visit on the

Peninsula. "Now we have a true Virgin in the air." Mr. Stone told him. His friend smiled.

For the first in a long time worldwide flights came in regular and left on time from Lagos, Abuja, Kano and Port Harcourt. They were relatively affordable and most of all they flew green white green.

A few years later, terribly angry and frustrated with politicians who sought bribe for everything they did. He pulled out and he called it the last Nigerian Virgin. But when he remembered the voice of his friend saying, "patience, patience my friend," he smiled. He needed a lot of patience to work in the country. Mr. Stone had told him. He had told him to set for himself goals that were neither cheap nor easy to reach. That was one. But the venture brought him closer to his friend. That was also a goal achieved.

Mr. Stone did not lose the piece of poem from Karim his former cellmate. And after he arrived at the Peninsula, he went through it a number of times. It reminded him a lot. Twelve months later a group of international lawyers some of whom were acquaintances of Mr. Stone began fighting for his Somali friend. The conviction was overturned. He was acquitted and he was a free man. His wife was the happiest. She didn't know whom to thank. "It was a favor from a friend of another friend." Karim told her. He had promised he would wed again her once he was out. He did. But he had one final fling before the ring. Several months later when he met with him his first words to him were, "may the odds forever be in our favor." That friend of his was the first to come to living and work in the country. He lived somewhere in the town not far away from them.

They had all gotten together when Mr. Stone was asked by his friend to suggest prominent world leaders to campaign on the need to protect the environment. It was during that meeting that Karim first saw the man whose organization had gotten him out. That day Mr. Stone went ahead to suggest names of some of the members of the Elders, as former as that was. A group backed with enormous financial strength and network to rid the world of problems. About venues, he said, "global warming is a reality and so is the threat to peace, but let them also enjoy the peace on the Island." That year world leaders, celebrities and business men from all over the world gathered on Necker Island discussing how to preserve the earth for the next generation.

When he was knighted Mr. Stone joked about it. He sent him a three page congratulatory letter at the end of which he addressed himself as Sir Lord Sylvester Stone. In the letter he congratulated him on his book "Losing My Virginity" and commented on "Long Walk to Freedom" and the "Inconvenient Truth" which he sent him as gifts. He hoped he would become mayor of London soon.

When Branston got a letter from a young Sudanese girl who has lost both of legs to land mine Mr. Branston wept. He called Mr. Stone and told him. He was involved and going back was not an option. It was Africa. Its' bad and its' goods had a way of captivating the mind. He decried the situation in the country. For three day he refused to eat. Worried about land mines and nuclear weapons worldwide, he launched the Global zero campaign. He renewed his call on world leaders to end the race for nuclear arms. He recruited soldiers of peace who day after day went removing land mines in places where young girls like Zefina were in danger of losing limbs. Mr. Branston made himself available whenever the Elders needed him. At the end of his fast, he told Mr. Stone it connected him to his true humanity. Mr. Stone was very proud to have him as a friend.

CHAPTER
≈89≈

Mr. Stone is pleased with Sylvester Azuogu Stone. He was home before commencing his campaign tour. The old man had some strategies that would benefit the younger man. S.A. Stone was worried about his father's health. He spent time talking to his mother concerning his father's health. He observed that his health was taking a toll on her. He encouraged her to get more help from the family doctors. His mother was not worried, though she knew that she was doing a lot of the jobs for which the doctors and the nurse were paid. She was happy to be by his side. It was the duty of a wife she recalled telling her son during his last visit. That duty has not changed.

Mr. Stone over the years has lost all his teeth and his wife has got him dentures. They were used to fill in for the missing teeth and gum. Though they were artificial they looked very natural in his mouth. They helped keep him looking healthy. His wife has learnt how to help him with new prostheses. Of all of them she was especially grateful for the dentures. She often said the youth of her husband was gone but for the teeth that still gave him the magic of years.

She would tease him of his youth, when women in America and Europe flocked over him. She usually ended her joke with a sympathetic look on her face if he was looking. And she called those wasted years. Those were her assumptions, she recalled him tell her a few times.

With the arrival of every new device she learnt how to make living easier for him. They were both learning to live again. A new life was what aging and illness brought with it. And they have accepted it. On certain days she started her day with cleaning the dentures, which her husband removed during the night. Somehow Mr. Stone did not feel comfortable having the dentures on once he turned off the light in his room. Every morning she picks up the dentures. Once the denture cup was in her hands and she heads to the bathroom to wash them she hummed a song. She tried not to show her teeth. Her immaculate and white teeth were intact, a total contrast to her husbands.

After helping him brush his month, she helps him with his range of motion, exercising on his fragile and wakes bones. At times she thought of him as dying and there is a great pain in her heart. Though they shared a long life together, each time that thought came. She remembered the first time they met. There was the man whom several years ago had given her and her children life. There lay the man who fought death and drove it away that she and her kids would live again. At the doorsteps of death he fought death and waved it away. There was her husband who loved her like no other man ever did. Why was it that she considered wearing gloves and gown to touch that body that she kissed all over a few months before? "Is this what life becomes?" She asked no one in particular. As she finished changing him that morning he looked happy and filled with a sudden surge of energy. He put down his head on the pillow and closed his eyes.

The dry and dying hays of the field touched his ankle. She felt the sensation. He never felted before. He wanted to walk to a distant land. A place he did not know. A place his imagination could only take him to. That moment his gaze went to the Tai rice field he once visited. He was a man who knew that leaping towards the sun may not land him on the sun but it did take you off the ground. He wanted a world filled with harmony yet he saw in it imperfections and the impossible. In those rice fields were men, women and children who set out to the field before dawn. They cut the rice on the stones to bring out the seeds. Looking at those hungry looking farmers he saw death and time were violently written on each seeds of rice they plucked. Though still lying on his hospital bed he was a man who sought a borderless world. But the fear that it was the sweat of those folks who were being shortchanged every step of the way that fed the world shook him off his escape. Several years before his ideas had been sought on how to deal with the Cuban sugar politics. And he made money off of it.

He was a man who taught others that it was not what they achieved in life that made them. But what they overcome. He counted himself as having overcome a lot in the life. The glory he did not care about. But he believes the world must have a place for a man like him. That was the exact thing in his mind when he erected the first stone on the walls of his Mausoleum. The pyramid was an architecture that brought that feeling to life each time he thought of the names and lives of the great kings and queens embalmed in them. It was a symbol of life, life after life. A continuing cycle of something, each time he looks at he recalls his life's worth.

Every often he would go into the enclosure, make himself comfortable in it. There he has the opportunity to escape from the noise of the traffic of life and the youthful life of a moneymaker. He was simply being an old man waiting on his maker. He wanted to be remembered, though he has led a quiet life since his escape from prison. Mr. Stone was a great man. Looking at the stone of the walls of his tomb, he studied the life of men. Those he referred to as his bloodlines who were descendant of the queens and pharaohs of Egypt. "Who she that comes forth in the morning rising, fair as the moon, bright as the sun, terrible as an army set in battle array," He memorized that as a kid. It was coming back to him now. He voiced his belief in the natural marriage of Greece and Egypt. He talked about the marriage between the maidservants of Nefertiti and male servants of Alexandria and the intimacy the two enjoyed. He was a dying old man whose dream was to conquer the world. But there he has come home. He has passed on the torch. With the sunrise from the east, it's the rays and shadows pointing to and falling on the valley of death. His feet stretched out and his eyes looking in the direction of the sun. He called on the cycles of goings and comings not to forsake him, till the end of time. He was home.

CHAPTER
≈90≈

Mr. Stone lay on his bed with the rails drawn up to protect him from falling. He rolled from side to side and he was secure in the bed. The first time he fell from his regular bed they knew something had to be done. It was not a nice experience for any one near him.

There were phone calls and everyone blamed everyone. The doctor got the better part of the blame. The bed was especial piece of equipment ordered from Europe. It was a gift to the old man. It was from a friend of the doctor who came to the house to check on him from time to time. He was promoting the sales of his medical equipment. When he heard about the patient, he aimed at using the man to convince his friend and friends of his friend, of another wonderful invention yet to be seen in the country. He was sure the national hospital did not have such equipment. If he became the supplier it meant he had a vast area to cover.

The medical equipment seller was at the airport when his friends called him to say he was in trouble. He needed to find a solution his patient was falling off his bed. He got a promise. The bed would be in the country in a few days. That made him happy. He was not planning on losing such a patient soon.

As the seller finished the call, his mind went to the first time he encountered a patient in a hospital bed. It was not a very good experience. It still brought tears to his eyes. He tried to distract himself. His mind was wandering into what seemed like a horror scene in a movie. He struck up a conversation with the girl standing in front of him. A beautiful girl, Rita was traveling to US.

The brief talk with her made him scan every face on the line waiting to board the Lufthansa airline to Amsterdam.

"Brain drain," He said to no one in particular. 85 percent of those travelers were not likely to be happy in the next four years. The similes on their faces would vanish within the first three weeks. It will not only be as a result of the cold weather. It would because that the dreams that they were after would soon turn into nightmares. They would have abandoned their true dreams. The soft touch of the girl brought him back to reality. He looked at her.

Rita was a chief prosecutor in a highly populated district. Single, beautiful and in pursuit of the American dream. He counted her as one of the victim of the new era. She did not understand him or the look on his face. On his face it seemed boldly written-

"This one will soon face the waking moment that followed every dream."

Twenty years earlier, he was on that line for the first time. Things were not that bad then in the country. But he was a new graduate with his master of business administration, and a very beautiful position in the bank and tons of female admirers. Then the lure of foreign travel and dreams of faraway places came calling. And he would be lost forever, the moment he walked away with a visa stamped on his passport from one of the embassies on Victoria Island.

He wished the young girl in front of him could read his mind. It would not make any sense if he told her that the future of the country rested in her hands. He was not a good example and that would not be convincing to the girl. As far as that girl was concerned the country had no place for her, than it has for her little brother. His school had been on strike for the past six months. Her little brother was frustrated with the country and the school system. The opportunity to escape was a welcomed one.

But Rita was not thinking pass the first few weeks of her travel, nor beyond the beautiful pictures on television and

in movies from Hollywood. She did not know that it was the exact opposite of what she heard of Hollywood that was shown of the district she was leaving. Though a respected prosecutor the image of the place she was leaving was what she did not know of. The perceptions of her country and its people had not really bothered her. It has not made her think of how she would fit in a foreign land. She did not think of the reverse side of the images she saw in the American dream nor the disappointments akin to the human nature. As single girl the seller knew what she was getting into without her knowing it. He was sympathetic.

When he arrived in the country several years before, he lost his first three years there. He stayed without proper work permit or identifications. He was depressed and had thoughts of killing himself. If he left the country, he would not be able to come back. He had no place, going back, he no longer, had the job in a bank. The thought of an early retirement from the bank had disappeared. His options were limited.

He moved from hostel to hotel, thrown out from room after rents were overdue. As a banker, he did not think of selling medical equipment. The thought did not come till he went to work as a nurse assistant. A job he never thought about. He could have become a medical doctor or a senior nurse, if he was thinking of the medical field. But he did not think of it then. He knew what he wanted to become. And he had become that, before he lost it. He threw up, till he became sick on his first day, as a nurse assistant. He wanted to serve humanity. But not changing diapers, washing shit and vomit off men and women, who thought nothing of him.

It is human to lose one's dream. But to be woken by nightmares, night after night and to face days of uncertainties was a world entirely different. It was not the world, in which he went to sleep, and dreamt of the good country. It was not the good life, he thought of. People thought he was a happy man.

One day he ran into the teacher. The teacher was a man who most people came to for rescue. He had come to known as a friend and one that could be trusted. When he first found himself lost in that void it was the teacher who made his life bearable.

The teacher had a philosophy. "The teacher was ready once the student was." He often said. And he waited for that time and only that time to teach. There was always deep revelations and powerful flow of thoughts when he was around. He gave his fellow men lifelines. With him it was in an unlimited supply. But there are those times he would become an intentional stutter too.

"They who dwell in the gardens the companions listen. For you- let me hear it"

The medical supplier recalled.

They may have ears, they may have eyes. But may not hear or see. It was from the book of old. A man of great wisdom, the teacher sought it from beyond the reign of the first and second earth. The present he said was physical, beautiful and ending. He sought to reign where men belong to the eternal.

When the time came, the teacher knew it was time to go home. He could no longer babysit. All he had in that once flourishing day care center were two adults who wouldn't even be able to pick him out from a line up, be able to say his name or tell what it was he did for them.

Going home, it was a call of duty. His people needed him. Those young vibrant minds hungered for direction. There, it was the future. He was happier than he had been in years. He provided needed services to those who would pass it on to generations to come. But some would have counted those initial years as wasted if it wasn't for his house. He was at home. He was happy. He would return to his creator a happy man.

The supplier lacked the discipline of the teacher. At times it bred envy other times remorse. But when he must mine, the depths beyond his own limits, he found a way to make it to him.

He was one of the men he could never completely understand. But he loved and respected.

The medical supplier eyes went back to the young lady. "She would understand when the time came." He concluded.

Brain drain became cancerous. It was worst in his country than anywhere else. The inflation rate remained on unchecked. And all ports were points of exit. She still had a smile on face. And his eyes were fixed on his black shoes, maybe she will get used to it sooner, he thought.

CHAPTER
≈91≈

"The sensitive shoe" was the title of one of his short video recordings. The medical equipment seller made it years after keeping dairies on his encounter in the states. He has known the cities and countries beyond what MTV and music videos shown. He has gone downtown and made his on video recordings. He interviewed drug addicts who littered those streets. He spoke with people who stayed on the streets twenty four hours a day, seven days a week, from Elijah's kitchen to saint Mary's shelter.

Downtown compared in many ways to Boundary Market. The only difference between the two was that most individuals in latter hawked one visible item or the other and everyone seemed to be shouting at the top of their voices at the same time. Most of those on the streets, on the former, seemed to be enjoying the air of freedom. Those who had things to sell had large posters. Some just came out of the prisons, so they cherished the open air. The prisons in both worlds could not compare. One was a modern warehouse, the other, was a dungeon, second only, to hell. But they shared some similarities, all prisoners could all pass as someone's slaves. They functioned both ways; they had the ability to make the inmates hardened. On both sides they constituted part of those on the streets.

He showed those short movies to his friends. Those who have come to see them were moved. One of such friends was Ms. Hills a former New Yorker film critic who just moved to the LA Times.

After seeing the one of the short films the next day she did a little piece on it in her column. They were his stories. They were his lessons. The final part of the film was with the camera focused on a piece of work he called the creed. He had drawn out the creed in those days when he was a single man, when he battled it out in mind, body and spirit. It was dictated to all his countrymen sojourning in foreign lands. It was on a beautifully designed square frame with spiraling patterns engraved on each side. Ms. Hills reproduced it exactly the same way in her column in the newspaper.

"The creed of the Exile,

Coming to America.

Packing up your belongings

Your take home pay cannot take you home.

You knee and you pray.

Your dream merges with visions

It is blurry.
But your country pisses you off, you must go.
On- arrival it's a dream not a promise
Get the papers, your voluntary slavery
We should have left it the way it was
Here you're no colonial lord or privateer
You have no military
All my unpaid bills.
Your learning;
Compassion, humility and care
First job; you regret the day you stood
on the long line for visa.
Here you clean vomit, feces, blood and bath
one who wishes you don't breathe.
Who would spit on your face when he can't bite you,
Told you thank you a million times
without thinking about it.
Lucky you get away without infection.
Second job mea- guard,
security day or night watchman;
You learn to respect the Aboki
who used to open your gate for you
And you would bark at him like he was your dog

But he is probably where you can no longer say
"am sorry bro"
Third job, cleaner; you wish you never
beaten your house girl.
Farmer and gardener, he owned a small farm
Not vacancies; Mexicans only landscaping company!
Teacher nah professor; you remember,
Mama Nkechi your nanny you did not paid her.
Prince nah 419.
What did I forget?
House wife abi nah husband, it's intense, congrats.
You open a shop, own a shop,
Wal-Mart drags you under or Medicare drags you in.
Beware
You never had 419 in you dna
Even when jails are filled they find space for you
They know kirikiri is worst.
It was no malpractice it is fraud my friend
On whose papers,
Accountant's, letter writer's, tax doer's, and doc's
Prodigious. We had to leave.
9ja nah helele! Insatiable,
10/15 on a job, car na luxury, house na dream

Pikin go even go school.

To all those who milked our cows

Those who shared our national cake

among friends and families,

God is watching,

The Asylee will return."

"The film stayed on the frame till it the lights went dark, there were no other credits." Her commentaries in newspaper attracted a lot of attention and response to the work.

Some dreams became big and some overshadowed reality. A few weeks later Honey Merchant Companies bought the rights to the film. They distributed it widely and made a huge profit from it. It was the idea of a little known intern who was also carrying her own cameras around.

CHAPTER
≈92≈

Back then Timmy, friend of the Medical equipment seller, made a few quick steps which seemed to fix things. But there were no permanent fixes with quickies. When he got to the new country, things were not as he had expected them to be. They did not look like the stories he has been told. Things did not look like the pictures on the big screen. It was neither like the TV nor the movies he saw. When they told them there was a place called America, what they did not tell them was that the beautiful clothes, fancy jewelries and cars were only for those trips home. They did not work with them, and neither were they used by them in America. He was disappointed. He was however not frustrated, he was a determined and honest man.

It was nursing, they said. He said yes. A job he did not dream of, not even when he was caring for his father. His father was sick for six month before he died. It did not bring him to the thought of becoming a nurse. He did not think of making money doing that job, though he was already doing it. Making money caring for people was not on his raider. Of course it would not be. He made money trading in stocks and brokering deals in the banks. He got used to wearing his suits, ties and dress shoes every week day. On weekend he found it hard to find what to wear, his social commitments on the weekend required him to dress up. How could he fit into the scrub category?

One morning, he got dressed like he did every day. He stool feeling a bit odd. Something was the matter. Yes he was not the man he used to be, where was he dressed to go to? He was in a different country, an unemployed man.

His phone rang. It was his friend from Abuja. He picked it. It was news about a man they know. The business man for years he sought links to medical equipment tycoons around the world. He eventually met one who was not willing to do business with him. He however introduced him to a charity in New York. The charity was willing to help hospitals in Nigeria. He quickly went home collected contract funds from government. And signed papers and never came to pick up the equipment. The business man was in the country and would be in his office that week. Timmy was not surprised. He was thinking hard on what to tell his friend. He would call him back, he told him.

Timmy took the phone and dialed Eliza. She seemed prepared for most things. She was a strong woman. Eliza was prepared for the job they did. After she left primary six with a not so good result, she decided caring was her calling. She went to the nearest hospital in her home town in Aba. There the clerk took down her name and asked her to come back the next day. She came back in a white dress, a gown that showed her beautiful features and a head tie that the doctor liked. She hadn't added much weight then. For fifteen year she assisted the staff nurse. In her seventeenth year she was promoted to a staff nurse. It was the same year that America came calling for Nurse Eliza. Chime came home from Atlanta, Georgia. He paid her dowry and she went back to America with him. Two years later she earned more money than Chime. It changed the dynamics in their home. To Timmy she seemed to have the right answers.

CHAPTER
≈93≈

A little before the elections a vice chancellor of one of the nation's premier university resigned. He was interested in an elective position. A professor who has spent most of life in the class room, people wondered what was behind his decision. Some said he had been assured of a position by one of the political parties in a state. No one was sure, but the bird dancing by the edge of the forest something in the forest must be drumming for it. The ministry of education had to find a replacement for him immediately. It was an order from above. It was not an easy task.

In the past Ulu who has been given several invitations by the university was called upon again. The minister pleaded with him. He knew he was likely to refuse the offer. It was not the first time. He spoke to him about the wind of change in the country. He explained to him why the university and the country needed him. Before the minister hung up, he told him in a tone which seemed more like an order, that he could not disappoint the country in such a time of need.

Ulu in his years of intellectual and academic sojourn has enjoyed relative peace. And he wanted it to remain that way. He did not want to be involved in boardroom politics. He believed an academic could make impact from anywhere in the world. He was just fine with his teaching and researches. But as he replayed the desperation in the minister's voice, he began considering it seriously. Going back to that country meant a lot of sacrifice, he told himself. He needed more time to consider the offer.

Ulu goes on the net, picks up the newspapers, turns the news and documentary channels. It seemed bleak. Something needed to be done.

The nation seemed a lawless state without total chaos. The economy was growing at a snail speed. The GDP was a shame to talk about. Poverty was growing faster by the minutes. It was spreading faster than anyone in the population could move from one spot to another. A few individuals still had monopoly of the import, and sale of certain food products in the country. And a hand full of families and their friends owned and controlled the country's oil blocks. Their rewards from presidents and heads of states, with unlimited powers, to allocate rewards and favors.

It was a very fragile state. Maybe it was the suffering and smiling syndrome that kept from the Arab Spring, The Occupy Wall Street, The Zeitgeist and many other movements. Capitalism was imploding on itself around the world. States were failing and maybe there were no clear indexes to follow to see the nation's rate of failure. But it still pumped oil. And there were attacks on the facilities. The companies still used the private army and killed. The world moved on and seemed not to worry. Oil flowed to the markets. There was either no reason to cry foul or they were engaged elsewhere. So the cry of the Ogoni and Niger Delta people went on unheard. Men whom hunger and the sun had already beaten and deformed the explorers added all forms of pollutions. They were at the brink of extinction. But there were some sympathetic minds. Looking at the faces of those supposed to be the future of the place in schools there was empathy.

Some citizen with the help of Transparency, Amnesty International and lawyers from across the globe had been able to get law suits against the oil companies in Abuja, London, New york, Paris and The Hague. The Igbos were still pushing in many fronts. MASSOB was still calling for the actualization of the state of Biafra. They got fired up especially after every riot which destroyed their merchandise and places of worship. They had their cases at UN, hoping it would be heard. The Odouwa republics were calling for all forms of conferences, sovereign and non-sovereigns. The area boys got away with whatever they laid hands on whenever they could. Many called for a weaker center and stronger economic unions within the sections of six geopolitical zones. In the North a young governor had played up the sharia, a more central role in their legal system. It became another excuse for a heightened theatre of religious zealousness. Many groups came up. Boko Haram went into action. They forbid anything not their own, yet unaware what the heritage truly was. They held the rest of the people at ransom. And the Arewa big boys held sway to the country's economy. Political meetings were held in churches and mosques. A few small states within the country were already running a separate cause. They were still within the union it seemed. But their people had a different mindset. In a state a group was busy fighting for one mile military corridors, onshore and offshore gains from faraway deserts. They sought to turn their camels to sharks.

For their lack of faith in the paper and debt based currency the bankers on Wall Street told their clients to turn the money into gold. Economists and countries agreed on ways to check starvation. And OPEC thought of exchanging crude oil for gold to give people more rights. The Arewa big boys were again not yet ready. There was great love for sitting behind those little bureau de change in Garki counting dirty notes laced with anthrax. In secret they gave money to boys who shouted in the streets burning houses and properties. Many went about with no care. It seemed life was normal. But it was far from normal.

After reading through the previous letters and several articles Ulu realized that career development for him was no longer a personal goal. He would have achieved that, if it was. There were voices to be given a voice. He had a flash back.

"Olaedo; Found in home of kings. Was he the king? No. But nature would bestow him with riches. And kings seek him. Olaedo." Those were words of the old woman who handed down the royal beads.

It was a call. It carried with it duties. It was that call, and its glory, that he has carried with him all those years.

There was an overall stampede in development, in infrastructure and politics in the country. And he saw those students are the tools, capable of achieving the needed change. He could reach the unreached. "He would work in sync with established modes of operation, whiling exploring concepts that embraced change." He scribbled down in his diary.

Some days later the minister called again. He told him he would be coming home. The minister was delighted.

Before Ulu left the United States he attended one of the weirdest dinners of his life. It was hosted by BP at the Waldorf. There he met politicians, diplomats, executives, past and present board members of multinational corporations. Those men and their businesses were bigger than the countries they did business in. And they sought to control them. For the first few minutes he was lost. He could not immediately make sense of his invitation to the dinner. Then the friend, an executive of one of the oil companies who had hand delivered the invitation to him walked up to him. As he introduced him to some of the people there, he told him, "You will be meeting some of these men in the future."

CHAPTER
≈94≈

Ulu came back and was ready to begin work the next day. He did not want the fanfare of welcoming a new vice chancellor. The registrar and the principal officers of the university gathered in the conference room. They were there to welcome him after he has been shown round the university. A few students from the student union body were also there at his request.

When he came in he did not waste time. He told them a little about himself, which he was sure they already knew. Then he began to address them.

"I am only here for four year tenure. And it was because there is work to be done, a lot of work that is why I came. And you are here; we are going to do it. Nobody expects me to perform any magic, we are all going to do it, and we have to work together.

Here what I wouldn't have is our own students shooting at each other on campus or elsewhere. If anyone does we help them find a better place for their career. They certainly do not belong here.

And this year JAMB will be sending us splitting images of our society, of ourselves and more so of God. It is our duties to correct those mistakes and failings. It is a huge task. The best amongst them come in here empty as nothing. They have no idea of how to realize their talents and potential that they have got. Society has taken it from them. They are mere walking shadows, excited about the opportunity of a higher institution. And many of these institutions have continued to let them sleepwalk back to society. They leave a little older than they came in, a little less excited and may be a little able to read road signs.

Today it is our duty to know that we are here so that society does not continue to recycle failure. There is only one thing which we can guarantee society today. We owe that to this generation and to posterity. It is change and that change begins today. We will wake the sleepwalkers; make genius of the best that have been sent to us. It begins here."

The ministry of education was happy. They have done their part of the job, they felt. Three days later the minister sent him a congratulatory letter. He has known him for many years and believed in what he can do to better the system. He replied with a thank you letter. The letter contained a list what needed to be done in the university. The budget needed to be worked on for there to be meaningful in impact. "Time was short," he ended the letter with.

CHAPTER
≈95≈

The election was approaching. Campaigns were on and many of the candidates seeking public office were busy relating to their people. S.A Stone called meetings, went to rallies and was convincing the people of things, they shared in common. At the end of the day most of the people attending his rallies were somehow convinced they shared a lot in common. Politicians traveled to places they have never been to before. They went to places they never heard of before. It was a season for adventure. Adventures they had to take if they were to get the votes of the people. The campaigns went to places, any place as long as there were people who were going to vote living in those places. They took their messages to the people.

Two former governors in the race dropped out. They were under investigations for financial crimes by the EFCC. They offered millions of dollars to end their investigations. But the young man heading the Agency had a name and he believed in it. In courts at home they called the shots. But days later those former governors from Delta regions would be singing, confessing and pleading guilty to the same crimes in court rooms around the world. The world was on a rescue mission. And they delivered. The guilty pleas were heard. Billions of dollars stolen and put away in foreign accounts were exposed. At home their people died of hunger and mosquito bites. The money they toy around with could provide their people health care system comparable to the best in the world. But those honorable men who are now common thieves when they became sick flew abroad. They preferred death in hospitals abroad. They died where their loots were. At home through first and second terms of four to eight years they were lords over their people. Were they no governors, they would be seekers of sovereignty. Were they heads of their sovereignties, their crimes would go on for a lifetime. They would be kings forever over small island peoples. But their crimes caught up with them. The other candidates forgot about them and went with their campaign. The mention of their names was dispiriting.

CHAPTER
≈96≈

Sylvester Azuogu Stone Jr. was one of those candidates still in the race. He touched the hearts of men and women of his party. He won their nomination. And more importantly he was now a married man. His beautiful young wife went on those campaign trips with him. She was a great help. There was no doubt that the moment she lets go her husband was thrilled. He did not stop to find out why she had agreed to go on the campaign, which she fought against at first. She was not a politician and did not hide her dislike for the game politicians played. But she just caught on. She added flame to the fire. At first she was not feeling, she would be able to relate to the conditions of girls and women in the man places, she had never been to, but once on the trail it was fun.

Women came to her to bring personal messages and to bless the campaign. That she was beautiful, that appealed to most of the young people. She and her husband could represent them in many places, some of them said, without knowing what place those could be. Some of them were girls, who only met them at the club the night, she got engaged. They had been thrilled by that night and they never stopped following her. It was every woman's dreams. That night also brought out a lot she did not know was inside her. It was a night they went to the club. At the club Stone Jr. had excused himself to go the gents, but actually went and made a request from the DJ. He came back, his hands were washed. He looked relieved. They continue to dance. Then the DJ took the microphone "it is going to be somebody's big night." He began to play Black Eye Pea's "I got the feelin." The club was electrified and everyone was on their feet, couples, men, women and girls dancing and singing along with the song.

Stone Jr. puts his right hand in his pant pocket, took out a piece of a round 2.17 carat D platinum princess cut diamond and slipped it into her left ring finger. She felt finger, looked at it and yelled. The DJ put the music on pause. And the echo of her voice resounded in every corner of the club. S.A Stone. whispered into her ears, "we can wake or sleep, holding the beauty of our dreams and prayers." The DJ announced, "Diamonds are forever and somebody just got one." He plays an interlude with a small remix of "diamonds are forever" then continued blasting "I got the feelin." All night the club danced and toasted to the happy couple.

Those pieces of precious stones sealed almost every deal. For love, peace, war or friendship, gold and diamonds were offered. Even the small gods demanded for them. For them hearts beat and bloods flow. With a warm heart he has offered his to the woman he loves.

If that night happened to her, it could happen again in many different ways.

S.A Stone. had a lot working in his favor and a few working against him. The youth were the first of those things working for him. His youthfulness was a big charm to the growing population of young voters in the country. They were able to understand his message of change. They made sense of the fact that at that stage in the country's development, the people could no longer let tribal and religious politics derail the country. It was a message the old folks found hard to make sense of, no matter how hard, they tried. All their life tribal and religious loyalty has been their guiding principle. To tell them something different was like teaching an old woman to use her left hand, when all she ever knew was to use her right. Among other things, they could not understand, the idea of a Day of National Remembrance, for all the victims of Religious Riots. However the fact the new candidate was little known was a real pulse for him. He was to introduce himself to the young and old at the same time. And that was what he was doing, and doing so with his wife added charm to it. He had a message and had the presence. Standing on the stage, he filled the arena with words and their echoes. He was not corrupt, most of those hearing his name for the first time concluded. It served him well. Student volunteers took over his campaign on campuses and schools and street corners. They told people of the good things that he has done for schools in the country. They were pleased with him. So they urged their parents to vote for him. He was the only one among the candidates to have built and supported schools in all parts of the country.

CHAPTER
≈97≈

As the campaigns were going on Ulu was busy. He was trying to figure out what to do with the responsibility he has accepted to undertake. As the vice chancellor, he became all things to all men, that he may win some more. Running the university was an odious task. "He had been roped in," he thought. He was not going it alone. He woke up one early morning took out a sheet of paper from his bed side drawer. He wrote the first line. He wanted the ministers past and present, the presidents, the heads of states, leading businessmen in the country and outstanding individuals to be involved in impacting knowledge. He finished the first draft. It was not exactly what he wanted. But it was something, he could work on. He puts it down.

He wanted to be able to invite the men, to appear at the university campus as lecturers, guest speaker and as professors. He wanted them to pass on the secret of their success firsthand to the people willing to learn. Some of them had failed. He wanted the students to figure that out as well. He wanted to engage the past rulers intellectually. He wanted to give them a post-office routine that would be meaningful to the society. "They could make better leaders of the students they teach." He included in the letter. When he got the final draft, he knew it was not going to be easy to convince those men, to come to the classroom after leaving power. It would make them feel lesser than the gods they played in while in power. They were myth and would not want to be demystified. Some simply will not know what to teach. But he wanted those to know, it was simply what they were doing in office. That was all, they were to come and have conversations with the students about.

It was both dangerous and would require extra security measures. But he believed leadership had to make itself more accessible to the society, at least to and through the student body. He wrote in the letter that it was a task they owed to society, to teach the ideals they aspired for and to effect the change, they crave for the country. He appealed to them. He knew that if it became a career after politics, some would consider well before venturing in. They would be paid for the service, the lectures, their speeches and seminars. But the university could not afford that. He would make it a symbolic fee. It was the kind of fee for which they would not bother to pick up the check, but would not say their time and intellect were not appreciated.

He finished typing and addressed the letters. He made copies of each letter. They would be used over and over he knew.

It was Monday. Wednesday, was the council of minister of states meeting, the letters have to get to those men as soon as was possible. He called the minister of education to remind him. He was on his way to his office. He has explained the content of the letter to him. He wanted him to hand deliver them, to stress their importance at the meeting.

CHAPTER
≈98≈

In the ministry's waiting room the Television was on. Someone in the room was busy toying with the remote control. He flipped from channel to channel, American, Chinese, European and local stations. TV ads sold gold morning, afternoon, evening and night. Wall Street's speculative buying was on. The end of paper money and debt based money had come. It was to be resourced backed. On another station end time prophets told their tales. They gave dates and time when the world would come to an end. Many of it came from the same ground where men played god and claimed to proclaim his messages. They have come with different names.

Some stations were in languages no one in the room understood. Like the rose gradually opening its petals at dawn, the world got free and freer. More and more people moved and connected faster. Communist China was busy. They were giving more and more loans to the capitalists around the globe. But that was not all they did. They sent entrepreneurs who spoke little or no language save for their own into every corner.

At a corner of the room he saw a look alike of the Chinese minister in charge of drug administration and food safety. The striking resemblance of the man to Chinese minister who was beheaded touched a part of him. He smiled to himself "this is it," he said. It could be him or another man, after all don't they all look alike. The man who committed the crime might have been beheaded or his look alike might have taken his place. His crime was serious, and frowned at by the constitution and the people. He could not have gotten away the same way those ones he aided did. For many years he was in charge of the food safety and drug administration in the country. He was accused of using his position to enrich himself, while turning a blind eye to the manufacture and sales of fake drugs. The drugs were for both domestic and international market. They made it to all corners of the earth. People died from their use. As depressing as his crimes were they said he was never remorseful. Most of the guys who manufactured the drugs went underground once their heinous crimes were discovered. It was having great effect around the world. The worst case was in places like Africa where it was not easy to discover what was wrong. People died in larger number in hospitals. It was hospitals, happy, when they heard of sources for inexpensive drugs. They made deals with the merchants of death, and were getting their supplies.

In the minister's office he handed him the letters. He thanked him for accepting to hand it to the men and woman of the country, whom according to him were duty bound to oblige the request. Once he was done with the business that brought him there, he inquired about the man he saw in the waiting room. He knew he had already taken the minister's time, but asked that last question out of curiosity.

The man's personal problems were getting compounded. He considered killing himself. He did not have anything to do with his look alike. That did not bother him. It was his daughter. He had gotten her in the wrong place at the wrong time.

Like any girl her age, once in a while, she wanted to be smart. She wanted to help. Even play god. She heard the man was influential. Any man her father was so worried about, must really be powerful. Her father, her country's minister of commerce was in Nigeria. Her country was in need of partners and expanded markets. It was a world tour for her. The old man's mistake was to have travelled with her that way six months earlier. Fresh from college, he made her his personal secretary.

To Ade the minister of education's son, she was the most beautiful thing he had ever seen. Ade was a young man at risk. At risk of falling in love, "There is no way he can make the right decision in that environment." His mother told his father when she heard he was seeing the Chinese minister's daughter.

"It was supposed to be only a formal evening and nothing more." The minister was in his room at the Embassy Suits fighting it out with his ex-wife and mother of his only child over the phone.

After the formal meeting, the two kids decided to keep seeing each other, without their parents knowing about it. The fight was about her pregnancy. Boi was four months pregnant for the minister's son. And they were in love, they claimed. And they found time to sneak around to give the baby in the womb more love. But both parents think it was a national embarrassment. In fact one thinks it might cost him his job, even his privilege of being a father.

His ex-wife was getting ready to hang him. He was there again, to talk to the minister to see what they can do. It was the only thing that made sense to him. Yet he did know what it was he wanted to do. He didn't mind if it meant revoking all the favors he got and exposing their business deal. To talk about it would give him some relief. It would buy him more time with his ex-wife. Of everything he was, being a father seemed to matter most. And according to his wife's score sheet, he was failing badly at it.

CHAPTER
≈99≈

At the political rallies many were still thrilled by the oratory of Stone Jr. Some people, who were not able to follow the speeches, just gave him and his wife a pass mark for appearance. At restaurants people were all talking about the couple. Those dating started off with their dates, discussing the couple or the rally they attended, when it seemed they had nothing in common. For some such discussion was their first adventure into politics. If one got the other to agree to volunteer, it meant and guaranteed another date.

Stone Jr. was increasingly becoming liked and hated at the same time. He was not surprised by this. He knew it was the pattern and geography of life on earth. His aim was to bring about change and that was his focus, any other thing would be to take his eyes of the prize. He tirelessly spoke about change that the country desired and needed at any campaign stop. In some places his campaign posters were repeatedly being defaced, pulled down and put back. Because of the hate messages received, some thug mobilized for him. But he made it clear he did not believe in winning at all cost. He appreciated the love they showed him.

He urged them to be involved in civilized campaign. But most in the group tended to understand the language of power, money and thugs in the country's politics. They had to face their opponents whether he was aware of it or not. And they did, making it able for them to have those posters up again, each time they were torn down. A few among them expressed frustration, at his lack of understanding, that, they had to match their opponents, whatever they came up with. They encouraged him to understand the politics of the place he got involved in.

"Politics was dirty and money never lost it power," they said. In the country party affiliation was strongly based on ethnic and religious sentiments. Ideology and philosophy were nowhere, near what the people considered, when they held the ballot paper in their hands, or stood behind the picture of a candidate. Many found it hard to listen to campaign massages, it did not help them, they told anyone, who cared to ask. What many cared to know was what tribe the candidate was from. It did not make sense to ask what the gender of the candidate was, since they always knew their politics was dominated by men. That question was taken for granted. It was the unwritten law, the female were to be seen, not heard. So the second question, naturally was, that of the aspirant's religion.

Mr. Stone understood the concerns of some in his campaign team. Those were the ills that plagued the country, which he hoped, would be broken by education. And he has put a lot into education in all parts of the country. He did not fail to give credit to the little effort and achievement of the schools and teachers. That the massage of a little known candidate like him, would be received that well, was a good sign. "The political atmosphere was getting better day-by-day", he would tell his people. He did not set out to become a politician, when he started his investment in education in the country. A victory in a free and fair election, would be, reward on his investment. His winning was a dividend of democracy, as it has come to be known in the country, though that phrase has been greatly abused.

Gains of democracy included those who became rich during the campaign. Many hoped to and did. Tribal and religious leaders, head of market women groups, heads of unions, and many others had their definitions of the term. Several of them met with the campaign manager at the request of the campaign. Others sent in their demands. They had the card with which they played. "Getting the party's message through, they met a lot of resistance." They asked for money out rightly. They talked about how much the other campaigns were willing to give to get them to work for them. The campaign knew the importance of having the backings of the groups. At Mr. Stone's campaign headquarters, they would come back with ridiculous, yet serious discussions about the campaign decisions. It took a long time, before they agreed to mobilize money, for some of the demands. It came from what they called contingence fund.

The manager knew the brutal forces they were dealing with, than the candidate did. He has been in the country longer and worked for different candidates. Some of those candidates were successful and others not. He knew what worked and what changes were needed, he said. He met with the leaders secretly and their spoke openly in the language they understood. They all believed in change and how to get it, that they agreed. The present situation was not the best, they believed in what had to be done.

CHAPTER
≈100≈

For the first time after months of preparation and campaign, Sylvester Azuogu Stone met with his major opponents. It was a radio and television organized presidential debate. Somehow they managed to organize a debate. It was a rare fate, which the announcer and his friend spoke about with pride. It brought them joy. A wealthy investor friend of the radioman was the happiest. He is a man who all his life, has called for the nation's political discourse to be elevated. But what he sees rather is sound political discourse replaced by political assassinations and massacres. And the nation reduced to mediocre and headline state. The political future was stunted. He knew it and believed it could be redeemed.

The public was excited. But they did not stop expressing doubts. At every corner the "seeing is believing," cliché came back. To their surprise, they saw the contestants on TV ready to debate.

The amphitheater's sitting arrangement was careful planed in a manner that it did not reflect support for any of the candidates.

The people were anxious to hear, what the presidential candidates were planning to do to with the mandate, they want to govern the country. The hall had no empty seats, it was filled to capacity. It was calm. One could hear the sound of a pin drop on the floor. Anticipation filled the room. The sound of the waiver bird was heard outside. And simultaneously, the announcer read out the rules of the debate to the candidates. The three contestants sat facing the crowd, while the moderators backed the crowd. The moderators were two, one from radio and the other from television. They sat facing the candidates.

At homes and sport bars, and restaurants millions were glued to the radios and TV sets. It seemed the whole country was quiet, the street seemed empty. And the world seemed to have shifted its attention, to that theater in the middle of a nation that had for a long time, refused to live up the expectations of the rest of the world. The debate was being fed to TVs and radio stations around the world via satellite.

Among the crowd were students who were members of debating societies in schools and elsewhere. They went to debates in high school where debates were mostly for fun. They 'marshaled' out points and defense, while planning dance moves. Most times, it was their first official dance and possibly first kisses. Then after, there was the usual back and forth flow of love letters and opinions. But when debates really mattered in houses of legislatures and political offices their people became like the caterpillar.

Caterpillars great beginnings, holding firm to the tree, but then they grow and fall face down, flat on the ground. Some of them believed it was the other party whose fame came through recitals on holy podiums. "It wouldn't fit their politics." They joked. The young men and women in the auditorium were tired of physical fights and chair throwing. They were excited about the good, sound debates would do the country.

The crowed listened as the moderators introduced the candidates. With a baritone voice, the radio announcer introduced the candidates from right to left. The first candidate was the erodent scholar and international business mogul Dr. Sylvester Azuogu Stone. He shed light on his bio and his philanthropic life. He proceeded with his lists of achievements stressing what the number of school he has established nationwide. He ended the introduction with mentioning that S.A Stone was the front-runner candidate of the National Congress Party. The next candidate was Alhaji Aka Togoh a multi-national businessman and renowned political warrior. He gave a list of his achievements that were mostly, how he built his business empire, single handedly. He did not fail to mention the bills that he has sponsored as both a member the lower and upper houses of the legislature. He was of the National People's Congress and has represented them in many capacities.

The last candidate was that of the All Progressive Alliance Otumba Balogun. He beamed with smile and had a lighthearted laughter as he was being introduced. He had an air of a man who had no qualms about the outcome of the debate or the election.

The announcer read out the rules of the debate for the benefit of the listeners. The politicians have had weeks of debates themselves over the rules. The crowds were cheerful it was an opportunity they can use to ask questions of the men who over the past months have dominated the airwaves, with their promises of heaven on earth.

The first of the candidate to give his open speech was Mr. Stone. He was time conscious, brief and straight to the point. He said as the moderator had instructed. "My name is Sylvester Azuogu." He spoke about his education, where he was born and where he rose from, about his beautiful wife and the baby they were expecting.

"The country is burning today and we all know it, we can begin today as it offers us that opportunity of change. We can begin with this election to say no to the things that divide us. We can embrace this wind of change. We can say no to old politics and laws that leave us going to bed hungry each night."

"To all those we have disappointed or let down, to them we may not have just or acceptable excuses, but we can only say we have been human." Those were the opening words of Alhaji Togoh as he took the floor. The crowd remained silent. He cleared his throat. The atmosphere was set. The people were ready for more. "Was he going to make a confession and resign his position at the senate?" People wondered. "Politics has disappointed us all", he continued. "The nationalist who fought the white colonial regime handed this country to us. They fought and the white men packed the baggage and left us. Many years after look at where we are, the colonial system itself has refused to leave us. We the politicians have looted public property." Everyone in the room kept their ears to the floor listen waiting for the moment of truth.

"Alhaji cannot count himself as having been disappointed by this system," someone mumbled from the back. The man who made the statement could not control his shock at what his ears were hearing. It was the first time a politician from the part of the country was heard talking about the national struggle that way. He continued speaking, longer than the time allotted for his opening speech. But no one bothered.

"Our people are hard-working," he continued. "At five in the morning the Lagos crowd flows out into the streets like the Bar Beach overflowing its banks. At six in the evening from Lagos Island they are again dispersing. They leave in cars, buses, boats, canoes and half the population on foot walking miles to get to the nearest empty bus. Each day the traffic flows back and forth like the waves of the Bar Beach in every city in the country. It is men, women and children as young as eight with their wares on their heads yelling and advertising their products. They brave harsh weather conditions, they must survive. They have all almost lost every hope in government and their legislatures, but in God and in themselves. The eight year old has no hope of changing government. He has no voice to be heard. He follows his sister with his tray full of bananas on his head. He calls out to the passerby like his sister to attract buyers. His early childhood education has begun. If he makes it today he would be out of college with a degree at twenty six. If no luck he would be walking into the office of the same folks who have failed him with his dusty shoes and already worn out heels with his job applications. Let us change the future today."

Mr. Stone's presence has changed the game. And he was a challenge. If he was to remain relevant he knew it was time to change the tune. As a member of the senate and one of the longest serving members, he has learnt the tactics and had to use it. Togoh went on to speak about his alliances with some very few respectable names in the senate. It was to stress the effort he has made to clean up the country and rid it of corrupt politicians. His efforts were yielding fruits and what the country needed was time to see that effort mature. Alhaji was an experienced politician. He was no stranger to talking the talk.

The crowd was happy. It seemed like substance has been finally added to the political dialogue in the country. If people like Alhaji could come to the crowd to explain what it was that they have been doing in the legislature, there was progress. In the past, he refused to talk to the media. To him interviews were a waste of time.

Again Alhaji cleared his throat. He went straight to his list of achievements. He started; that the country- enjoyed electricity to it was a bill that he helped pass. The states could boast of good roads, it was his handiwork. Though there were no roads anywhere to lay claims to. At least not in the south of the country, but Alhaji laid a bogus claim. After all it was politics. He moved on to investment climate in the country. Several foreign and local investors invested in the country because he attracted them.

His opponents were new in the politics and do not understand the workings of the country. They did not understand the rudimentary of game and that is why he should be voted. He should be voted for, a vote for him was a vote for experience, he said. The word experience was not what he wanted, but it came out however. The crowd cheered and clapped their hands for him as he finished.

Otumba Balogun was a man given to flamboyance in everything. He first adjusted his white Agbada and a matching hat. He face beamed with smile, adjusting his clothes as he took an appraisal of the crowd. Rumors had it he was addicted to clothes that he frequently went on oversea trips just to pick up tailored pieces for himself. The one he was wearing was probably a special oversea collection for the debate. Otumba Balogun was also a member of the national assembly. But he was said to spend more time in Dubai than on his seat at the senate. The fashion magazines got tired of his weekend trips that they stopped using his picture in either front or back pages of their publications. They loved him for one thing. He was handsome and took good care of his family, so somehow they were still able to write good stories about him.

After his introduction of himself he wasted no time to lunch into an attack. He attacked the experience of his senate colleague and the young Dr. Stone's lack of it "It was the experience of people like Alhaji Togoh that left the country in the terrible hole it was politically and otherwise." He said. He accused him of being a man who could not be trusted in the senate nor in his private business dealings. He accused him of pursuing bills that when passed only awarded contracts to his business interests. "Alhaji apart from bills through which you awarded contracts to yourself and your friends mention any other thing worth of note you done." He challenged him. The statement attracted applauses from the crowd.

For Mr. Stone his educational banners were quite impressive. And his eloquence were still needed in the classrooms in the universities in the country. It was not the right time for him to enter politics. The day would come when he would raise his hands and wave them and the country would welcome him, Otumba Balogun said. For the time being, it was matters of political restructuring and reconstruction that required people like him to captain the boat.

Though he neglected whatever it is that makes him the best qualified of the three. Otumba's attack seemed to have taken the attentions off the list of achievements of the others. He kept the crowd waiting. They waited to hear what it was, he achieved in the senate for his two terms there. Finally he mentioned the name of the committee, which he chaired in the senate. He mentioned the achievements of the culture ministry. It was their duty and responsibility that the country remained a united one. It was the duty that the people had the right orientation. He gave a long list of functions, which the people found very hard to pin down its relevance to their lives. But he kept on run the commentary, he was running. He kept taking attention by constantly attacking either of his opponents. The audience wanted more. But the time was up for that session of the debate.

CHAPTER
≈101≈

It was question and answers session. The questions were to be from the moderators and the audience. The microphone went from hand to hand. And questions ranged from experience to the meaning of experience in a country struggling in almost every facet of its existence. A student from one of the universities had a question for the Alhaji. "Alhaji Togoh, do you have any plan of action beyond this election campaign?" She wanted to know if he had a blue print, something, anything that could determine the direction of things in the country for at least a year. People thought she knew the answer to her question. But her emphases on the beyond election also gave another impression. The question on reparation was a question thrown to Otumba Balogun. The man who asked the question simply identified himself, as "Christopher." He wanted to know if he would push for reparation from the international community on the ills done the nation. Another man in the audience had the microphone. His hands had been in the air from the moment the floor was opened to questions. Finally got the microphone. He was from the Niger Delta. His question was for Dr. Stone. "Dr. Stone."

He said. With the air of a man about to broker a deal, "The wealth in the Niger Delta, its distribution and the environment will continue to be an issue dominating political affairs in this country for the next twenty years. If elected how do you wish to tackle that?" He handed back the microphone to the man sitting below him.

As the microphone made its way back to the moderator, Dr. Stone took a quick look at area where the question came from. There was an air of relief on the faces of the people in that corner of the theater. The man who asked the question was a youth leader. His group was one of the groups in the area that made it clear at different meetings that they did not believe in violence. But violence perpetrated in the area leaves them no options than to defend themselves. "He was a power broker. He is the reason the area was enjoying the cease-fire it was enjoying." Someone in the crowd told his friend. The size of the room made him so little. He would have gotten no answer to his question had he directed it to any of the other candidates.

His question was a launching pad for Mr. Stone. It was the avenue he was looking for to attack the failed politics in the country. He ferociously attacked both senators. "The Niger Delta was a test on the country's nationhood," he said. For that country to continue as a nation, it was one question that needed to be answered. He thanked the young man who asked the question. "It could not be asked at a better time," he said.

For anyone who knew the country, it was the politics of greed and corruption that has left that and other parts of the country in their present state. In the parlance of the country the Niger delta was the goose that lays the golden egg. The egg unfortunately has never been allowed to hatch before it is taken away from the goose. The goose left no water to swim in. "Greed, corruption and ignorance were the only things that could reduce a country to a single source of economic dependence," he pointed out. Those qualities were not lacking in the country's present crop of politicians.

"The dependence on oil was due to the destruction of the groundnut pyramid in the north, the cocoa in the west and the palm produce, coal mines in the east. It was the lack of desire to explore the land. God blessed the land abundantly natural resources and people. "The oil in the Delta and its distribution was never an issue years ago. But it is today ladies and gentlemen," S.A Stone said.

Looking straight pass the crowd to the place where the young man from the Delta sat. His eyes filled with sympathy.

There he sees a future destruction. And a people who in the next three to four years would be told to evacuate their land, ignored to be submerged or wiped away by ecological disaster. It was a no good news. But that was imminent. It was a problem he saw as more dangerous than those created by disgruntled politicians.

Looking straight into the camera.

"Ladies and gentlemen there was a time when this country harvested from every region. Then the strength of our currency matched and stood above those of other major world economies. Today that is history. Look at the experience. We have been devalued by blind and corrupt rulers. This country we have still wealth. The problem with Nigeria is still how to spend the country's money, more than 35 percent on every project is still spent on bribes and tips for loyalty and another 10 percent to our collective devaluation and inflated contracts cost."

He employed the audience and viewers to shun selling their conscience and their vote. Those who buy your vote continue to impoverish us while amassing wealth for their selfish use. The same old politicians that passed laws they never read nor discussed have signed the future of this country away to the oil companies. They have sold the homes you live in. The land our brothers sit on has been bought. The wells in your back yards and doorsteps leave you no breathing space. The air you breathe is polluted and something has to be done now. No one has asked what the effect of the mass scramble in the delta has on the health of its people.

Africans we are blessed with oil, mineral and human resources. The curse of oil is the continent's corporate explorers exploiting everything for more resources. The drill and kill. They pollute the earth, our land and the rivers with spills. They drop their leftover on us in every front as our reward. Like dog dying of starvation we fight over their leftover. They cursed our water and food and call us names. We kill ourselves.

"If elected I will diversify the economy. Explore hundreds of unexplored natural resources. The land and waters were flourishing with them. To those who say we will not sleep in peace. I plan to meet terror head on. "If you don't meet terror head-on, it will meet in your home, in your kitchens or meet you running." Stone Jr. would install scanners capable of dictating bombs, explosives and illegal arms at toll gates. Highly dangerous areas would be watched by both manned and unmanned armor vehicles. When illegal activities are suspected, the suspects would be escorted to designated areas. The occupiers or driver of the vehicle would then be required to go further inspection or face being met with force. It was more like a vow. He would bring back value to life and living in the country.

"All we need is the will to drive the ship of this country aright. The treasure in agriculture would once again be discovered. Our human resources would be developed to the prime standards. I will make loan available for research at every level. Our schools will no longer produce graduates who come out to seek employment. Our schools and students will be employers in the future I foresee for this country. My people come let's make our dreams come true. Let us build the future together. Let us build the Nigerian Dream. We are one people joined together by the fountain that flows within. The dawn is now. Vote for me."

Dr. Stone end his answer to the question asked him.

The moderator thanked the candidates for coming and the audience for their conduct. To the listener and viewers at home, he reminded it was their chance. It only comes ones in four years. "It is up to you the people to decide, go out and vote."

The debated ended with the candidates shaking and exchange pleasantries. They told each other how they looked forward to beating them at the polls.

Mr. Stone went to his wife who was sitting in the crowd and hugged her. She remained a valuable asset to him everywhere. During the debate her eye contacts acted as guide as in many other occasions.

CHAPTER
≈102≈

As the crowd was dispersing two men exchanged pleasantries. It seemed to draw a lot of attention. Everyone including the press rushed to the scene immediately taking photographs. It was two old formidable forces in the land, always on the opposite sides on any issue. They sat through the debate listening to issues and arguments. Their different positions escalated issues. Their wars were over and their time was up as shown as they noticed that evening. It was age of reason. They chatted like two friends on opposite sides of a school debate. The press watched with eagerness being careful not to disrupt the conversation with their questions.

As the old rivals were leaving the theater the moderator announced to inform the studio of the presence of the two during the debate. The announcer knew what to do with the information. The moderator regretted not noticing them on time. It looked like it was carefully planned to avoid disturbing the debate with sentiments from the old war. Many journalists missed the opportunity. Their presence was a major part of the story that evening and would remain till the end of the election. Those journalists who missed out on the opportunity tried to make up. The next morning the newspapers and magazines with the photos of the two leads at the venue of the debate sold out. Some journalists received their last paycheck from their employers. The photographers and cameramen were most affected they did not capture the moment.

Amongst them were journalists who loved their jobs, loved to quote those past leaders. But they were fed up with pretentious claims made on a two page newsletter. One had written an article about their presence. His take was not what the editor wanted. He had ended that article referring to the leaders as, "Men who several years after they left office, have not been able to sit down and articulate. Tell their people what they did with their resources. Tell them how they tried to make their lives better. Men who all those years have never cared to prove they were not just ordinary criminals who hijacked power. Yet they want to dictate the way this election goes."

The presence of the two former leaders was a game changer. Men shifted loyalty at the last minute. A lot of water went under the bridge. The leaders and the coverage from the press changed the dynamics of the election. It was no longer just a symbol to fill an empty office or an about to be vacated office. It was the election to elect the president, of a nation that was fast, coming to know its history. A wake up call, a new dawn had arrived.

CHAPTER
≈103≈

It was Election Day. The candidates went out to the poll station in their wards to vote, with their supporters behind them. They voted and made the rounds to nearby poll stations, booths and community halls. As the evening came the sun was returning in the west. Party agents and polling officers were counting ballots under heavy security.

The results were trickling in. People were anxious. Mr. Stone who was little known months ago seemed to be doing very well. There was a mixture of suspense, anxiety and jubilation. People prayed and waited. The supporters, of the candidates, who lost the election in places, where they hoped to win, looked for what or whom to blame. They tried hard not to resort to violence.

That night people went to sleep with their radios and televisions on. The ballots were being counted. In many places, people hoped on hope. Something, anything could change the whole game. By afternoon the next day Mr. Stone was declared the winner. He won with a landslide. In the second place was Alhaji Togoh, who at first found it hard to concede defeat. Otumba Balogun quickly called to congratulate Dr. Stone the winner. Congratulatory calls and messages began pouring in from around the globe.

One of the calls which almost moved him to tears was from a friend and son of one of the continent's long term serving leaders. In their telephone call, he reminded him of the burden of ruling in Africa.

He told him how sometimes he watched his father struggle with the trauma of the years of independent struggle.

"I sympathize with him, when I hear those voices in his voice. But still those forces, he fought against do not go away. They are constantly coming back in many forms. They are like ghosts in his dream. But these ghosts are still alive. The ghosts of the living can do more harm." He said.

It is the Post-Ubuntu syndrome. His father is not alone. The nationalist fighters who fought for independence from colonial regimes suffer from it. It is a post war trauma. The trauma forces them to cling to power, even when they lord it over their own citizens. They tend to see themselves as commanders, still engaged in a long guerrilla war. They are in constant fear of foreign corporate interests in the country. The fear is re-enforced by the kinds of cut throat business practices that the countries engage in, even after they left the countries. The enemy is no longer your enemy. He is a friend far worse than an enemy. It is the Post-Ubuntu syndrome. No longer we, it was I.

Dr. Stone was supposed to be celebrating his victory. But the call gave him a lot of concern. "Nothing breeds despotic leadership in Africa more than this syndrome." He said and kept listening. During his campaign tours he read the book, "Inside the brain of a former freedom fighter." It was given to him by his friend Joe Scott. He is a popular fiction writer he has read over the years. The book was his latest and his first attempt at nonfiction.

S A. Stone Jr. mentioned the name, began to tell him about a section in the book "In it he studies the psyche of the occupiers and natives. His inspiration came from a song "we piss the angry bird off" in which a friend of his, a scholar and rapper documented, the sufferings and braveness of the Mau Mau Movement."

Ote himself has read the book. And he had it translated to make it accessible to his countrymen. "It is our experience." He agreed. "I am gripped with fear at the sufferings of the kikuyu people. How the foreigners came, took over their most fertile lands and made their people so poor they were forced to work as low wage labor. They held them in camps far worse than those of Hitler. My father has this nightmares he wakes up at night perspiring."

Dr. Stone felt a notch in the stomach, but continued, "Scott's girlfriend was born in captivity in an all women detention camp at Kamiti in 1955."

Dr. Stone met Joe Scott and Mary, and his friend at the other end of the phone, a few years before, at a dinner party in South Africa. It was before he thought of a career in politics. That evening and the friendship helped put things in perspective.

Just like that evening, the night of victory was turning into another of remembrance. The words, of one of the guests at the party, attended by over two hundred celebrities, resonated with him. It was the words of Jay Z. He and Alicia Keys had just gotten on the stage after Eminem. Alicia was filled with life and energy. She had given the people water when they were thirsty. He said, "The imbalance and inequality in the world would never go away. It is a trauma we all suffer. Africa we are a dispossessed people, whose death are certain, but by installment. Our leaders are leaders of structurally impoverished and dispossessed people. They find it hard to hand over power. They fear everyone else knows little, or nothing, of these journeys by our people. This hold on us, is worse than slavery, we are in our own lands." The two friends repeated the lines together. The rap star had gone ahead to point, "We all want to sing of beauty and love, but our wounds are raw, we say it as it is." Those were Abu's lines. He was just repeating them for emphasis. Abu had opened the show that night.

Ote congratulated his friend again. He was happy with his friend and the country. And convinced, his friend knows, what is wrong or right. He dropped the phone.

CHAPTER
≈104≈

Celebrations were on everywhere. People were jubilating. Alice and Michael were excited. They were on the phone as well. They were at that party that evening. They walked the walk from the beginning. And had remained friends with Dr. Stone, Ote and many others they met there.

Though her father was a well-known politician, Alice was not always the one to talk about politics, or take too much interest in it. But somehow she seems to have transitioned.

Alice was talking to Michael. They have known each other in the past, but have found a way to remain friends. Michael was surprised about what she was doing in South Africa and at the party. She partied but that was not her circle. Michael was always aloof she always complained. When she first met him years ago, she was not sure, if he was single or not. But even if he wasn't she would not have bothered. He was a handsome young man, with a successful career. He had the best Mercedes Benz in the neighborhood. They said he waited for the latest version to come out each year, before he got it. But unlike the persona with that much lust for cars. He seemed very restrained when it came to women.

His best friend Ramsey was unlike him. He was famous among the women, a son of a traveler. His father was a traveler fond of the continent. He had a son whom he named after Ramses11. The son became an actor to fulfill the dreams of his father. The Egyptian ruler was said to have been an incarnate of a god. But how could he a mortal fill such a big shoe. First he took to dancing. He entertained on the streets and get money, and then his stars began to shine. He was smooth and good with the ladies. Alice knew him too. Once he approached a beautiful girl, he was meeting for the first time. To her surprise he began "If ever these dreams of mine don't come true, please for once gimme, the opportunity of telling, you how, I would propose." She lets him buy her a drink. Before the end of the night she was on his bed. He might not be a god, but he was the son his father he wanted.

Micheal's neighbors sometime pried, they were not sure what his deal was. Alice told them he was as straight as can be. They were seen hanging out together. Alice seemed ready to give up some habit for him. Her friends said she did. Michael did not seem impressed. He saw a wounded girl. Michael himself like his name sake, MJ, was a man of whom, it could be said, has got it all, yet he hasn't got it. Somehow

Alice had become interested in politics and his current affairs. She thought it was boring at first. And Michael could never get her into a real political discourse.

She had campaigned for Barack and Michelle, she told him. "The black president campaign," she and her team, had called it. As they stood there she seemed to be the one talking. And he was listening. He has raised an issue about warlords in Africa and movement to bring the wars to an end. She had taken part in the "Kony 2012"; it was a campaign to capture Joseph Kony of the LRA in Uganda. It was led by American youths.

"It is a great movement," she said.

"Because the world cares today, the world should hear the cry of that child who has lost both parents to Boko Haram. The call for good governance in Africa is everyone concern."

"Yes," Michael was interested, he urged her on. He wanted to hear more about how he could be of help. Listening to her for a while he told her. "While we strategize on how to prosecute the book haram. Let us also consider how we got here. Are we able to see it from the eyes of history, from the eyes of the other? Let us negotiate our ways out of these stupidities."

Her voice changed, "yes, but these are a bunch of mad and murderous crowd, sinners who have no business with god, nor god any hands in their dirty dealings, yet sinfully they chant god is great. Enjoined to pursue knowledge, but knowledge is the last thing on their minds. Wasn't it the hope, knowledge would bring understanding and peace. But the fools left behind with the sword continue to shed blood."

Michael was more impressed when she continued to offer suggestions. He took a glass of wine from the server. And walked across the room with her and introduced her to another friend.

Everyone was celebrating the victories. Dr. Stone had called on them during his campaign. And they remained resourceful throughout. The victory was theirs. They congratulated each other.

CHAPTER ≈105≈

It was a quiet day at the peninsula. Ngozika, the granddaughter of the antelope woman, was attending to her sick husband. Her husband's radio was on and she was expecting to hear the outcome of the election. His condition was very critical. She managed to keep her mind off the immediate trouble, thinking about the election and the commentary on the radio. The election had managed to keep their spirits high.

That night Mr. Stone called his wife to bring a chest case from the closet in his room. When she did, he unlocked the case. He took out a number of documents. He looked at each of them carefully. He handed her what looked like a map or building plan. She looked at it and he took it back from her. He gave her another, this time a document with his signatures on it. He handed her another one, similar to the one she just gave back to him. They did that for some minutes. When they finished looking at the documents, he asked her to lock the case.

Mr. Stone took the key from her. He felt its smooth and rough edges, then handed it to her. "Give this key to my son" he said. "Tell him, a man is not a man without secrets. And a man with too many secrets, may die with his own memorials" he concluded.

That treasure box has been gathering dust, since Mr. Stone placed it in a corner of the closet, on his arrived at the peninsula. When she dusted it, what she did not know, was the amount of time, it would take to dust the content, of the documents in it. In those where millions of dollars, in cash and gold, still stacked away in banks, safes and abandoned warehouses, in different locations around the world.

When he handed her the key, he smiled. "Gold for oil," he said. "The bag of money was not, the bag, with which the land of Golgotha was bought. But still, give to Caesar, what is his and to my people, what is theirs." For long he and his friends, had diminished and devalued the worth of Africa. In several ways, they retarded the growth of the continent and her people, with inflation and paper money. It was not the politics of Western Union or IMF. He did not see, how Africa would not, trade itself out of its present sick state with gold and silver, as legal tender. With that son, he had paid his debt. There was a man, capable of fighting, the global economic and financial dictatorship. He was proud of the day he broke away from prison and the day he met the black woman. He remembered the song "swing low sweet chariot." He felt the song's true meaning, knew he was home. Mr. Stone sr. was pleased. He has given all he has. It was what he took. He has given himself. The reparation was paid. He was a man who has completed his journey.

Ngozika had a bright smile on her face. She was amazed and bewildered. She wanted such much to ask the man with whom he has shared flesh and blood, if he was her god or his messenger. And if there were there more, she did not know about the man?

He knew that someday, soon, he was going to have grandchildren, who would not be satisfied with his cash or wealth. They would want more. They would ask for more. He bequeathed his diaries to his grandchildren. They were part of his treasure. When a man had gotten a thing, anything, he seeks more from that thing. When it cannot offer more, he gets too used to it. Next he discards it, to search for that which offers freshness or newness. So Mr. Stone found a way not to be tired of those things, he once hungered for and now had in surplus. Those were part of what made his diaries valuable. He was not a man to leave anyone, asking is that all?

CHAPTER
≈106≈

After his election quoted stocks of companies doing business in the country went up. It was a good sign. Dr. Stone's promise of bringing home Nigerians scattered all over the world seemed to be materializing. Many delegations foreign and local, who came for the election, indicated interest of a longer presence.

Big corporations in the country knew there were going to be changes in the way they did business in the country. They began to announce immediate changes. They were to pay careful attention to the laws on the environment. It was one of the companies, which had operated in the country for many years, with disregard to the laws. It said it was studying the laws. This was company, that had for fifty five years, applied the divide and rule system, on the people and their land. They had dealt with kidnapping and fuelled the flames of unrest in the delta. They had their private police. They were lords in the land.

Those men would have preferred to die, than support independence, if they had the power, they later came to acquire in the land before 1960. They were the ones announcing changes. They did not want to be sued. The citizens of Nigeria were empowered and they knew it. Their voices were being heard loud and clear. Their messages of congratulation, which carried the changes, were videotaped in their corporate offices in London and New York. One of the drug manufacturing firms sent its message from its world headquarters in New York. It wished the government and the people of the country well, while it hoped to do business with them. But with a new government, those who were listening knew that they meant well.

Oil refining was not to be done far away from where the oil was drilled. It would save cost in terms of transportation. That meant there were to be refineries in the south. There would be immediate over haul in labor, employment and prison reform in the country. Those were to be more productive and efficient segments of society. The institutions were to be goal oriented and no more waste of human resources. That came from the office of the president-in-waiting. It was selecting and screening candidates for various positions in the new administration.

At the inauguration, many of the heads of governments and businesses who had sent messages or called to congratulate the country were present. They came from all corners of the world, From the kingdom of Arabia, Accra, Beijing, Berlin, Johannesburg, The white house, The British Prime Minster was elated, he had gotten to know the new president as a friend. From Dubai the Emirate flew in young enthusiastic royals. Buckingham palace, was not left out, the queen had sent a delegation. In her beautifully hand written message, on a fresh smelling card, the queen wrote. She was rescheduling her yearly visit to Canada. That year it was going to be Nigeria. "Nigeria is a common wealth member nation, a worthy member."

The new President was overjoyed at the friendship the rest of the world had offered him.

CHAPTER
≈107≈

Amidst tears of joy, as she watched her son on TV, sorrow filled Ngozika's heart at her husband's condition. Mr. Stone Sr. could still hear his wife singing mixed songs of joy and sorrow, and the voice of his son on the TV in the background. The last words he heard, was his son thanking his parents for giving him life. He raised his arm, and placed the left palm of his hand over his chest, and then placed the right on top of it. He slept, like a man, who has accomplished his entire mission on earth.

She placed her forehead on his, murmured a word, and looked at beautiful smile on his face. "Sleep on my love you have led a fulfilled life." She said.

Death is strong, but her love was stronger.

She picked up the telephone. She places a call to her sons and daughter. Ngozika wiped away tears from her eyes. She smiled as she looked at the body on the bed with great admiration.

Eight days later Sylvester Stone Sr.'s interment took place. He was buried in the mausoleum he built for himself, in a private ceremony, attended only by family and close friends.

Ada attended the burial with her husband and two years old son. She was six months pregnant. Ihuoma was also pregnant. The women could see it from her looks. Her mother was at the burial as well. Ulu's fiancée could not attend the burial. He discouraged her. It was not the best time for her to meet his family.

Mr. Branston was glad his family invited him. Despite his billions of dollars in investments around the world, what he called his greatest achievement, was the day, he handed the man lying there, a tiny piece of paper signed by the US president. His friend was pardoned. Being around during his friend's last days on earth was a great achievement.

His life and death were testaments, to the words of the woman who came to the pond. "A man will come from a distant land. Amongst our people he will find a home. In his sleep he will find peace. The meek will drink from this pond and find healing and peace." As she foretold, Stone Sr. began a cycle of life in the area.

www.ingramcontent.com/pod-product-compliance
Lightning Source LLC
Chambersburg PA
CBHW071111290626
47170CB00018B/52
9780988780217